The Winter Sorcerer and
the Summer Witch

Books by D. Lieber

Minte and Magic

The Exiled Otherkin

The Assassin's Legacy

Intended Fates Trilogy

Intended Bondmates

Intended Strangers

Intended Enemies

Council of Covens

Dancing with Shades

In Search of a Witch's Soul

Also by D. Lieber

Conjuring Zephyr

Once in a Black Moon

A Very Witchy Yuletide

The Treason of Robyn Hood

The Curse of Moonseed Manor

The Goblin King's Mischief

Bitten by the North Wind

The Glass Moth

The Winter Sorcerer and the Summer Witch

D. Lieber

Ink & Magick, LLC
Kenosha, Wisconsin
contact@inkandmagick.com

Hardcover ISBN: 978-1-951239-34-3
Paperback ISBN: 978-1-951239-35-0
Ebook ISBN: 978-1-951239-36-7

✗ HUMAN AUTHORED

   Reg #: 8146443, https://authorsguild.org/human

Cover by GetCovers
Edited by Olivia Kalb at oliviakalbediting@gmail.com
Proofread by Samantha Talarico

Special Thanks

Thank you to my beta readers John and Amy.

Chapter One

Whit smiled to himself as the two-hundred-year-old floorboards creaked beneath his weight in the front hall of his grandfather's house. Today was his lucky day. He could feel it.

He glanced around the parlor as he passed through. Everything from the dark wainscoting on the lower half of the walls to the spindle-legged couch to the sconces on either side of the heavy stone fireplace was either original or had been carefully restored by him.

He knew every inch of this house, every iron nail, every cobweb. He loved everything about it, had loved everything about it since he was a small boy. And it loved him right back. Even the ghosts of his ancestors, who sometimes popped in and out to check on things or impart messages, welcomed him here.

To everyone else, it was just a house. A Georgian

colonial, beautiful in its craftsmanship and valuable in its age. But to Whit, it was home. He'd lived with his grandfather for a while to help take care of the place, and today, it would finally be officially passed down to him.

Lifting his hand, he knocked gently on the library door. "Grandfather?" he called out.

After hearing his grandfather's voice beckon him in, he entered.

The small room had taken very little work to restore. While he'd had to replace the bookshelves, which covered one wall, the windows behind the desk, and the desk itself, were original. The reading lamp was a reproduction though that was to be expected since it was electric. The armchair tucked into the corner near the fireplace was also new. His grandfather was old and needed a comfortable place to rest his joints.

He grinned at the old man, who sat at the desk with his fingers laced and his head bent. "Good morning, Grandfather. It's a good thing you caught me this morning. I was planning on jumping into research for the shop. The veil is thin, so it's the perfect time."

Grandfather raised his chin, and Whit's smile faltered at the serious expression on his face.

It wasn't that Grandfather didn't usually wear a serious expression. In fact, most of Whit's family, most winter sorcerers and witches in general, were quite serious as a rule. One needed to tread carefully when worshipping the dark gods and goddesses, when working with the dead and the depth of winter's chill.

Still, Whit had expected a warmer reception, and his grandfather's frown made him a little nervous.

"Have a seat, Whittaker."

Whit flinched at the moniker. *Oh, gods. What did I do?* He lowered himself into the armchair—the leather creaking in protest.

Whit forced himself to hold onto his smile but didn't dare say a word.

"I drafted a new will with Caldwell last night," Grandfather said solemnly.

Whit grasped the stiff arms of the chair as his heart skipped a beat.

"I know you have only ever wanted the house, and you have taken good care of it." Grandfather sighed heavily, and his dark eyes met Whit's. "But I cannot give it to you."

Whit's chest tightened.

"You will get your share of the inheritance like everyone else, but the house will go to Caldwell."

Whit shot to his feet. "Grandfather! That's unfair. Caldwell doesn't know a thing about taking care of a house like this. He's a lawyer, for gods' sakes. You know I would give up every dollar of my inheritance money if I could only have the house."

Grandfather glared at him, and Whit clamped his mouth shut. Then Whit sighed a steadying sigh and continued more calmly, "Why are you doing this? You know how much I love this house. I love it more than anyone else. And I have spent my entire thirty-two years learning how to properly take care of it. I've studied art, architecture, history, restoration, carpentry, everything. Are you really going to give it to Caldwell because he's older?"

Grandfather shook his head. "That's right, Whittaker. You are nearly thirty-three years old, and what do you have to show for it?"

Whit flinched as if he'd been slapped. His face flushed. "What do I have to show for it? A successful business and more skills than I will probably ever need."

"But no family," Grandfather said severely. "No wife. No children. This home has been in our family for generations. You expect me to leave it to a confirmed bachelor? What then? Who will it go to when you die?"

Whit frowned. "Why would that matter? As you said, Caldwell has children. Why wouldn't I just leave it to them? What's the difference if I have it first? Either way, it would go to them."

Grandfather shook his head. "They do not yet appreciate it. They don't love it. I feel they will have to grow up here for them to truly understand it."

While Whit hated his grandfather's logic, he understood what he meant about his cousin's kids. They had absolutely no interest in anything related to the house.

"Grandfather," Whit said reasonably. "I've done everything you've ever asked of me. Are you really going to keep the only thing I've ever wanted from me?"

"It's time to grow up, Whittaker. You don't understand what it means to be a winter sorcerer."

Whit clicked his tongue like a child who'd been

scolded. "Grow up? I've never been called immature in my entire life. Aren't self-reliance and introspection pillars of what it means to be a winter sorcerer? Do I not have both?"

Grandfather stared at Whit for a long moment, then sighed heavily. "All right. I'll make you a deal. I'm going on this cruise today—the one your grandmother had planned for us before she passed. I'll be back before the solstice. If you're married before I get home, I'll give you the house."

"You can't be serious. How is that the adult thing to do? Where am I supposed to find a random stranger who'll agree to marry me in such a short amount of time?"

Grandfather shrugged. "Should I sign the deed over to Caldwell before I leave, then?"

"No! I'll…think of something."

Grandfather stood slowly, his knees popping as he steadied himself on the desk. He held out his hand. "*Marry a witch before the winter solstice, and I'll sign the house over to you.*" He spoke with the intonation of an oath.

Whit clasped the old man's withered hand, their magic swirling together in a binding contract. "*If I don't fulfill your conditions, I'll concede the house to whomever you choose.*"

As Whit exited the room, he left the smile he'd entered with on his grandfather's face, exchanging it for his grandfather's frown.

Chapter Two

Clover's pocket vibrated as her cellphone rang. She knew it was her best friend; Ari was the only one to call her at this time of day, especially when it was so late in the year and the sun was barely up. Hell, she and her parents were only up so early because they'd needed to prepare for an early delivery.

Clover shut the back door of the van and flipped her dumbphone open. "Good morning," she said without looking at the screen.

"Good morning," Ari answered in that sweet voice she always used when greeting her.

"How are you this morning?"

"A little sad to be honest. Another summer is over, and my magic is so weak with the season change that I could barely extend the hot water in my shower this morning even with Rhys there to help me."

Clover frowned as she opened the driver's side door and climbed in. "At least you have Rhys there to help you. I had to seal a good luck charm I've been charging for months on my own yesterday. I still don't know if it'll work. Maybe I waited too long. I probably should have sealed it when it was high summer and my magic was at its height. Then I wouldn't have needed help."

Ari tutted in sympathy. "Do you feel luckier?"

Clover sighed, pressing the speaker button and setting her phone on the center dashboard before starting the van. She looked down at the pendant that hung just above her breasts. She'd painted a three-leaf clover onto the flat side of a cabochon, then painted over it with glow-in-the-dark paint. She couldn't see the glow now that it was daylight—it looked like a simple clover on a plain background—but she knew the specialty paint had worked because it had glowed bright green the night before. She could feel the sun's magic faintly shimmering about the charm— mounting as she'd charged it in the sun over the last few months—but whether it would stick or slowly fade away, she didn't know.

Clover pulled out into the street. It was still early, so there was hardly any traffic. "I guess we'll see if it works or not. I could use a bit of luck."

"Now that you brought it up... I haven't said anything because you didn't seem like you wanted to talk about it. But you've never done a luck spell before—not that I can remember. Are you all right? You've seemed out of sorts for a bit now."

Clover sighed. *Of course, Ari noticed.* She'd tried to keep her feelings of unease to herself. She'd tried to be the same upbeat, carefree Clover she'd always been.

Her parents, her brother, and even her sister hadn't seemed to notice. They treated her the same as always. But her best friend obviously hadn't been fooled.

"I don't know. I'm fine. It's not like there's anything *wrong*. It just feels like something isn't quite right. Does that make sense? Something needs to change. I don't know what, but I'm hoping this good luck spell will shake things up a bit."

"The gods of summer will provide as they always do," Ari said with confidence.

Yeah, as they always do…for everyone else. Clover scolded herself the moment she had the thought. It was much too dark for her. *That's not fair. I have a job and a loving family. Everyone is happy and healthy. So what if I'm just the delivery driver? So what if Erie will inherit the business? It's not like my sister will fire me. So what if I want more? We have food on our table and a roof over our heads.*

"I'm grateful for whatever the gods of summer provide me," Clover said humbly, stopping at a red light.

"Hang in there," Ari encouraged. "Change is one of the only things we can count on in this life after all. So if it's change you want, then you'll certainly get it eventually."

"I know you're right," Clover agreed. But it still felt like things had been the same for so long—not that she'd been unhappy with that until recently.

"You sound like you're in the car. Are you out making deliveries already?"

"Yeah." Clover started again as the light turned green. "Someone's wedding."

Clover could hear Ari's scowl in her voice. "What kind of winter witch bullshit is that? Who gets married on Halloween? What did they order—black roses and funeral lilies?"

Clover chuckled. "You're half right. But I don't think it's the winter witches. It's on our side of the woods, and they never order flowers—at least not from us."

"Ah, so some amagical ordinary playing up the witchy origins of Forest Haven, do you think?"

Clover shrugged. "Who knows? I just make sure the delivery gets there intact and on time."

"Right. So actually, I called to see if you're coming to the farewell-to-summer party out in the woods tonight. You're not on social media, so I thought you might not have heard about it."

Clover hesitated, her shoulder muscles tightening. She didn't feel like partying, and she worried her mood might bring the others down. "Uhh… Isn't it going to be really cold tonight? I heard it might snow."

"You're thinking of it all wrong. You're focusing on the negative. It might be just what you need to reconnect and cheer you up. There will be food and a bonfire. We'll play games and sing songs and give the summer gods a proper send-off. Maybe I'll break out some lingonberry cordial. You *love* lingonberry cordial."

Clover's mouth watered as she thought of her friend's homemade drink. She did love lingonberry cordial, and she wasn't above taking a bribe in cases like this. Clover smiled. "Okay, fine. Text me the details."

Ari squealed with excitement. "It'll be fun, I promise. Oh, and don't forget to wear a costume. Okay?"

Clover groaned. "But it's going to be freezing!"

Ari's chipper tone was unaffected. "Then wear something warm."

Chapter Three

Whit sat at the work table in the back room of his antique shop, carefully polishing the tarnish away from a silver trinket box. The swoops and swirls of the carved filigree flowed into images in his mind—a Christmas present from a loving father to his precious little girl, an heirloom to a favorite niece who'd just lost her beloved aunt, one of the few valuables clutched tightly on a treacherous ocean voyage, and on it went. The images of the many emotional moments that had been imbued into this box. The love, the tears, the eventual abandonment.

Those moments weren't enough to have made the box an anchor object for a ghost; it hadn't been loved quite that much or witnessed something truly horrible. But its long history and its many experiences were enough to give Whit flashes of where it had been and who'd owned it. And, most importantly in his business, how old it was and where it had been created.

This was Whit's job, his life. Every day, he cared for the once-beloved things that were left behind or discarded. These things, this touchable history, were people's lives to him. So much energy went into acquiring and using them that he could see entire lifetimes in their surfaces.

He loved each and every piece in his shop, whether someone had sold it to him directly or he'd found it at an estate or garage sale. Each one was precious to him, and he especially loved finding them a new home with the right people.

He was so absorbed in the images of the box that he didn't hear the bell above the door chime as someone entered the shop.

"Hey!" Alexandre popped his head into the back room a few minutes later.

Whit's heart jumped as he nearly dropped the box. "Jesus!"

Alexandre's dark face brightened as he flashed a smile. "You haven't called me that in a while."

Whit snorted at his friend's joke.

"What are you doing back here?" Alexandre glanced around. "Chatting with the dead? I don't see anyone."

Shaking his head, Whit placed the box on the work table. "Not today."

Alexandre crossed his arms and leaned against the doorframe that led into the shop proper. "You okay? Your phone was off, and you didn't answer when I called out to you."

Whit sighed. "Sorry. I didn't really want to talk to anyone."

Alexandre stared at his friend for a long while. "What happened? I haven't seen you look so serious since your grandmother died. Is your grandfather all right?"

Whit nodded. "Yeah, he's fine. He…he called me down this morning to tell me he's leaving the house to Caldwell."

Alexandre lifted one side of his lip as his nostrils flared in distaste. "You're getting evicted?"

Whit sighed again before continuing, "If I don't get married before the solstice, I guess I am."

"What?" Alexandre's voice rose in surprise. "That's crazy! You're not even seeing anyone… Are you?"

Whit shook his head. He would have to do the math on how long it had been since he'd had a date.

"Why would he make that a requirement to stay in the house?"

Whit shrugged.

"Where are you supposed to find someone to marry before then? Unless…" Alexandre grinned. "Are you going to Vegas? Take me with you."

Whit just stared at his friend. Nothing in the years they'd known each other should ever have made Alexandre think Vegas was a place Whit would go. "No. And in any case, I need a witch. He was specific about that."

Alexandre raised one eyebrow dramatically. "You think you're going to convince a winter witch to marry you on the fly? That's impossible. Those women are way too serious to do something like that." He groaned suddenly. "You're not thinking about calling Faustina, are you? Don't *tell* me you're getting back with her. Do I need to remind you how much she messed you up? I'll lock you in a basement and feed you under the door until New Year's if that's what you're planning."

Whit hadn't thought about Faustina in a while. As far as he'd last heard, his ex-girlfriend had gone to visit extended family in Europe. He'd never been as ambitious as she'd hoped. She wanted that high life, and the fact that he didn't become a doctor or lawyer or politician disappointed her to no end. But despite everything she'd put him through, he'd been absolutely decimated when she'd left him.

Whit shook his head. "Not if she was the last woman on earth." He needed a woman quickly, but he didn't need one like her. The hopelessness of his situation crashed down on him again. How could he even get to know someone well enough to ask her to marry him before his deadline?

Alexandre sighed in relief. "Thank the winter gods! So…are you still going to your family's ritual tonight?"

"I don't know. My mom will be mad at me if I don't, but I'm just not in the mood." Whit tilted his head as he looked at Alexandre's expression. "Why…?"

Alexandre's eyes gleamed with mischief. "I don't have to visit my family for Fèt Gede until tomorrow…"

Whit knew that look in Alexandre's eyes too well.

It had gotten him into more than his share of trouble over the years.

"Okay…"

Alexandre grinned. "So I thought you might like to go to a party."

"Ugh, a Halloween party? I don't have the patience for ordinaries tonight."

Alexandre raised a finger and wagged it. "Not a Halloween party. The summer sorcerers are celebrating the end of summer. I heard they got a campsite in Forest Haven woods."

Normally, Whit would have avoided such an outing at all costs. Even with his magic on the rise and the summer sorcerers' magic waning, even with him having the advantage, it wasn't worth the potential fallout if they were caught.

The hostility between the two factions had been going on for centuries. They likely never would have come together at all had it not been for the mutual threat of puritan witch trials—not that their treaty was entirely peaceful or long lasting. The animosity between the two factions had cooled to a rivalry rather than a proper war in modern times. Though every now and then, things went too far, and someone really got hurt.

But the thought of going home that night and being surrounded by people he wasn't particularly happy with at the moment made him reconsider his standard rejection.

Sensing his hesitation, Alexandre doubled down. "We don't have to do anything big. Even just showing up is prank enough for me. They'll never know we were there. You know they're going to have tons of food and drink. A good party is a good party. You won't have to go to the ritual, and you won't be sitting around moping."

"I'm not moping," Whit grumbled.

Alexandre raised an eyebrow, clearly unconvinced.

"They'll recognize us as winter sorcerers. They'll at least know they don't know us."

Alexandre lifted his chin with pride. Then reaching behind him outside the door, he held up two masks. "I got you."

He handed Whit a silver masquerade-style mask. It covered only the nose and above and had the ears and spiral horns of a ram; the surface featured etched floral designs.

Alexandre nudged Whit with his eyes.

Finally, Whit gave him a small smile. "All right. Who can say no to free food?"

Chapter Four

Clover straightened the cloak over the dress she'd borrowed from her mother. It had been made for the founders' day play a few years ago. It was a little scratchier than what she was used to, being made of wool, but it was warm, especially with the petticoats underneath.

She'd planned to pull her long hair up and put a cap over it as her mother had done for the play, but she figured it would be warmer if she left it down and simply covered it with a kerchief.

Clover was plunged into darkness as she stepped out of the parking lot lights and onto the path through the woods to the campsite. She could distantly hear the sounds of merrymaking, but she couldn't see the bonfire she knew would be burning.

The good luck charm, still hanging around her neck, glowed brightly in the night though not enough to see by.

Pulling her phone from her apron pocket, Clover

flipped it open and found the flashlight icon. The LED light illuminated the mulched path before her, and she strode on with confidence.

The nocturnal creatures were quiet this evening, and the only sounds were the wind rattling what was left of the dry autumn leaves hanging from the branches above and the distant murmur of laughter.

Clover shivered. She never much liked the night, especially at this time of year when the days were getting shorter and each dawn felt like a miracle. Too much was hidden from sight; it felt cold and dangerous. She knew she wasn't alone in that feeling; many summer sorcerers and witches felt the same.

She gathered her skirts in her free hand and quickened her pace. A few minutes later, she finally saw the warm flicker of the fire surrounded by a circle of tents. Ari hadn't said whose party it was, not that it much mattered. It was always an open invitation to all summer sorcerers and witches for things like this.

As she approached the fire's glow, she could feel the dimming magic of the sorcerers and witches around her. It was there, no mistaking it, but it was sleepy—a faint hum to what it had been over the last few months.

There were probably fifty people there from what Clover could see—talking and laughing, eating and drinking—in the area around the campsite. She scanned the costumed figures for Ari.

"Clover!" Ari cheered, hopping up from her seat on Rhys's lap. She flitted over to Clover, the bells hanging from her lace fairy wings tinkling as she walked. Her short golden hair shined in the firelight, as did her summer tan, which had yet to fade.

Embracing her best friend, Clover relaxed as warmth spread through her.

Ari pulled back, grinning at her. "You're glad you came, right? I can already tell. Come sit by me."

After taking Clover's hand, Ari led her back to where Rhys sat. Rhys nodded and waved in greeting, which Clover returned.

"Babe, would you get Clover a drink, please? I brought that lingonberry cordial just for her."

"I see how it is," Rhys grumbled. "Your wife is here, so I'm thrown to the wolves."

The women chuckled at the long-standing joke.

"Love you, babe!" Ari called loudly after him as he headed over to a picnic table bursting with food— even the benches had platters on them.

"So how was your day? Did you—" Ari started.

"Babe!" Rhys interrupted. "Which one is it?"

"It's right there. The one labeled lingonberry cordial."

"I don't see it."

Ari sighed heavily. "Ugh, I'll be right back."

Clover snorted, quirking a smile at the couple's dynamic. It had been a while since Clover had been in a relationship, but she'd never found anything like what Ari and Rhys had. She could never quite mesh with the men she'd tried dating—sorcerer or ordinary.

Clover settled herself onto a log near the fire, glancing around to see who else she might know. She recognized a few faces from open rituals and dipped her head at them if they made eye contact. But many of the people there looked closer to her brother Llew's age, which was probably why they seemed only vaguely familiar.

As she nodded to the youngest daughter of the potter family who made the vases they used in the flower shop, someone sat down beside her.

Clover jumped, surprised at the arm suddenly pressed against hers. Her head turned to see the slicked back hair and high-collared cloak of a Dracula costume.

"I vaunt to suck your blud," Rune said in the worst impression Clover had ever heard. Then he flashed a set of plastic vampire fangs at her with a hiss.

Clover's stomach rolled. *I wouldn't have come if I'd known he was going to be here.*

Rune laughed and removed his false teeth, smiling that predatory smile he always seemed to wear. She couldn't believe she'd ever given him a chance; even one date was too good for him.

"Hey, Clover, how have you been? I haven't seen you in a while. If I didn't know better, I'd say you were avoiding me." He smirked as if he knew that wasn't possibly the case.

You'd be right.

The sense of peace and belonging Clover had felt upon arrival dissipated. "Hello, Rune," she said flatly.

He kept going as if she were happy to see him. "Wow, that's a great costume."

Clover cringed as his green eyes flashed with lust. She didn't want to know what he was imagining while his gaze traveled over her.

"What's that?" he asked, reaching toward the three-leaf clover charm glowing at her chest.

She flinched away from him, jumping to her feet. Sighing in relief as Ari and Rhys headed back toward her, Clover stepped away from Rune without another word.

Chapter Five

Whit stood near the picnic table with all the food, watching the summer witches and sorcerers mingle amongst themselves. They wore a variety of costumes—everything from grotesque zombies to the good witch of the north.

"Dude, this party sucks," Alexandre whispered beside him before shoving half a piece of pumpkin bread into his mouth.

Whit shrugged. He'd never crashed a summer party before, but he took Alexandre's word for it. There were a few tents around the central fire, and the picnic table had good food. But the summer sorcerers and witches mostly just stood around talking.

As it was, it was pretty close to a winter party in atmosphere. Although, winter sorcerers and witches tended to celebrate with family and close friends only, unlike the summer faction who invited anyone and everyone. A typical winter party was a dinner with maybe some games afterward. Charades was as boisterous as the winter faction got.

"At least they know how to cook. Oooo, pie!" Alexandre turned his attention back to the food table.

Whit snorted at his friend. Even though the party was a bust according to Alexandre, he was glad he'd come. Well, he was glad he wasn't with his family or sitting alone in his shop, anyway.

"I vaunt to suck your blud," a man in a cheap Dracula costume pronounced to the woman beside him not far from where Whit stood.

Whit watched as she shrank away from him, clearly uncomfortable with his attention. She jumped up from her seat a few moments later and started walking toward Whit. With the fire behind her, he couldn't see her face. She was a silhouette, her long hair fluttering in her wake.

Whit took a sip of his hard apple cider, turning toward Alexandre as he returned.

Alexandre looked down at the cupcake in his hand, then back up at Whit. "Did you want one?"

Whit shook his head. "No, thanks." He'd eaten more than enough already. He'd have to get up early to run for a month straight to counter what he'd eaten tonight.

Once again, he marveled at Alexandre's stamina when it came to food. *Where does he put it all?* And the fact that the man was still as skinny as he'd been as a teenager was just annoying. Whit's only solace was that Alexandre was a foot shorter than him.

The sound of a tambourine jangling sliced through the night, and everyone turned in that direction. It came from a man in a chef's hat, a fake mustache, and a bow tie who stood on a stump with the tambourine raised high.

Whit tilted his head. *Is he dressed as a Muppet?*

"All right, everyone. It's time for us to say goodbye to summer. Let's make a circle around the fire," the man dressed as the Swedish Chef instructed. "We'll raise our energy by singing, but feel free to dance as well."

He jangled his tambourine again, then hopped down from his stump.

Whit glanced at Alexandre, who shrugged by way of consent.

As they were told, the summer sorcerers and witches formed a large circle around the fire. There were enough of them that, even standing close together, there was room for dancers in the middle.

The Swedish Chef started out the first round, and the others picked up the song a few words in.

> *"Hail ye gods of summer,*
> *Mother and Father to those gathered here.*
> *Hail ye gods of summer,*
> *Thank you for another fruitful year.*
>
> *"Goodbye gods of summer.*
> *Your gifts were bountiful and sweet*
> *Goodbye gods of summer.*
> *Until at next we meet."*

The song repeated over and over—raising in strength and volume as the summer sorcerers and witches combined their voices—and a cone of magic surrounded the fire.

A woman with short golden hair, her fairy wings chiming as their bells jingled, grabbed the hands of a woman near where Whit stood—the one who'd earned Dracula's unwanted attention. The woman needed little encouragement as she followed the fairy into the circle to dance.

She wore a historical-style dress—late seventeenth century from what Whit could tell—under a dark cloak. She smiled, laughing as she twirled, swaying her hips to the song of farewell. Her long hair, flaming in the firelight, fluttered and swirled around her as she and the fairy danced.

A glow at her chest winked at Whit like a green firefly as he watched her twirling motions. His eyes lost focus.

Finally, the song reached its pinnacle and stopped. The magic zipped all around the circle, but the only sound was the soft crackle of the fire and the breaths of the summer sorcerers and witches around him.

Quietly, the dancers stepped back into the circle, the woman in the cloak slipping in beside Whit.

The Swedish Chef stepped into the center of the circle near the fire. "Our ritual will be short tonight. I know you all want to get back to the party. So a quick prayer to whatever gods you worship, and we'll be on our way."

Silent understanding answered him.

"Tonight, we bid farewell to summer. It's a sad time for all of us. Another year is gone, and we face the cold darkness ahead. But remember, when your magic is low and you shiver from the New England wind, the light will return. The sun will get warm, the leaves will grow back, and our magic will get stronger. For now, it's a time of rest. So thank your deities, whomever they may be, for the bounties they have given you. Shout their names to the skies so they may know you still worship them even when they're at their weakest."

Shouts came from all around the circle in a mingling of voices. "Apollo! Freyr! Demeter! Lugh! Mercury! Ra!"

"Brighid!" the woman beside Whit called.

Whit didn't say anything and neither did Alexandre on his other side.

"Farewell ye gods and goddesses of summer! We will keep our fires burning to strengthen your return," the Swedish Chef proclaimed.

With a sudden gust of wintry wind, the warm campfire was blown out, and everyone was plunged into darkness.

Gasps and murmurs traveled through the group. "A bad omen," someone whispered near Whit over the sound of Alexandre's snickering.

Of course, Alexandre wasn't about to let an opening like that go.

"Don't worry," the Swedish Chef said. "Even the darkest night comes to an end. Take the hands of those on either side of you."

Whit took Alexandre's hand and squeezed it in warning. *That's enough. Even if their magic is waning, they could mess us up with this many of them here. We aren't at full power either.*

Whit stiffened as a jolt ran through him when the woman on his other side slipped her hand into his.

Her hand was small and thin but warm.

"*Fear not the darkness, fear not the night,*" the Swedish Chef said.

Everyone else, including Whit and Alexandre repeated his words.

"*We spark this fire with inner light.*"

As everyone repeated the spell, the magic of the summer witch holding Whit's hand flowed into him. It was heady and intoxicating like a humid rain in a garden bursting with violets, lilies, orchids, and gardenias. The sweetness of honey and plum were mellowed by the depth of amber and vanilla. Whit's head spun as her magic filled him with giddiness.

He turned his head toward her while the fire sparked back to life, reawakened by the collective magic.

Her face tilted up at him, and their eyes met in the dim flicker of the fire's glow.

Chapter Six

Clover stared beyond the horned mask of the man beside her, her hand still in his as their gazes met. He was tall and wore a sleek black suit. In the dim light of the fire, she couldn't see the color of his hair or eyes, but she saw the strong line of his jaw and the plump curve of his lower lip. His facial hair was short, maybe a week's stubble—certainly not long enough to pull off the goat mask he was wearing.

Did I imagine it? For a moment during the conjuring of fire spell, she'd exchanged magic with him, and it had felt like nothing she'd ever experienced before.

Small snowflakes drifted lazily down from the sky, sparse but unmistakable.

She squinted, trying to see past the mask in the firelight. But she was already sure she didn't know him. At the very least, they'd never done magic together.

"Now that the ritual is over"—Brandr, who was dressed as the Swedish Chef from *The Muppets*, grinned—"we're going to play satyrs and nymphs."

Clover's fixation on the sorcerer beside her broke with this announcement, and she pulled her hand from his, her face heating at having held it for so long.

Her eyes found Rune across the circle, and she marked his progress toward her. "Hey, I think I'm going to head out," Clover told Ari, who stood next to her.

Ari frowned even as Rhys wrapped his arms around her from behind, nuzzling the back of her neck in anticipation of the game. "Aww, already?"

Clover nodded. She didn't want to be anywhere near Rune during a game like satyrs and nymphs, though she was a little disappointed to let him ruin what could have been a nice party. "Yeah, I was up early anyway. Call me tomorrow, okay?"

Ari agreed.

Lifting her hand in farewell, Clover gave her friends a little wave, then turned to head back to the van. She could feel the excitement in the atmosphere growing as the summer witches giggled, some of them already running into the woods with happy squeals—completely ignoring the freezing temperature and drifting snowflakes.

Clover reached into her apron pocket for her phone as she stepped out of the circle of light the fire provided.

"Clover?"

She flinched at hearing Rune's voice call out for

her. Shoving her phone back into her apron, she decided walking carefully along the dark path was preferable to being easily found by Rune.

Her heart pounded in her ears—as loud as the shrieks of mirth echoing into the night. She could feel the mulch beneath her shoes, and she knew as long as she stayed on the path, she would reach the parking lot. Concentrating on her footing, Clover slowly made her way.

"Clooooveeeeer," Rune called cheerfully after her, farther than before.

She clicked her tongue. *Dude can't take a hint.* Shaking her head, she sighed and glanced up at the sky. Now that she was deeper in the woods, well away from the light of the campfire and not yet close to the parking lot, she saw the night wasn't so dark after all. The moon was two days past full, and it shone through the trees, their branches crisscrossing over its surface like veins.

She still didn't like the night, but she understood its allure. There was something so mysterious, so magical, about the moon's distant glow. It filled her with wonder as well as fear. It was indirect, providing no warmth, and changeable. Did its shadows hold truths or simply illusions? It was beautiful. It was dangerous.

A stick cracked nearby, and Clover jumped.

"Clover? Is that you?" Rune asked, much closer than Clover expected.

How did he find me? Glancing around herself, her eyes dropped to the green glow at her chest. She cursed internally, clutching her pendant in her fist to cover it.

Out of the night, a hand gripped her wrist, snatching her off the path.

She gasped and filled her lungs to scream. Her eyes whirled around to her attacker.

"Shhh," the sorcerer in the horned mask hushed, putting his finger to his lips.

"Hey! Where'd you go?" Rune said, not far away now, his light flashing as he searched.

Clover's heart ran wildly as her body pressed against the solid warmth of the masked sorcerer. She lifted her chin to gaze up at him, trying to see more than just his outline in the moonlight.

Releasing her wrist, he laced their fingers. "*Shadows surround us, hide us from sight / let us be one with the darkest night,*" he whispered.

Magic swirled around them, flowing between them in an alluring but unfamiliar exchange. Clover shivered as his magic poured into her. It was sharp and refreshing like balsam fir and cedar wood and had the sweetness of candied apples and winter berries and the spice of cinnamon and clove, tickling her stomach like sparkling wine.

"As long as you don't make too much noise," he murmured to her in an intimate low voice, "he'll walk right by us without seeing us."

Clover strained her eyes to see the masked sorcerer. She was sure now. She'd never felt anything like his magic. *Who is he?* It was strong and serious with just a hint of mischief.

"Clover?" Rune's voice was uncertain now, and it came from not five feet away.

Clover hunched her shoulders, curling into the sorcerer who still held her hand. She strained her ears, closing her eyes as if that would hide her from Rune's view more effectively.

Rune groaned in frustration before retreating back to camp, his light dimming with distance.

Releasing the breath she'd been holding, Clover pulled back a little from the shelter of her savior's arms though she didn't yet release his hand. "Thank you," she said in a hushed voice, still trying to see something of him in the darkness.

"You're welcome, Clover." His voice caressed her name.

She smiled as her stomach fluttered. "I'm at a disadvantage. You know my name, but I don't know yours. Who are you?"

He hesitated.

Clover huffed a laugh through her nose. "You want to stay a mystery, huh? Well then, I'll just think of you as a merry elf out for a stroll while the veil is thin. Shall I? That way, I can excuse you not sharing your name. What would you have in trade for your assistance? I'd hate to be in debt to one of the Fair Folk."

Silence answered her question. But a moment later, he unlaced their fingers and brushed his thumb over her cheek, wiping away a stray snowflake.

Her breath caught at the gentle stroke. There was something so tantalizing about not being able to see him properly. It made his every move, his feathery touch, his soft breath, all the more vivid.

She tilted her face upward, wetting her lips. "Would a kiss suffice, my merry elf?"

She could hear his smile. "A kiss is far more precious. That is not a fair exchange."

A tingle ran over her skin. "I'm fine with that," she murmured. Clover waited, her breath slow but shallow, as anticipation mounted within her. For a shadow, he was solid and warm. And though the cold night blew its promises of winter around them, she felt flushed and feverish.

His soft lips met hers in the darkness, fleeting and delicate as the memory of a dream.

Clover's heart leapt, and her chest swelled as she tasted his sparkling magic—his essence as a sorcerer—on her lips.

He was the dancing fire on a snowy night. He was the twinkle lights shining off the silver and blue baubles on their solstice evergreen. He was the creamy melted marshmallow in a steamy hot chocolate.

And as Clover languidly opened her eyes, he was gone.

Chapter Seven

Whit pulled his cloaking spell with him when he stepped away from Clover, watching as she slowly opened her eyes to find him gone.

He could see her clearly by the moonlight as she blinked rapidly into the darkness in search of him.

His heart still raced in his chest. He'd seen her slip into the night after the ritual, hadn't taken his eyes off her for a moment. It was obvious she didn't want to deal with couldn't-take-a-hint Dracula. The green glow at her chest had been easy to follow through the night. He'd told himself he only wanted to see her safely to her car; it was the decent thing to do.

He hadn't planned on casting a spell with her, sharing his magic with her. It was far too risky to do so. He wasn't supposed to be there. And who knew how the summer faction would retaliate if they found out two winter sorcerers had crashed their party?

He'd done it without thinking, pulled her close and held her in the shelter of his arms—of his magic.

Never in a million years did he expect to be offered a kiss for his trouble.

He shouldn't have taken that offer. But in that moment, with the moonlight shining in her eyes, the warmth of her magic swirling around him, and her face tilted upward expectantly, he couldn't stop himself.

She was the cool ocean breeze that broke the summer heat. She was a pink and orange sunset that painted the dusky sky. She was the sweetness of cherry ice cream with chocolate chips.

He'd felt summer magic before; of course, he had. But that magic had been different, oppressive like desert heat or gusty and loud like a hurricane.

Never had he felt summer magic be so sweet, never had it been shared in good will. He watched as Clover smiled softly before turning back to the path.

She pulled out a light and started toward the parking lot.

As he trailed after her, careful to make as little noise as possible to keep his spell in place, he wondered if all summer magic was like hers.

He could still feel the echo of her lips on his, still hear her soft intake of breath as his face neared hers. His chest swelled with the memory of her curling into his protective embrace. He shook his head. He couldn't believe that all summer witches were like her. It wasn't possible. Besides, every witch's magic wasn't quite the same. Everyone had their own special signature.

Still, he was glad for one thing. At least he had the wherewithal to keep his identity to himself. With a name like Crawford, and especially because it was shared by his antique shop on the north side of Forest Haven, it wouldn't be hard for her to figure out he was a winter sorcerer.

A few steps ahead of him, Clover's foot struck on a root. She stumbled, and Whit flinched—reaching out to her by reflex. But she caught herself before she fell.

Whit froze, his hand uselessly extended toward her, and the absurdity of the situation hit him. Here he was, under a cloaking spell, following a summer witch he'd just met—and just kissed—to her car. Why? To make sure she wasn't accosted by unwanted attentions, sure. But she felt safe enough that cheap Dracula wasn't following her to turn on her light. So why?

He frowned. There was no accounting for it. Perhaps because he'd never felt magic quite like hers, he wanted to analyze the feeling by being near her a little longer. Perhaps he was just fascinated by a woman who would kiss a complete stranger in the dead of night. She'd clearly not wanted anything to do with cheap Dracula. So why would she offer a kiss to him?

Her reaction to him had been a surprise, but his reaction to her was infinitely more so.

Maybe she had history with dollar-store Dracula, and that was why she was avoiding him. Maybe it wasn't uncommon for her to kiss strangers.

In any case, it was certainly uncommon for him to kiss someone he'd just met.

In truth, he wasn't much different from most winter sorcerers. He valued a well-laid plan, organization, and quiet contemplation. He didn't mind solitude, and he was predictable if nothing else. There were the occasional pranksters—trickster gods were usually winter gods after all—within the winter community, Alexandre for instance, but most were solemn and hardworking like Whit.

He wasn't one to run away with his emotions. He had goals and benchmarks to meet those goals. He'd studied hard, worked diligently, and built his business from scratch.

Sure, he'd had a few relationships along the way— mostly just a handful of dates other than his stint with Faustina. But it didn't take him long to figure out that those emotional entanglements were more trouble than they were worth. Ordinaries were too much drama; he couldn't even talk magic with them. And as for winter witches, well, what he wanted from his life just didn't match up with what they wanted, so they simply parted ways.

Did women—and a few men for that matter— proposition him on occasion? Yes, but he never took them up on it.

So for him to follow this summer witch through the woods, for him to kiss her, was so out of character that he hardly recognized himself.

As they approached the parking lot, the streetlights provided enough light for Clover to see. She shut her phone and stuffed it into her apron pocket. Whit tilted his head at seeing that it was a basic flip-phone. He didn't know they still made those.

Staying in the shadows beyond the lamplight, Whit watched as Clover took out her keys and approached a white van with the words "Bronwen Floral and Gifts" decaled on the side along with a telephone number.

A loud "Caw!" shrieked into the night. Clover jumped, dropping her keys as a result. She retrieved them from the pavement and raised her head to find the source.

On top of her van stood a crow—its beady eyes glinting in the overhead light. She stared at the crow, and the crow stared at her.

Clover spoke to the bird, and Whit strained to hear her words, but he couldn't make them out.

After another tense moment, the crow let out another call, then took flight.

With a wide smile, Clover climbed into the van and closed the door. Whit shed his spell and pulled out his phone to text Alexandre that he was in the parking lot and ready to leave.

He wondered if Alexandre was still raiding the food table or if he was playing some joke on the summer faction as they romped through the woods. He hadn't bothered to look once Clover had caught his eye.

Chapter Eight

Clover sat on the window seat with her elbows resting on her knees, staring out her attic bedroom window at the trees in her backyard. It was still dark outside, daylight savings having yet to take effect, even though it was already time to be up and about.

The temperatures had dropped overnight. She could tell by how hard the furnace was working, her vents rattling as they pumped warm air into her room. The bundled herbs hanging from the exposed crossbeams of the ceiling swayed in response to the circulation.

The slanted walls were made to look squarer by bookshelves lining the width of the room. Jars packed with dried herbs and blended teas neatly labeled took up more space than actual books on the shelves. At the center of the room was a round table with two chairs, currently holding an open paper bag and a bowl.

The scent of dill hung in the warm air. Clover had planned to harvest her dill seed, the drying flower heads waiting in the paper bag. But something on this cold November morning made her restless. It was a mindless activity, pinching the dill seeds into the bowl, but she couldn't seem to force herself to do it.

Why staring unfocusedly out the window should be any better, she didn't know. A sense of expectation fluttered in her chest and tingled across her skin.

Most of the trees outside were already naked, but one blazing maple still shone brightly amongst its fellows—speckles of last night's snow glittering on its colorful leaves.

The bright orange reminded her of the bonfire from the night before and the way it had shone off the silver mask of the sorcerer she'd met.

She smiled to herself as she thought of him again, not that he'd been far from her thoughts since she'd first felt his magic travel through her.

What a deliciously summer encounter. Just the way to end the season.

Their exchange had been beautiful in its fleetingness. No name, no expectations, just a gentle kiss with no farewell spoken.

The fact that her unnamed sorcerer hadn't even said goodbye left the door open in her mind. He was so mysterious, swooping in at her moment of need and gone without a word. But even though he'd left her in the dark, she hadn't felt alone. On her way back to the car, she got the feeling she was still safe, safe enough to turn on her phone flashlight anyway.

And then to find a crow waiting for her. Well, it

was almost too good to be true. Something was changing. She could feel it. She always interpreted crows as a message of change.

She wondered who the sorcerer was and if they would meet again. Her heart leapt with hope and expectation. It was the feeling of the unknown, a joyous summery feeling. That small hope one feels when they plant a seed in rich soil and wait to see if it sprouts.

If for nothing else, Clover was grateful to her masked sorcerer for giving her this feeling. Was he the herald for the change that was happening or its cause?

A shout came from downstairs. "Clover!" Her mother's voice was high with panic.

Clover's heart jumped into her throat as she raced toward the stairs leading down from her attic bedroom to the second floor.

She flung open the door.

No one was there, but she could hear a commotion coming from downstairs.

Her slippered feet thumped heavily as she ran down the stairs and rounded the corner to find mayhem in her living room and chanting filling the space.

Llew sat on the couch, his teeth chattering despite the heap of blankets wrapped around him. Mom knelt before him, her hands hovering over his exposed foot. Even from the doorway, Clover could see there was something wrong with her brother's foot. His baby toe was nearly black.

Standing behind Mom, Dad rested a hand on one

of her shoulders, and holding his free hand was Ash, then Royer—two of Llew's longtime friends.

Clover had no idea what had happened, but she knew what to do. Stepping forward, she broke into the circle, taking Royer's hand and resting her other on her mother's shoulder to complete the circle. Then she joined their chant.

"Willow, rowan, elder, and ash,
Summer winds blow and waters lash.
Primal forces of sun and sea,
Bless and heal him, we ask of thee."

The magic of summer swirled through the circle. Clover was filled with the sounds of lazy summer days, when cicadas chirped and the gentle wind blew the full trees. She could feel the sunbaked earth under her feet, and her eyes swam as if distorted by hazy heat.

This was the summer magic she knew well, and as it entered her, she pushed it into her mom to aid in her work.

After a few minutes, Llew stopped shivering, and Mom sighed in relief.

"It's gone," Mom announced.

There was a collective easing of tension, and the inevitable exhaustion that followed. Healing someone was always a difficult job, but it was far worse when their magic was waning.

Mom glared at Ash and Royer and pointed to the couch. Clover hovered nearby to find out what had happened.

The three grown men sat on the couch with their heads hung low, looking very much like children who'd broken a window with a baseball.

"Explain yourselves," Mom demanded with her hands on her hips. Dad stood over her shoulder, silent and serious.

"It was just a joke," Llew said, his voice tired and quiet.

Mom squinted at him. "What was? What did you do?"

Royer, a very tall man with blond hair and a lampshade mustache, lifted his blue eyes guiltily. "I mean, if you really think about it, we were doing something nice."

Ash nodded, his sloppy topknot bouncing as he did so. "That's right. Those snowman fuckers are in the wrong here."

Mom's voice was quiet, which made it that much more terrifying. "Someone better tell me what you did, or so help me—"

"We went to a graveyard on the north side and made flowers grow on some of the graves," Royer said in a rush.

"You made flowers grow?" Mom asked flatly.

The men nodded.

"On Halloween? When there's snow on the ground?"

They didn't respond.

"In a graveyard frequented by winter witches?" she raged.

They flinched—even Clover jumped, and she wasn't getting yelled at.

"What would make you do something so—you are grown ass men! Why—?" Mom was so angry she couldn't even finish a sentence.

Dad rested his hand on her shoulder. "Then what happened?" he pressed, calmer but not gentler.

Ash sighed. "I guess we should've assumed those corpse lovers would be hanging out in graveyards after dark. They caught us and blasted us with something."

"Must've been a frostbite spell," Llew said. "I got hit, and I felt really cold. Then I started losing feeling in my foot."

"I should have let you lose the whole damn thing!" Mom snapped. "You're going to sit there and tell me you didn't think the winter faction would be in a graveyard last night? When you know very well that's when they honor their dead."

Dad shook his head in that look of disappointment that was somehow worse than Mom's ire.

Clover sighed heavily. *Some things will never change. This is why the feud will never die.* She turned on her heel to head into the kitchen for breakfast.

Chapter Nine

Whit stared at the cheery brightness of the glass of orange juice on the large dining table. The sun was just starting to come up outside the east-facing windows of the dining room, and it seemed to dye everything in happy morning colors.

The year had turned to the dark half, his magic was on the rise, and he could feel it would be unseasonably cold today. But he wasn't thinking about that this morning.

He'd left the party the night before with the resolve to keep his encounter with the summer witch in perspective. It was interesting and fleeting. And it was over when he'd stepped away from her. He had a good life—an easy, fulfilling, mostly calm, steady life.

That's what he'd told himself. That's what he knew to be true. That's what his brain wanted for his life.

But when he'd slipped into sleep the night before, she'd invaded his dreams. They were filled with hope and a happiness he didn't know he could feel. Bright summer days, cozy winter nights. Even now, he could still hear her voice as if she were humming in the other room—her clear sweet tones playing over and over in his head as she sang the fire back to life.

He couldn't remember ever being afraid of ghosts. As most winter sorcerers, he'd learned to coexist with them at an early age. But finally, he understood what it meant to be haunted.

And unreasonably—unthinkably—he'd awoken that morning with an idea. If a summer witch was okay with kissing a stranger, would she be okay with marrying one?

It was a crazy idea—absolutely absurd—but he hadn't thought about anything else since he'd opened his eyes that morning.

It was an obsessive little thought he couldn't seem to shake, that no logic could shoot down.

Oh, he'd asked himself real questions, brought up real concerns. They didn't know each other at all. What if they hated each other in the light of day? She was a summer witch, and her upbringing, her way of thinking—her magic—would be totally foreign to him. His friends and family would have a hard time accepting a summer witch into the fold, and who knew how seriously hers hated the winter faction. And yet…the outrageous pact he'd made with his grandfather—the pact he'd agreed to only to delay the inevitable—hadn't specified a winter witch…

Had he wondered whether the rest of his life was worth a house, a house he loved, sure, but still just a house? Of course, the thought had crossed his mind.

But for some reason, it didn't seem to hold much sway.

In any case, he didn't want a *real* marriage—no matter what had happened in his dream. He could approach this with logic and reason. He imagined the whole thing would be like having a roommate. He'd have his life, and she'd have hers.

What's the harm in asking her? He considered the idea as he drained his orange juice and picked up his empty oatmeal bowl.

He moved through the dining room to the kitchen. The house was much too quiet for this time of day, his grandfather usually up and puttering around. But he'd left earlier that morning. Whit had found a note on the refrigerator with his grandfather's goodbyes. Grandfather had an early flight to get down to Florida and didn't want to wake Whit. He'd promised to send a postcard and said he hoped to meet his new granddaughter-in-law when he returned.

Sticking the glass and bowl into the dishwasher, Whit knew what he had to do next.

Heading out into the hall, he started up the wide, polished staircase. Then he turned left into his bedroom, where he passed his bed and settled into an armchair before pulling his computer from the side table onto this lap.

It didn't take him long to find the website of Bronwen Floral and Gifts. It was pretty standard and neatly organized.

He clicked on the "About Us" page and was greeted with a photo of his summer witch and her family. There was a short description underneath talking about how it was a family business and when they'd opened.

He gazed at her as she smiled from the screen, her brother's arm around her and her sister's head on her shoulder as they stood in front of their parents, who sat on the counter behind them.

Though none of them looked quite the same, they all looked related. The siblings all had the same cheeks—their mother's cheeks—and their father's nose, which was small and slightly upturned. Clover's hair was a dark auburn, which framed her fair face—making her skin appear that much lighter. Her sister's hair was blonde, while her brother's was a bronzy red. Her mother's was a strawberry blonde streaked with grey, and her father's was a muted white. Her brother was bigger than her, muscular but lean. Even her sister had a few inches on her.

They must be a tall family. From the night before, he remembered that she seemed of average height.

Her eyes, a cornflower blue, sparkled as if her sister had just said something to make her laugh.

He clicked on a social media icon at the bottom of the page to see more pictures.

Their social media page was mostly a series of posts about sales and specials or pictures of flower arrangements. He scrolled for a while before finding a picture of Clover. She held a vase full of pink roses as she lifted her hand to the brim of her baseball cap—embroidered with the name of the shop.

The caption read: Want to send something special

to someone even more special? Our resident delivery girl has you covered.

Even better.

Clicking back to the shop's website, a banner flashed across the top of the screen. "Order in the next four hours for same-day delivery."

Whit's mouth quirked in a smile.

Scrolling the page, he clicked on the first flower bouquet that caught his eye—something yellow. The label said they were camellias. He didn't really care what they were as long as they brought her to his shop.

A sense of satisfaction flooded Whit as he completed his purchase and closed his computer. Everything would be settled by the end of the day. He would have his answer one way or the other.

Chapter Ten

Clover was just entering the shop to grab another package to bring to the van for her morning deliveries when her sister came in for work. Mom was at the counter, and Dad was in the back, cutting flowers for the day's ready-made bouquets.

"Good morning, family," Erie greeted cheerfully.

Everyone returned her salutation.

"How was trick-or-treating?" Mom asked her eldest.

Erie shook her head. "It's not what it used to be when we were young. It seems like everyone is just doing trunk-or-treat now. Hardly anyone on our block was giving out candy. Crane's pillowcase wasn't even a quarter full. She had fun, though."

"What did she go as?" Clover asked.

Erie smiled, pulling out her phone. "Oh, she was so cute. She dressed as a little alien with spring antennae and everything. Look."

Clover glanced at the picture of her niece's green-painted face, all of her baby teeth on display as she grinned. Clover smiled at the image. "Did Antony go with you?"

Erie sighed. "No, my lovely husband was not there for yet another occasion."

"That's not fair, Erie," Mom scolded lightly. "You know how hard he works."

Erie frowned. "I know. I just wish he wasn't missing so much of his daughter's life. She's already in the second grade. If he keeps going like this, he'll miss her whole childhood."

A feeling of unavoidable sadness settled over them.

Erie tried to put on her best I'm-all-right smile as she made her way to where Mom was. "That's why I'm so grateful for my baby sister. How would I ever have any free time if it wasn't for the best aunt in the world watching her very favorite niece on occasion."

Clover snorted. "What do you need?"

Her sister smiled prettily at her. "Would you mind watching Crane tonight? The moms in her class are getting together to plan holiday pageant costumes."

Just when Clover was about to tell her sister that she didn't have plans that evening, their mother jumped in. "I think you should ask Llewellyn to watch her instead."

Erie blinked in surprise, and Clover flinched. It was never a good sign when Mom used their brother's full name.

"Is there a reason I should ask him instead?" Erie inquired.

Mom nodded seriously. "Yes, I think he needs to spend more time with family, and he clearly needs more responsibility. So I'll pick Crane up from school, and then we'll all stay in for the night."

Erie met Clover's eyes with a question, and Clover shrugged and shook her head.

"Well, then," Clover said. "I better get going. I'll see you all later."

Clover gritted her teeth against a blast of cold air that nearly blew her over when she exited the shop and hurried to load the package she carried into the van. Just as she moved to close the back doors, an icy drop landed on her nose.

She looked up into the grey sky overhead to see little flecks of white drifting toward the ground.

Snowing again.

Like other summer witches, Clover didn't like snow. Sure, it was beautiful when she was tucked inside under a warm blanket. But it was a clear sign of winter, a physical reminder that her magic was weak and would be for months to come.

But for the first time in Clover's thirty years, she smiled up at the fluffs of white. For the first time, she saw the promise that the first snow brought.

Closing her eyes, she breathed deep the cold air and tilted her head back to let the sparse flakes land on her face.

She had to admit there was something refreshing about the cold water that melted on her skin the moment it touched her. It was as if the snow was kissing her warm skin before ceasing to exist.

Clover smiled to herself, her heart thumping as she suddenly felt that this snow promised new things for her.

She closed the van doors and climbed into the driver's seat, turning the heater on high to melt away any chill before it got into her bones.

What should I do this weekend?

She still didn't have an answer when Ari called her on her lunch break. She was parked in the lot of a local drive-thru, about to take a second bite of her cheeseburger when her phone rang.

She glanced at the screen and saw it was Ari calling. "Hey, what's up?" she asked as she flipped the phone open and pressed the speaker button.

"Hey, you on break?"

"Yep," Clover confirmed around a mouthful of burger.

"Good. I was just checking to see if you got home all right. I heard Rune was making a pest of himself last night. He didn't bother you, did he?"

"I'm fine."

"I feel like we should have an intervention with him or something. Dude just can't take a hint."

Clover paused with her cheeseburger halfway to her mouth. "I think, next time, I need to be clearer with him. If he can't pick up on it himself, then I just need to tell him to his face to leave me alone."

"That's a good idea."

Clover nodded as she swallowed. "On another

note, I wanted to ask you. Do you know that guy who wore a silver horned mask last night?"

"A horned mask?" Ari went silent for a moment. "I don't remember it."

"He was standing on my other side during the ritual."

Ari hummed in thought. "Was he? Sorry. I guess I didn't notice."

Clover blinked. *Surely, he couldn't* really *be a fae… right?*

As many summer witches did, Clover often encountered the Good Neighbors. She made offerings to them and sometimes even asked for their help. But never had she seen one so clearly and solidly as she'd seen the man from last night. If she ever saw them in solid form, they were usually out of the corner of her eye. She'd certainly never physically touched one and definitely never kissed one.

"Why?" Ari asked. "Did something happen?"

Clover bit her lip, hesitating. "Okay. This is going to sound crazy, but stick with me."

Chapter Eleven

Whit tapped his pen on the notebook in front of him. His shop was silent and deserted, and the rhythmic tapping seemed to ease his tension.

Normally, he would have put on a record for the customers—most people were unsettled by silence. But when he'd put on a Dion record earlier that morning, he found it only made his nervousness worse.

The website had said same-day delivery, but it hadn't said when.

Every time the bell above his door chimed, his heart jumped, and his head snapped in that direction. But, so far, Clover had yet to appear.

The fourth time this scenario played out, he wondered if this wasn't a good idea after all.

This was a crazy plan, a stupid plan. What if she said no? What if she called the cops? For gods' sakes, what if she said yes? Was he really ready to marry someone he'd only met yesterday?

Was he ready to bring a summer witch into his life? Into his home?

By lunch time, he'd convinced himself he wouldn't propose to her when she arrived. That would be too absurd. No, what he would do was he would talk to her, feel her out.

If he thought she wasn't going to freak out, maybe he would tell her he was the man she'd kissed the night before. That was a much better plan. He'd see how she reacted first.

He had two months to try to convince her. He shouldn't just spring something like this on her. But then, did he really want to drag this out? If he was trying to meet his grandfather's conditions, shouldn't he try to find a winter witch in those two months?

He was certain he could ask Alexandre to hook him up. He could even ask his mother if he was desperate. Maybe he'd finally ask out the daughter of what's-her-name that his mother had hinted at a while back.

As he pictured what he would say, it dawned on him that he was going about this all wrong. What if she sensed he was a winter sorcerer and felt threatened? He'd called her into winter territory and was going to spring a marriage proposal on her? It was sort of creepy.

Groaning, he took out his phone and looked up the number to the flower shop.

"Bronwen Floral and Gifts," a cheerful female voice answered.

He swallowed around the lump in his throat. "Um… Hello, I'm sorry. I ordered some flowers earlier today for same-day delivery, and I was wondering if it wasn't too late to cancel."

"You don't want the flowers anymore?" she asked.

He hunched his shoulders. He knew how inconvenient it was for a customer to cancel. "It's not that. It's just…well, I'm not going to be at the delivery address much longer today, and I thought maybe I could just pick them up instead?"

"If you ordered same-day delivery, then they're already on their way. If you'd like, I can call our driver and see how close she is."

"No, that's all right. I'll figure something out."

"Are you sure?"

"Yeah. Don't worry about it."

"All right. Well, thank you for your order, and have a great day!" The woman hung up.

This was a horrible, stupid idea.

And the more he thought about it, the more he agreed with himself. It was too late now. He'd already ordered the flowers, but he would not ask the summer witch to marry him. That would be just too much.

Under the fluorescent lights of his shop with his dreams from the night before fading from memory, he wished he'd had more sense that morning. What was he even going to do with a bouquet of flowers? The winter faction didn't mess with flowers unless it was for a funeral.

He threw his pen down on his notepad in disgust. This was all his grandfather's fault. He shouldn't have let him get inside his head. So what if Caldwell got the house? He'd move into the space above his shop. It was storage at the moment, but there was a bathroom. He could renovate anything else he wanted, maybe put in a kitchenette.

He glanced at the grandfather clock near the door. There wasn't even an hour left before closing time, and he'd neglected most of what he'd wanted to get done that day.

Maybe I should just close early.

The lights inside the glass jewelry case he was sitting behind flickered, and a sudden chill raised goose bumps on his arms.

He froze, recognizing the ghost's presence immediately. "Grandmother?" he asked.

But as his eyes swept the shop, he didn't see even a wisp of her.

He thought about getting the spirit board he kept in the back.

His grandmother hadn't been dead long, and she wouldn't be strong enough to manifest as a full-body apparition, especially without an anchor.

But when he stood from his stool, he heard a whoosh followed by a thump as if he'd knocked something onto the floor behind him.

Glancing back, he knelt down and picked up a tattered deck of tarot cards—the lamination peeling around the edges from longtime use.

It was the deck his grandmother had given him for his tenth birthday. He smiled as he bent to pick them up. She always used to say that anxiety came from the unknown, and that, as winter sorcerers and witches, they had more than enough foresight to avoid it. She'd taught him how to read the cards—his mother favored a pendulum, and he had a talent for scrying. But every so often, when he felt particularly off-balance, he would bring out his tarot deck and pull a few cards.

He slipped the old deck from their torn box—thinking it was about time he got a bag or chest for them. The cards were winkled and hard to handle but oh so familiar.

He shuffled them on the glass case with difficulty. They stuck together, and he wondered if he couldn't get them resurfaced. He'd clearly neglected them for too long and would look into fixing them as soon as he could.

As he continued to mix them, he could practically feel his grandmother hovering over him—her cheek pressed to his head—as she had done when his hands were still too small to properly shuffle the cards.

A shiver went through him again, telling him to stop. "All right, Grandmother. What is it you want me to know?"

Flipping over the top card, his stomach dropped. As much as other sorcerers might fear the death and devil cards, those had never much bothered Whit. But as he stared at the ravaged tower—on fire from a lightning strike as rain pelted its surface and people jumped from its heights in the hopes that gravity would somehow be kinder to them—fear coiled in his gut.

As a man who planned wisely and treaded

carefully, he hated the tower card the most. It was chaos, upheaval, and destruction.

It was supposed to be a needed change, a change that was for the better overall, a change that would make one stronger and wiser and better equipped for the future. At its core, the tower warned that he was on shaky ground, and if he didn't make some real changes soon, the gods of winter might just force the change on him.

Chapter Twelve

Clover sighed in relief as she finally found the address of her last delivery. It was already dusk, and she should have been done for the day.

Her parents had been pleased to get an order from the north side of town. They primarily served the south side, which she knew without the help of GPS. But the winter faction didn't do flowers, and there was a flower shop on the north side for the ordinaries.

Dad thought that this order was a sign they had a leg up on their competition. Maybe the preservation spells they cast on all their flowers to make them last longer were making a difference.

Just this last delivery, and then I'm free for the night. She cheered the end of her work day as she turned off the van and zipped up her thick, down coat.

Her muscles tensed when she opened the door and set her rubber boots onto the still-wet street, hunching her shoulders against the cold. She knew the snow wouldn't last long. It was still early for snow that stayed, and it had already melted from everywhere but the grass. She gritted her teeth, promising herself a hot cup of tea and a game of pirates with Crane and Llew.

She pulled out the bouquet of yellow camellias—smiling down at the flowers. *Someone will be happy to get these.* She wondered if they knew the blooms represented destiny and longing.

As she tucked her clipboard under her arm to close the van doors, she glanced at the side of the two-story building at the very end of a row of connected storefronts. The sign above the door declared the shop Crawford Antiques.

Adopting her usual, friendly smile, she entered the glass door—a bell chiming cheerfully overhead.

For an antique shop, the space was neat and well-organized. Every inch of the walls not taken up by a shelf was covered by paintings or mirrors. There were antique furniture and lamps, dishes and silverware, and more salt and pepper shakers than she thought existed in the world.

Her smile faltered, and she tilted her head. Something about the space seemed familiar, like a song playing in another room. She heard the notes distantly but couldn't hear the melody clearly enough to name it.

There was magic in this place. Not an active spell recently cast, more a buildup of remnant energy.

She could feel it. It tickled her stomach and made her want to reach out with her aura to identify it.

Glancing around the space, her gaze fell on the

clerk who stood behind a glass display case filled with jewelry. He clutched what looked like an old tarot deck in his hand, but his dark brown eyes were fixed on her.

He was not what Clover expected from an antique shop. He looked more like a carpenter—about six feet tall with broad shoulders and toned arms. He had a square face with a strong jaw, and his dark brown hair was styled in a medium quiff. Her wore jeans and a plaid button-down.

Something about his gaze felt familiar although she was sure she'd never been in his shop before.

She glanced down at her clipboard. "Are you Whittaker Crawford?"

His eyes seemed to warm as she spoke his name. "I am," he said smoothly.

His voice… Something about it…except more hushed and intimate.

Clover stared at him uncertainly for a moment.

"These are for you." Clover stepped closer slowly and placed the flowers on the glass case.

The clerk didn't take his eyes off her face, nor did he move to pick up the bouquet.

Tentatively, she reached out with a little tendril of magic, extending her aura toward his. Even in the dead of winter, she was able to do magic like this. This was basic survival stuff. She wasn't manifesting anything into being or plucking the strings of fate in her favor. She was simply pushing her awareness outward, tasting the air around him.

As her magic reached him, a familiar sensation flooded into her—a warm fire on a snowy night, winter berries, warm spices, and mountain evergreens. She blinked in surprise. "It's *you*! *You're* my helpful elf?"

He smiled back at her. "Hello again."

If she wasn't so surprised, she might have felt like a right idiot. She'd even suggested to Ari that she'd kissed a real fae the night before. As it was, she was nearly as surprised to learn she'd actually kissed a winter sorcerer.

When she let out a disbelieving laugh, the winter sorcerer blinked. "No wonder you didn't want to give your name. That's quite the joke you pulled, crashing our party and blowing out our fire. You're lucky I'm the one who caught you and not someone else."

Clover placed her clipboard and pen on the glass case between them and pointed to where he was supposed to sign.

He frowned. "Actually, that was my friend who blew out the fire. He shouldn't have done that. And you didn't catch me... I ordered the flowers from you on purpose."

She snorted, raising an eyebrow. "Oh? And why's that? Got a little taste of summer witch and couldn't forget?"

But her smirk faltered as he watched her seriously.

"Will you marry me?"

Chapter Thirteen

Whit flushed at the look on her face. Clover's fair cheeks blossomed like pink tulips, and her cornflower blue eyes widened.

Why did I say that? he screamed internally.

Initially, that *was* why he'd called her to his shop. But then he'd convinced himself not to. That was, until he saw that tower card. Somewhere in his heart, he felt the change the card promised involved him getting evicted. And then when Clover reacted so good-humoredly to discovering her rendezvous the night before had been with a winter sorcerer, it just sort of slipped out of him. He grabbed at it like a kite string that was barely within reach.

But the expression on her face now had him stumbling over his words. "I-I mean… Let me explain. I—"

"Okay," she said seriously with a sharp nod.

He squinted at her, uncertainly. "Okay…?"

"Okay. I'll marry you."

His mouth dropped open as his insides seized. "You will?"

She gave him a polite smile. "Yes."

"But…you don't even know why I asked." He honestly couldn't believe it, and he wondered if she was having him on.

"I'm sure you have your reasons," she said simply.

He'd known he'd never met someone quite like her, but this was next level. "I do have my reasons, and I think it's important for you to know them."

She nodded again, patiently waiting to hear what he had to say.

Taking a deep breath in, he sighed heavily, trying to order his thoughts. "You see, the thing is, my grandfather told me that if I don't marry a witch before the solstice, he's going to evict me from our ancestral home and will it to my cousin instead. I'm very attached to this house, and I'd like to inherit it as I always thought I would."

"Okay," she said again, clearly hearing him though the words didn't seem to affect her.

Whit hesitated. This all felt way too easy. He knew why he would do something so crazy, but he didn't know why she would.

"Can I ask why you said yes? I don't have to tell you we don't even know each other, not to mention the winter and summer faction stuff."

Clover's lips spread into a warm smile. "Because you ordered camellias, and I talked to a crow after we kissed."

He could hear in her tone that she thought these

were omens of some kind. It wasn't surprising. Many witches felt that way. Whit wasn't one of them.

"You'd make a life-altering decision like this over a flower I chose at random and a bird you saw on your car?"

Her eyes brightened. "You'd marry a summer witch you don't know because of a house?"

"A house that I love and has been in my family for generations."

"A bird who heralds change after I asked for it and a flower that signifies destiny."

Whit stared at her. From her words, he knew she felt this proposition was part of her fate somehow. His shoulders tensed.

"You…" Everything in him told him not to say it. She'd already agreed. He could easily fulfill his grandfather's conditions before the solstice. But he said it anyway. "You know I'm not in love with you, right?"

She sighed indulgently as if nothing was more obvious in the world. "I know."

"You're not…in love with me, right?"

Clover smiled and shook her head.

"Okay…as long as we're on the same page."

Silence settled between them as they stared at each other across the glass display case. "We should… probably keep this a secret until after it's done. Don't you think?"

Clover nodded. "I agree. My family would try to stop me for sure."

Whit's throat tightened as the word in-laws came to mind.

"Do you know any priestesses?" she asked.

"Do we need a priestess? I thought we'd just go to the courthouse."

Clover tilted her head. "Will your grandfather count that as a real marriage? If we aren't spiritually bound?"

Whit frowned. He knew she was right. His grandfather would have enough reticence about her being a summer witch even though it wasn't against the pact's terms. "A priestess who'll marry a winter sorcerer and a summer witch on the sly? No. Winter sorcerers and witches go through a long and thoughtful process before getting married."

Clover raised an eyebrow. "Do they?"

Whit shrugged. "Usually."

She hummed, and her eyes grew distant in thought. "I might know someone. She can legally sign the documents, but she's pretty new to the spiritual ceremony part of it."

"When can she do it?"

"I can give her a call tonight and find out. We wouldn't be able to get a license until tomorrow anyway. The County Clerk's Office is closed or will be soon."

Whit nodded. "All right. The sooner the better."

"I'll let you know later, then. I have your number from the order form."

With a plan in place, Whit's mind reeled. *Am I really getting married?*

He looked down at his fiancée, and the memory of her pressed against him in the dark surfaced in his mind. *She's beautiful.*

"Um…" She looked up at him expectantly.

His heart thumped.

She broke into a smile. "You still have to sign for the flowers."

His face flushed as he reached for the pen. *What does it matter if she's beautiful or not? This is a marriage of convenience. Keep your wits about you. You have your life, and she'll have hers.*

Taking up her clipboard, she tucked her auburn hair behind one ear, then held out her hand. "Well, I guess, I'll see you later, Whittaker."

Whit reached toward her, clasping her hand in his. "You can call me Whit."

Her smile was as sweet as her kiss had been. "Okay, Whit."

A tingle ran through him when she said his name. Her hand felt small and soft in his.

Her hand slipped away—and he had no reason to stop her—as she clutched her clipboard to her chest. "Don't forget to put those flowers in some water."

When she turned and left, he picked up the camellias and brought them to his nose. But all he could smell was the lingering sweetness of her presence.

Chapter Fourteen

Clover's cheeks blazed as if she faced the full summer sun. But when she stepped out of the antique shop, she cooled down immediately—a blast of cold air assaulting her.

Her mind whirled, replaying the bizarre conversation she'd just had. After climbing into her van and shutting the door, she stared out the windshield, her eyes fixed on nothing in particular.

Did I just agree to marry a near-complete stranger? This is crazy.

And even though she knew as much, her intuition assured her this was the right choice for her. She'd never ignored her intuition in her entire life. And even when her mind argued with all its power of logic and reason, her intuition always turned out to be right. She'd never once regretted following it.

"I asked for change," she murmured, her breath visible in the freezing van. "And the gods of summer have provided. I appreciate your blessings. I will not squander this chance you have given me," she pronounced to whatever entities happened to be listening.

Her heart swelled with excitement and anticipation. A new, untrod path lay before her, and she was nothing if not adventurous.

She smiled as she turned on the van. The decision had been made, and for the first time in a while, everything felt right in her world.

Taking out her phone, she texted Ari—asking for Rhys's sister Rania's number.

Ari must have been busy with work because Clover didn't receive a response until after she was already pulling into the driveway at home.

Clover turned off the van but didn't climb out. Instead, she thanked Ari and called the number provided.

It was a few rings before a hesitant voice answered.

"Hello…?"

"Hi, is this Rania? This is Clover, Ari's friend. We met at Rhys's birthday party earlier this year."

"Oh! Yes, hello, Clover. How are you?"

"I'm good. Thanks. You mentioned last time that you were studying to be a priestess and you've already gotten your license to perform legal marriages. Have you done any handfastings yet?"

Rania's tone was a little sad. "Not yet. No one I know has needed an officiant, and everyone else just goes to Lady Wanda."

"Well, I know someone who's interested in getting

married in a hurry. Do you have time in the next few days?"

"What? Really? That's great! Oh my goddess! Thank you for recommending me. Sure, I have time. Let me see. Um…I have yoga tomorrow morning"—she chuckled—"Actually, I take your brother's class at his studio. He's great. Thanks for telling me about it."

Clover frowned impatiently, wondering if she shouldn't turn the heat back on. Rania had a way of getting off topic. "No problem. Anything this weekend?"

"Hmm. I'm free Friday night. Does that work?"

"That's perfect. Where should they go?"

Rania laughed again, the giggle she made when she'd been a little silly or forgetful. "Right. They're going to need that, huh? If they don't have a venue, they can come to my apartment. You said they're in a rush, right?"

"That's right. Could you text me the time and address, please?"

"Sure, no problem. Oh, gods! I have so much to do if they're coming here. I've got to—"

"Thanks so much, Rania," Clover interrupted so she wouldn't have to sit on the phone for an indeterminate amount of time. "I'll hop off so you have enough time to do what you need to."

Rania giggled. "Good idea. Thanks again, Clover. I'll let you know how it goes."

Clover shut her phone and started toward the kitchen door. She didn't feel bad for not telling Rania that she was, in fact, the person getting married. She needed to keep this as quiet as possible for as long as possible, and Rania wasn't exactly discreet.

Clover wasn't under any impression that this road would be easy. Why, Llew's graveyard fiasco had only happened the night before. She wasn't doing this to heal the rift between the summer and winter factions —or for any higher purpose.

Clover was marrying Whit because it felt right. Whether he was a winter sorcerer, whether her family and friends didn't approve, it didn't matter. In her heart—her heart that had felt the warmth of his magic—she knew it was right.

No one would convince her otherwise, but that didn't mean she wanted to make it harder for herself. In this situation, it was far better to tell everyone after the deed was done, when it was too late for them to try to dissuade her—especially when that would just be a waste of time anyway.

She heard the squeals from inside before she even opened the door. Her mother was sliding a baking sheet of what looked like her famous stuffed lemon cookies into the oven.

"Avast, ye hearties!" Llew called from the living room. "Hoist the sails and flibber the gibbet!"

"Aye, aye, Captain!" Crane answered. "The gibbet be flibbered."

Clover raised a finger to her lips when Mom looked over at her entrance. She slipped her coat off and hung it on a kitchen chair as she sneaked toward the living room.

Llew was standing on the couch, one foot raised

on the arm like Washington crossing the Delaware—his pool-noodle sword raised dramatically.

"What's all this, then?" Clover demanded. "A mutiny, is it?"

"Zia!" Crane cheered upon seeing her, breaking character to hug Clover. She wore a newspaper hat, an eye patch, and a stuffed velociraptor named Parrot on her shoulder as she always did when they played pirates.

Clover embraced the little girl. "Ciao, stregina," she said affectionately. Though her family was not Italian, Crane's father was second generation, so they tried their best to speak what little Italian they knew as much as possible.

"Mutiny! Mutiny, you say?" Llew shouted, puffing out his chest. "What scurvy dog boards my ship and speaks thus?"

Clover stood up straighter. "*Your* ship! I think not, you scabby scalawag! It is *my* ship. I am Captain Tickle, and I have ravaged the seven seas since before you were born!"

Llew pointed his noodle at his sister. "If you would have command of this vessel, then I challenge you to a duel!"

"A sword!" shouted Clover, holding out her hand.

With laughter and sparkling eyes, Crane passed Clover her noodle.

"En garde!" Clover pronounced, lunging toward her brother.

Chapter Fifteen

W hit maneuvered the ring in his hand so it caught the light of the flickering flames from his parlor hearth.

He'd pulled it from the display case at his shop earlier that evening after Clover had left.

It was a rectangular amethyst with gilded flowers etched into it—two tiny diamonds at the center of their petals. From what he could tell, it had to be over a hundred and fifty years old. It had seen much joy and hardship, but it had always been given in happiness.

Will she like it? He hoped she would.

After the initial shock of Clover actually agreeing to his proposal, his emotions settled within him. This was not what he'd planned for his life, but he could handle it.

She'd agreed to it with such ease—even acknowledging that they didn't have feelings for each other. He couldn't believe his good luck. He didn't know a woman like her existed.

As gratitude had filled his heart, he'd thought he should give her something nice as a thank you. He would inherit the house like he'd always wanted, and no one would ever nag him again about his relationship status. She'd saved him, and he would be able to maintain his calm life because of her.

What better gift for his fiancée than a ring? The gold flowers and purple hue of the stone spoke of warm summer twilights. It was perfect for her.

Not long after he'd returned home, he received her promised text, asking him to meet her tomorrow during lunch to pick up the license and Friday evening for the ceremony.

I should prepare the guest room for her. It had been a while since someone had slept there. And though he cleaned it with the rest of the house, the bed would need fresh sheets. *Maybe I'll put the camellias in there on the dresser. It will be her room from now on. I should make her feel welcome.*

Sticking the ring into its velvet-lined box, he put it on the table beside him and rose from the armchair he sat in. She may effectively only be his housemate from now on, but a little effort on his part could make all the difference in making her comfortable and preserving the peaceful atmosphere he tried to cultivate.

He had one foot on the stairs when he heard a knock on the front door. He tilted his head at the sound. *Who could that possibly be?*

Whit turned and walked down the front hall to

the door. After opening it, he blinked in surprise upon finding his mother on the front steps.

Her salt-and-pepper hair fluttered around her in the wind. Her dark eyes were sharp this evening, and he knew he was in for it.

As he stepped back into the hall, she entered, bringing her barely restrained disapproval and the slightest hint of what Whit recognized as his father's magic. He could hardly remember his father; he'd been so young when he'd died that he remembered his spiritual presence more than what he was actually like in life. His father's spirit wasn't always with his mother, but he was there pretty often when she was upset, especially at this time of year when the veil was thin.

"Good evening, Mom," Whit said cheerfully, knowing that greeting her with a serious tone would only make things worse for him.

"*Is* it a good evening, Whittaker Crawford? I hope you're having one, at least, because I most certainly am not." Her tone was biting as she took off her coat, folded it over her arm, and strode into the parlor.

Ah, so she'll be here for a while. Whit followed after her, choosing to stand near the fire as she plopped into the armchair he'd so recently vacated.

"I'm sorry to hear you aren't having a good day," he said, trying to ignore the ring box not a foot from her. "What happened?"

She flattened her lips into a line, little wrinkles appearing at the edges. "You know very well. Why weren't you at the ritual last night? You know how important it is to pay homage to our ancestors and greet the winter."

As a younger man, Whit would have just shrugged and let her rage at him until she was exhausted. But lately, he'd learned she really did just want an explanation.

"I had some bad news yesterday, and I wasn't up for being with the family," he replied honestly.

His mother's irritation hesitated—teetering between the lecture she'd planned and her urge to comfort her son's hurt. "What bad news?" she asked.

He turned his profile toward her, directing his gaze into the fire. "It doesn't matter. I've taken care of it."

Mom's eyebrows scrunched. Whit could tell she wanted to know what had happened.

He met her eyes seriously. "Mom, you trust me, right?"

She blinked at his question. "Of course, I do."

"So you'll hear me out if I do something you might not agree with?"

She squinted ever so slightly, and her tone became hesitant. "Such as…?"

Whit shook his head. "Don't worry about it. I just want to know you'll support whatever decisions I make."

She gave him a reassuring smile. "You're a good sorcerer, Whit, and a good person. I'm sure any choice you make will be the right one."

Whit's heart warmed at his mother's words. This whole thing might have been way too spontaneous for his liking, but given the circumstance, it seemed like the best option. "Thanks, Mom."

She opened her mouth to speak but then closed it again without a word. He knew she wanted to ask what was going on but thought better of it.

"So how was the ritual?" He changed the subject.

Mom sighed heavily. "The ritual was fine. Nothing out of the ordinary. But I can't tell you how glad I am that when Alexandre took the apprenticeship with me, he also moved into your old bedroom."

"Why is that?"

She frowned seriously. "Last night, after everyone left the cemetery, I heard a commotion outside. I thought it was just Alexandre coming home late, but it turns out some summer sorcerers came onto the grounds and vandalized a few of the graves."

Whit flinched. "What? Vandalized the graves? Are you sure?"

Mom nodded slowly. "According to Alexandre, they were out there making flowers grow on the graves. I heard Alexandre shouting at them—that was the commotion. He said he hit one of them with a frostbite spell."

Whit clenched his jaw while trying to keep a neutral expression. This reminder of the feud between the factions couldn't have come at a worse time.

It doesn't matter, he told himself as doubt crept into his mind yet again.

Chapter Sixteen

Clover tucked a stray lock of hair behind her ear as she walked along the side of city hall.

It was warmer today, nearly sixty-five degrees, and all the snow had melted. Still, the breeze carried a chilly undercurrent.

She was later than she wanted to be. The trip had taken longer than she'd expected even though the county seat was only one town over from Forest Haven. She picked up her pace.

But as she rounded the building, she saw Whit standing on the front step not far from her.

His back was to her. He wore a white T-shirt and jeans that deliciously accentuated his backside. His shoulders were tense, and his head was bent over something in his hands.

Clover grinned, slowing her approach and stepping ever so carefully in her sneakers. She slid up behind him as quietly as she could.

"What's that?" she asked loudly.

He jumped, dropping whatever he'd been holding as he spun around to face her.

Clover's chuckle died on her lips when she saw that the man was not Whit after all.

"Oh my g—I am so sorry!" Her face flushed with embarrassment as she bent down to retrieve the man's clipboard. "I thought you were someone else."

The man smiled sheepishly at her. "That's all right."

Now that she was facing him, Clover saw that he didn't look anything like Whit. His hair was the same dark color and longer on the top than the sides, and he was probably around the same age. But he was a few inches taller than Whit, clean-shaven with blue eyes, thick eyebrows, and a sharp chin.

The part that embarrassed her the most, though, was that he was very clearly an ordinary. His aura held none of the magic a sorcerer would have. It was clean and clear of bad intent but entirely average.

"I'm really sorry again," Clover said, holding out the clipboard to him.

"It's fine." He reached for what she offered, his eyes warming as he took her in. "Actually, would you mind signing my petition?"

Clover tilted her head, looking down at the clipboard they both held. It didn't have many signatures. "What's it for?"

"I volunteer for a local cat rescue. We're trying to get a referendum put on the ballot that would make it illegal to declaw cats in our state. It's a horrible mutilation, which cuts off part of the cat's fingers and leaves them without necessary defenses. If—"

Clover nodded. "Enough said. I agree with you."

The man gave her a brilliant smile and offered her a pen.

She signed her name and filled out the necessary boxes. Then she handed it back to him with a smile.

"Good luck with your petition. I hope to see it on the next ballot…?" She offered him her hand.

He shook it. "Orion. And thanks"—he glanced down at his petition—"Clover."

"Orion. That's an interesting name. Beloved of the goddess Artemis, immortalized in the stars."

His cheeks turned a bit pink as he looked down at his feet. "Yeah, my parents are a couple of old hippies."

Clover smiled easily. "Nothing wrong with that. The earth could use more people who care about it."

"You're right." Looking up, Orion met Clover's eyes. "I don't know if you're interested, but my organization, Pets and Scritches, is having a volunteer orientation soon."

"Clover."

Clover glanced over her shoulder at the sound of her name to see Whit standing at the top of the stairs.

Oh, he was already here, and I'm late. She waved at Whit, then turned back to Orion. "I have to go, but sure. I put my phone number on the petition. You can call or text me with more details. Okay?"

Orion smiled warmly again. "Sure thing. I'll be seeing you, then."

Clover nodded, then raced up the stairs toward Whit.

"Sorry, I'm late," she told Whit, a little breathless from her haste.

Shifting his gaze from Orion to her, Whit dipped his head in understanding.

Clover started toward the door, moving into the shadows created by the classical roof.

"Wait," Whit called.

Clover hesitated as he moved toward her.

"Before we go in, I wanted to give you something." He reached into his pocket.

"Give something to me?"

Given the circumstances and the size of the small box he held out to her, she could guess what it was. She glanced up at him, a little surprised by the gesture.

"It seemed the right thing to do," he said, clearing his throat.

Taking the box from him and opening it, Clover beheld an amethyst ring with gilded flowers and small diamonds. The purple stone glimmered like the captivating light of an aurora borealis on a cold winter night.

Her heart skipped a beat. "It's gorgeous," she whispered, meeting his eyes.

His answering smile held a clear sign of relief. "I hope it fits. If not, I can resize it."

Taking the cool metal from its velvet slot, Clover slipped the ring onto her left hand. In truth, it was a little big, but not so much that it would fall off.

"It fits." She held out her hand to show him. But as she did so, the stone slipped to the side.

Gently, he took her fingertips in his, bending over her hand.

Her heart fluttered at his touch, somehow more intriguing in its feathery lightness.

His smile faltered. "It doesn't fit. I'll take it back and fix it before tomorrow. I have tools at home."

Clover snatched her hand away, suddenly protective of the gift she'd only just received.

Whit looked at her curiously.

"It can wait until later. We have more than enough time, right?"

Whit glanced around them, and she did the same. There was no one in sight. Though she hadn't seen Orion leave, he was not in view from this angle.

Whit held out his hand. "Give me your hand for a moment."

Clover didn't hesitate—her fingertips tingled as they brushed his palm.

Stepping closer to her, Whit covered her hand with his other one.

His voice was low and intimate, barely above a whisper, as his dark eyes locked with hers. "*Lovers, friends, kin, and allies*"—she murmured his words back to him as his magic flowed into her—"*a ring that binds us should be to size.*"

A pleasant shiver ran through Clover. She didn't dare look away from Whit's eyes for fear he would pull back from her.

She tingled all over and knew her face must be flushed.

Whit cleared his throat and let go of her hand.

She tempered her disappointment by looking

down at the ring on her finger—now a perfect fit. She couldn't help but smile up at him.

"Thank you so much. I love it."

He held her gaze for a long moment, his eyes wavering though she didn't know why.

"You're welcome," he responded, his tone a little more formal than she expected. "Shall we?" He motioned for them to make their way inside.

Nodding, she followed him toward the door. Her heart was light in her chest, and she believed with all her might in the bright future they would share.

He seems a little reserved. That's not so strange for a winter sorcerer, I suppose. Still, he's thoughtful in his actions.

Clover glanced at the face of her fiancé as he held the door open for her to enter city hall.

And he did kiss me the night of the party even though we'd never met, so he can't be too uptight.

Whit pointed to a sign standing in the marble vestibule that directed them downstairs for a marriage license.

Clover smiled to herself as she followed him down the stairs, then toward the clerk's counter.

I look forward to getting to know him little by little.

The clerk at the counter smiled brightly at them, pulling their attention toward her.

"Hello," she said cheerfully. "How can I help you today?"

"We're here to apply for a marriage license," Whit answered.

The clerk beamed. "Congratulations!"

Clover's stomach fluttered. For the first time, the

magnitude of the situation settled into her. She was getting married—legally and spiritually bound to the man beside her—and this stranger seemed genuinely happy for them. A giddy joy zipped through her.

"I'll need each of your driver's licenses or IDs, and some information about you and your families. If you have your birth certificates, that would make things go faster. The fee is one hundred dollars."

Clover placed her ID and birth certificate on the counter, and Whit did the same.

"Excellent." The clerk took the documents and started typing into her computer.

"Wait," Clover said, noticing that Whit had taken five twenties from his wallet as she was picking through hers. "I'll pay for half."

Whit frowned. "You don't have to," he said in a low voice though the clerk was close enough to hear everything.

"I want to," Clover insisted, offering him fifty dollars.

She knew that, given the reason why he'd asked her to marry him, they would be living in his house. So Clover felt she needed to establish things from the outset. She didn't want him to feel as though she would be a burden to him, financially or otherwise. It was only fair she pay her own way.

Clover could see the hesitation on Whit's face, but he relented and took her money.

"This is the best part of my job," the clerk commented with a grin, glancing at them only momentarily before going back to her computer screen. "How did you meet?"

Whit stiffened beside Clover, who couldn't help but let out a laugh. *Maybe a bit more uptight than I thought.*

"We met…at a Halloween party," Clover answered.

"Did you?" The clerk sounded interested despite her lack of eye contact. "So this is a sort of anniversary for you, then? Halloween was just a few days ago."

Clover glanced slyly at Whit, sharing the little joke between them. "It will be."

Chapter Seventeen

W hit tried not to squirm as he glanced at Clover in the dimly lit apartment hallway. It had been a while since he'd worn a kilt, and the fabric itched his legs. But even if he did nothing else the way he was expected to for the rest of his life, he knew it was a right, honored tradition for his family.

Beside him, Clover wore a long-sleeved green linen dress that laced up the back. She had a wreath of flowers on her head with all the colors of a summer's day.

His heart squeezed when her eyes met his, and he had to remind himself he wasn't in love with her.

"She's expecting us," Clover assured him, mistaking his staring for something else.

He nodded and turned his attention back to the crooked seven nailed into the apartment door.

Clover sighed and lifted her hand to knock again, but the door swung open before her fist met wood.

The woman before them had long blonde hair—her circlet a little askew—and wore a blue Scandinavian-style apron dress common to witches who worshipped the Norse gods.

"Hail and wel—Clover!" she started seriously before cutting herself off. She stared Clover up and down, her blue eyes wide with shock. "*You're* the one getting married! Why didn't you say?"

Clover grinned but shrugged. "Surprise!" she said.

The priestess laughed a giggle that was pure joy. "I *am* surprised!" Then she turned her eyes to Whit, who stiffened.

It won't take a priestess long to figure out I'm a winter sorcerer.

But if she knew, she didn't let on. She smiled broadly. "Come in! Oh, but watch your step, I didn't get to clean as much as I wanted to."

Whit bumped a tennis ball with his foot as he followed Clover into the cluttered space.

The living room they entered held more furniture than it warranted with a bookshelf stuffed with hastily folded fabric, a couch with a teddy bear head —the stuffing hanging out of its neck hole—a sewing machine table with a half-made project, and a sheet hanging over the television—before which sat a table with ritual supplies.

A high-pitched whine pierced the air, and Whit winced at the heart-breaking sound.

"Erik!" the priestess shouted. "That's enough." She turned to them, clearly embarrassed. "Sorry. Erik is my husky. He's upset that he can't meet you."

"Oh," Clover glanced at Whit. "We don't mind if you want to let him out."

The priestess shook her head seriously. "Oh no. He doesn't understand personal space. He'll jump all over you, and we'll never get the ceremony done."

The dog let out a pitiful howl that resulted in the priestess admonishing him again.

"So," the priestess said cheerfully, turning back toward them. "When will everyone else get here? I hope there aren't a lot of people. My apartment can't hold many."

"Oh, uh." Clover looked around. "We, um, we didn't really invite anyone actually… We just…" Her words trailed off.

"We just couldn't wait," Whit supplied, assisting Clover in a tough situation. It was obvious she knew this woman, and that it was strange for Clover to get married without telling anyone.

The priestess flushed, then grinned. "Ah, I see. A whirlwind romance." She sighed happily. "Well, you don't need any witnesses in this state, but if you want, I can ask one of my neighbors."

Clover shook her head. "No, that's all right."

"Okay. No worries. Do you have everything you need? Rings? Something to bind you together?"

"I have the rings," Whit said, offering them to the priestess after retrieving them from his sporran.

Clover dug into her purse and pulled out a long red knitted cloth—around three inches wide with a cable running down the center. "I have the cloth." She offered it to the priestess while looking at him. "I…made it a long time ago."

Whit's heart jumped into his throat. For the first time in this whole business, he thought about what Clover might be giving up. Had she hoped and dreamed of meeting a true love when she was younger? Of being swept off her feet, getting married, and starting a family?

He hadn't coerced her into anything. If she'd given up on all that, then she'd done so of her own accord. But he still felt bad about it in that moment. He couldn't be that for her, and therefore, she'd never have it.

"Great! We're all set, then," the priestess pronounced. "I'm so excited you're the first person I'll marry, Clover!"

Whit's suspicions of the priestess were confirmed. He hoped her credentials were legal at least.

"First, I'm going to cleanse you both." She turned her back to them to face the ritual table.

The sound of a lighter flicked multiple times before she turned back, holding a cereal bowl with smoldering rubbed sage. The priestess grinned unabashedly. "I forgot I used the rest of my smudge stick last week, but this will do."

Taking a deep breath, Whit closed his eyes and tried his best to get into the ritual mood.

The priestess walked around each of them, wafting the smoke over them to cleanse them and the space.

"Hail to the gods, the goddesses, the ancestors, and to any and all spirits who would bless this union and wish these two souls well. Be with us this day to witness and bless this binding of hearts." As she spoke the unmistakable energy of witchcraft, the heavy presence of otherworldly entities traveled through the space.

The priestess turned to Clover. "Do you, Clover Bronwen, enter this space with an open heart and of your own free will?"

Clover nodded seriously. "I do."

The priestess cast her eyes toward Whit. "And do you"—she lowered her voice—"what's your name?"

Clover stifled a laugh.

"Whittaker Crawford," he said as seriously as he could in the face of Clover's giggling.

The priestess's eyes widened, finally realizing he was a winter sorcerer. Her gaze flicked between the two of them. Clover gave her an encouraging nod. And, to the priestess's credit, she cleared her throat and continued as professionally as her ability would allow.

"Do you, Whittaker Crawford, enter this space with an open heart and of your own free will?"

Whit dipped his head. "I do."

Chapter Eighteen

lover could see how much effort it took Rania to keep her composure. If Whit had been an ordinary, no one would have thought anything of his name. But Crawford had the unmistakable sound of winter for a sorcerer.

Clover wondered if she should take his name or not. Did she want to be mistaken as a winter witch?

"Did you prepare your own vows?" Rania asked.

Clover shook her head and glanced over to see Whit doing the same.

Rania tried for a smile of reassurance. "No problem. I have some just in case. Please turn toward each other and join hands."

Clover faced Whit and offered her hands to him. He took her fingers in his, locking his gaze onto hers.

A shiver ran through her as her cheeks flushed. Not for the first time that day did she thank the gods for whoever had sent him to her.

She'd cast a good luck charm, and boy, did it work. She sure felt lucky seeing him in his kilt and peasant shirt. He looked like he belonged in a wall calendar she'd once had called Kilts and Kittens.

She knew they didn't love each other yet, but attraction was the perfect place to start in her opinion. She smiled to herself, looking forward to their honeymoon later that night.

Rania turned a serious stare to Whit. "Will you, Whittaker Crawford, take Clover Bronwen for your wife? Will you swear before the gods, goddesses, spirits, and ancestors that you will honor and respect her above all others? That you will care for her when she is ill and comfort her when she is distressed? That you will share her burdens and her joys from this day forward?"

Clover's heart jumped as she held her breath.

"I will," Whit declared, his eyes serious and true.

She tried to swallow, but her mouth went dry while warmth radiated from her chest.

"And will you, Clover Bronwen, take Whittaker Crawford for your husband? Will you swear before the gods, goddesses, spirits, and ancestors that you will honor and respect him above all others? That you will care for him when he is ill and comfort him when he is distressed? That you will share his burdens and his joys from this day forward?"

Clover gently squeezed his hands as unexpected tears blurred her vision. She smiled. "I will," she said breathlessly. "I will," she repeated with more strength.

Whit frowned, and a wrinkle formed between his eyebrows.

"You may exchange rings," Rania said. "Clover, remove your engagement ring first. It goes on after."

They released each other's hands, and Clover slipped her ring off. Rania handed Clover's ring to Whit.

The energy around them seemed to vibrate like a low hum. As Whit slipped the thin band of gold onto the ring finger of Clover's left hand, the air seemed to sparkle and tingle like cranberry soda. She slid her amethyst ring on after.

Rania then offered Clover Whit's ring.

Clover's breath was shaky and shallow as she met his gaze before dropping her attention to his hand. She carefully pushed the ring onto his finger.

"Now you will share of the cup of joy and sorrow." Rania turned back toward her table before facing them again with a glass of unknown contents.

Clover and Whit eyed the black liquid uncertainly.

Rania smiled. "I made a special tea blend with magical herbs just for the occasion. I hope it tastes all right."

Rania offered the cup to Clover first.

As soon as the brew touched Clover's lips, she wanted to spit it out. It was a horrific amalgamation of tastes that somehow carried the worst parts of everything put in—cardamom, chamomile, cayenne, lemon, licorice root, and the unmistakable zing of vanilla extract.

Clover swallowed a mouthful and started to cough, which set off Rania's dog in the other room.

"Are you okay?" Whit asked, putting his hands

out toward her as if he wanted to help but didn't quite know how.

Clover nodded, raising a hand to tell him she was all right.

Rania giggled that oopsie laugh of hers. "I guess it was a cup of sorrow more than joy." She offered it to Whit, who drew back—eyeing the concoction like it was going to jump out of the glass at him.

"Sorry," Rania said. "But you have to drink it to complete the ritual."

With a heavy sigh, Whit took the glass from her. He sipped it, managing to handle it better than Clover had.

Rania frowned at the cup, still more than half full. "It's bad luck if you two don't finish it…"

Clover shuddered, then nodded. "Okay, I'll—"

But before she could finish her statement, Whit downed the lot.

Clover's mouth dropped open. She knew how disgusting it had been, but he weathered it without flinching.

His face reddened as he held his breath.

"You good?" Clover asked uncertainly, wondering where the nearest bin was in case he needed to vomit.

He blew out his breath and nodded as he waved a hand. "You can go on."

Rania shifted her eyes between them. "Please join your left hands together."

They did so. Then, taking the strip of cloth Clover had knitted back in high school, Rania wrapped it around their joined hands and tied it in a fisherman's knot.

"Whittaker, repeat after me."

Whit repeated Rania's words, each one striking its way into Clover's heart like a blacksmith's hammer.

"I, Whittaker Crawford, promise you, Clover Bronwen, that I will stand with you in summer's blessings and in winter's bane, in times of plenty and in times of famine, while you are a bright-eyed youth, a nurturing mother, and a wise elder. Will you take me as your husband?"

Clover stared up at Whit, thinking she saw the hint of worry in his eyes. "I will," she assured.

Rania told Clover to repeat after her as well.

"I, Clover Bronwen, promise you, Whittaker Crawford, that I will stand with you in winter's blessings and in summer's bane"—Clover grinned as she purposely swapped the words for Whit's benefit—"in times of plenty and in times of famine, while you are a bright-eyed youth, a nurturing father, and a wise elder. Will you take me as your wife?"

"I will," Whit proclaimed, his magic shimmering like sunlight on a blanket of fresh snow.

Rania placed her right hand atop their joined hands. "From this day forward until your parting, whatever form that may take, I declare you two bound together as one. May Freyja the goddess of love and marriage—as she appears as Frigg—bless your union with love everlasting. I now pronounce you husband and wife. You may kiss to seal your promises to one another."

Rania carefully unwrapped their hands, being sure to keep the knots in the fabric.

Whit glanced at Rania, then stepped nearer

Clover awkwardly. His expression was tight and uncomfortable, and Clover smiled, finding it endearing.

She slipped her arms around the back of his neck and tilted her head up expectantly. "Come now, my helpful elf, this won't be the first time," she said with a grin.

With her little bit of encouragement, Whit slid his arms around her waist and lowered his face slowly toward hers. He stared at her so keenly that her stomach fluttered in anticipation.

As his lips met hers, a wave of magic burst outward, declaring their bond to all the powers that be.

Heat pooled in her core as he held her against him. She could feel him holding back, feel his solid, unyielding body pressed to hers. His kiss was so light that it teased her, filling her with anticipation.

Rania's dog in the other room let out the longest most sorrowful scream Clover had ever heard.

Clover burst out laughing, despite the animal having fully killed the mood.

Whit chuckled softly. And as Clover pulled back, she saw a small smile on his face.

Shaking her head in embarrassment, Rania said, "Let's sign these papers so I can let him out before my neighbors call the cops."

It took no time at all to sign their names, and Rania said she would file the paperwork on Monday. She also insisted on taking a quick picture of them with her cellphone. Not five minutes later, Clover and

Whit were standing in the parking lot near Clover's van.

She watched her new husband shift his weight from one foot to the other. But just when she was about to ask for his address in case she got lost following him to his house, he cleared his throat.

"I'm sure you have a lot of packing to do… You don't have to move all at once, but I planned to close the shop for the weekend to help any way I can. If you text me your address, I'll come by tomorrow…if you want."

Clover scrunched her eyebrows in confusion. *Tomorrow? Does that mean there will be no honeymoon tonight?*

She could feel the pout on her face as she looked at him in his kilt. *Does he not want to move that fast? It's true we don't know each other well, and winter sorcerers are more serious by nature. But we're already married…*

Clover sighed heavily, disappointment making her head drop instead of giving him a proper nod. "Thanks. I appreciate the help. I'll ask my brother to cover my shift so we can get most of it done this weekend."

"Do you need me to bring any boxes?"

"That would be helpful. Thanks."

Whit dipped his head in acknowledgment. "Okay, until tomorrow, then."

"I guess so," Clover reluctantly agreed.

"Goodnight."

After wishing him the same, she watched him

head to his car, and with a heavy heart, she went to her van and climbed inside.

She glanced at the overnight bag in her passenger seat. "I even wore my sexy underwear and everything," she grumbled before starting the engine.

Chapter Nineteen

Whit sighed heavily into what would be Clover's bedroom starting tomorrow. He sat at the foot of the freshly made bed.

The room was clean and tidy. He'd even wiped out the drawers of the dresser and vacuumed the upholstered seat of the only chair for good measure. But he'd forgotten the camellias at the shop. He didn't really have a vase in the house anyway. Winter sorcerers weren't known for their good relationships with flowers.

Guilt tugged at his chest. It had been steadily growing since Clover had produced the red cloth that now represented their handfasting.

His mind had toggled between how beautiful she'd looked in her wedding dress with fresh flowers in her hair—how bright her eyes had been, how lovely she'd smelled in the small cluttered apartment —and how scummy he felt for putting her in this situation.

He'd robbed her of her dreamed-of future, and his heart squeezed as he remembered the tears in her cornflower blue eyes when she swore to the gods, goddesses, spirits, and ancestors that she would take him as her husband. She'd tripped over the words. She'd trembled as they exchanged rings. And he didn't miss the confusion on her face when he suggested she move in tomorrow. And the sigh! The disappointed sigh that had left those pouting lips of hers.

Whit had always thought of himself as a good guy, but he was wondering now if that had ever been true. How could he see how much she was struggling and still let her go through with this marriage? He should have backed out the moment he saw her hesitation. He was selfish—selfish and cruel.

And though he censured himself severely, he also reminded himself she seemed to be doing it all on her own—despite whatever inner hesitations she harbored. An unbidden smile spread on his lips as he recalled how she switched the words of her vow for his benefit and how she'd encouraged his kiss.

He let out a loud groan and flopped backward onto the bed. He stared at the ceiling without really seeing it.

Maybe she wasn't as reluctant as she appeared. Maybe she just needs time to adjust. We don't have to move so fast. I'll text her and tell her she can take her time moving out. After all, Grandfather won't be back for a while.

He thought as much, but he didn't make a move for his phone. He glanced to the empty space on the bed beside him, wondering what she would have looked like if they'd had a proper honeymoon. He could almost picture her there, smiling that slow, heated smile she'd shown him after their first kiss.

He squeezed his eyes shut, banishing the fantasy as his manhood responded.

He blew out his breath in a loud gust, puffing his cheeks to steady himself. *I'll get used to it. Yes, she's beautiful, and she's legally my wife, but that gives me no right. This is a marriage of necessity. I already drew the line between us when I first asked her to marry me. I'm sure all this pent-up lust will wear off when I get used to her being around. She's my housemate, and I need to treat her with respect. I can do that. I'm not an animal.*

On the nightstand near the door, his phone beeped. He lunged at the thing, grinning when he saw a text from Clover.

He scowled at his own eagerness.

She'd sent him the address to her place along with the picture the priestess had taken of them.

His heart swelled as he stared at the image. He wore his polite smile, the one he wore when a particularly difficult customer finally left his shop. But Clover was even more breathtaking than he'd just pictured in his mind. She grinned happily, her eyes shining as she leaned her head on his shoulder as if this were truly the best day of her life—as if she loved him with her whole heart.

"I'll do everything I promised," he told her likeness. "It's the least I can do."

He saved the image to his phone, then opened the messenger app he used with his family.

Tapping on his grandfather's image—the dot

beside it telling Whit he was online—he attached the photo and pressed send.

The three dots jumped, indicating that Grandfather was typing.

Grandfather sent a GIF of Leonardo DiCaprio raising a champagne glass.

> **Grandfather**
> I'll have Caldwell draw up the papers and sign them as soon as I return.

> **Grandfather**
> And what is my new granddaughter-in-law's name?

Whit frowned. He didn't want his grandfather to know his new wife was a summer witch just yet, not that it really mattered because he *had* fulfilled the terms of the deal.

> Clover.

> **Grandfather**
> She's a lovely girl. I'll bring her something nice back from my trip as a congratulations.

> **Grandfather**
> I'm proud of you, my boy. Be good to her.

Whit could feel his grandfather's joy through the phone screen, and he frowned. He had to know he'd only gotten married for the house. He had to know it was all a farce.

More jumping dots hopped on his screen, and Whit choked on his breath as his mother's image appeared.

> **Mom**
> WHAT THE HELL IS GOING ON?!

The blood drained from his face as dread clenched his gut. He'd clicked on the first instance of his grandfather's name without realizing it was the family group chat.

Then the rest of the chat members started chiming in—his cousin Caldwell followed by his wife and mother.

> **Caldwell**
> Whoa, you actually got married?

> **Eirwen**
> Congratulations!

> **Aunt Cheri**
> What??? Whit got married? How unexpectedly wonderful! Love to you both!

Whit covered his face with his hands, and the

groan that escaped his lips didn't come close to reflecting the magnitude of his feelings.

"Idiot!" he called himself. Then picking up his phone again, he sent a message that he hoped would buy him some time.

I'll talk to you all later. I'm on my honeymoon.

Chapter Twenty

Clover silently ticked off the list of things she would need right away, picturing the suitcase she'd left upstairs as her chocolate chip waffles popped up from the toaster.

She spread them with butter and poured maple syrup on top before taking her plate and fork to the kitchen table.

Mom and Dad already sat at the table, eating and chatting about something they saw on their newsfeeds. There was too much horror in the world at the moment, so Clover tuned out their conversation in favor of basking in the atmosphere.

Though excitement thrummed through her at the thought of this new chapter in her life, a twinge of sadness accompanied it. This was likely the last breakfast she would have with her family like this. She hadn't expected it to be gone so suddenly.

Llew thumped down the stairs and entered the

kitchen just as Clover was bringing her first bite of waffle to her mouth.

"Ooo! Chocolate chip waffles! I think I'll have that, too," he said, heading toward the freezer.

"There aren't any left," Clover informed him after swallowing.

He groaned with disappointment. Clover frowned down at her plate.

"You can have mine," she offered her brother.

Llew froze, then leveled a squint at her. "Why...?"

Clover shrugged innocently. "Do I need a reason to be nice to my little brother?"

"Usually."

She scowled. It wasn't true to say she was never nice to him, but she acknowledged that sharing her food with him was a rarity.

"If you don't want them—"

"I never said that. I just want to know what they'll cost." He moved to the table and sat beside her.

She waited until after he'd already put the plate before him and taken a big, syrupy bite.

"Would you mind covering my shift today?"

Llew pursed his lips, and Clover half expected him to spit his mouthful out.

"Do you have plans?" Mom asked. "You didn't say anything."

Clover hesitated. She knew this was the right time to tell them everything—the only time really—but she still hadn't figured out how to break it to them. "I didn't know until last night," she said, buying herself some time.

She stood from the table. "I think there are some blueberry waffles in the freezer."

But when she turned away, a loud, insistent knock pounded on the front door.

"I'll get it." Clover's voice croaked with panic. *Surely, that's not Whit already. It's not even nine yet.*

She hurried through the living room to the door. But the relief she felt at finding Ari there didn't last more than a moment. Her friend's eyes blazed, and her face was red with rage.

"I can't believe you, Clover!" she yelled, storming into the house, stomping her feet the whole way. "How could you do this? And you didn't even say anything, not even to me!"

Clover blinked, following Ari farther into the living room. "Wha—"

Ari shoved her cellphone into Clover's face, pointing at the photo Rania had taken of her and Whit the day before. Clover's stomach dropped. *Isn't there priestess-client confidentiality or something?*

"You got married?" Ari shouted. "You got married by Rhys's sister, and you didn't think to mention it? Hell, you asked me for her number. I thought we were friends."

Ari's voice broke on the last word, hurt seeping into the rage.

"What does she mean you got married?" Mom asked, confusion on her face as she, Dad, and Llew came into the room—no doubt called forth by Ari's shouting.

"What are you talking about, Ariadne?" Mom turned to Ari, who handed her the phone.

Mom gasped, and Clover flinched at the sound.

"Clover, you *didn't*," Mom whispered.

"No way!" Llew grabbed the phone. "Who'd marry you? Who's this? I've never seen him."

Clover's mind whirled so much that she couldn't even respond to that little brotherly dig.

"Oho! Who?" Ari yelled, getting louder with every word. "Who, you ask?" She shook her head in disgust. "I can't say I'm surprised you kept this from me and even your own family." Ari turned toward Clover's dumbfounded family. "Clover married a *winter* sorcerer."

Silence settled over them like the dust from a shell-blast.

There it was. The truth was out, and there was nothing left to do. Clover took a deep breath, raised her head, and squared her shoulders.

The shock and horror she found in the faces of her loved ones twisted her heart. Even Dad—always so stoic—wore his surprise plainly.

"Clover, is that true?" Dad asked gently.

"Yes," Clover answered seriously. "Yes, it's true. Yesterday, I married a winter sorcerer."

"Fucking hell!" Llew exclaimed. "You mean, you married a corpse lover?"

Clover frowned. "Don't call them that."

Llew stepped forward. "You're defending them now?"

Clover sighed in exasperation. "This feud is stupid anyway. Why shouldn't I marry a winter sorcerer? Why shouldn't I marry whoever I want? Are they so different from us? Mom, even you tell Llew and his friends to leave the winter faction alone. You've always discouraged the feud."

Mom shook her head. She had that quiet anger— the ticking time-bomb that could go off at any moment. "Not picking a fight with the winter faction isn't the same as marrying one of them. How could you do this? Even setting aside betraying your faction" —Clover flinched at the word betraying—"you got married in secret without even telling anyone. You know very well anything you have to do in secret probably shouldn't be done. You didn't tell us because you knew we would stop you! You knew we wouldn't approve, and you did it anyway! If you truly thought this was the right decision, you wouldn't have hidden it from us!"

"Yes, I knew you would try to stop me," Clover argued. "I knew, and that's why I didn't tell you. But not because it wasn't the right thing to do. I know with everything I am that it was the right thing to do. And if you'd get over your own prejudices, you would listen to my reasoning."

A throat cleared from behind Clover, and she glanced over her shoulder to find Whit standing at the entrance to the living room.

He dipped his head self-consciously. "Your front door was open... I knocked...but..."

Llew surged toward Whit, his eyes blazing with fury. "Is this him? You winter fuck—"

Clover stepped between the two men, forcing Llew to halt his progress across the room.

"That's my husband you're talking to," she snapped.

Llew smirked darkly. "Not for long. You're about to be a widow." He moved to step around her, but she moved with him.

"If you think I'm not going to defend him, then you're sorely mistaken. Don't you dare."

"If you think I'm going to hand you over to some winter bastard, you don't know me very well," Llew snarled down at her.

"It's a good thing I'm a grown woman who can make her own decisions, then. I don't need you to *hand* me over to anyone. I don't need your permission, Llewellyn, or anyone's." Clover leveled her fiercest glare at her brother, then shared it with the rest of her family and Ari—emphasizing just how serious she was.

"Well," Dad said calmly. "You've made your stance clear. There's nothing else that needs to be said."

"Oh, yes, there is!" Mom raged. "There's plenty I have to say."

"Perhaps it should wait until everyone has had a chance to calm down," Dad suggested.

Mom bit her lips, looking very much like she did not want to reconvene at another time.

Clover backed down as well, turning to Whit— whose expression and demeanor were tense and tight. She tried to give him a reassuring smile. "My room is upstairs. I'll show you the way."

Chapter Twenty-One

Whit clenched his jaw. It wasn't his habit to turn his back to someone who was showing him clear hostility—especially a summer sorcerer who'd threatened his life. But as Clover started up the staircase, he went against his instincts and followed her deeper into enemy territory.

He hadn't heard the whole argument, but he'd heard enough. He'd heard her mother tell her that if she hid their marriage, it was because she knew it was wrong, and he'd heard Clover assert that she felt it was right.

Despite the clearly tense atmosphere, the fact that Clover believed marrying him was the right thing to do had made his heart flutter. And when she'd stepped in front of her brother and called Whit her husband, he'd thought his heart might explode. Whether she actually believed her words or was just saying so to defend her position hadn't factored into his physical reaction. At the very least, her words in the face of her family's reaction told him she was committed to this decision.

Whit watched Clover's back as they climbed the stairs. Her shoulders were tight and her footfalls heavy—stomping with every step. She practically vibrated with anger.

He frowned. This was one of those situations he'd promised to help her through in his marriage vows. And maybe if he knew her better—if they loved each other and had gone about this whole thing the proper way—he would know what to do. He would know what she needed. Did she need comfort? Did she want him to fight back? Let her handle it? Be angry along with her? Calm her down? He just didn't know.

On the second floor, they traveled down the hallway to a door, which opened to a set of stairs. She stomped loudly up these stairs as well.

The attic bedroom—Clover's bedroom—was a quiet haven. He took in his surroundings, trying to learn everything he could about her from how she chose to live.

Drying herbs hung from the rafters, and there were bookshelves full of neatly labeled jars. A door led to a small bathroom, and another set of stairs climbed to a loft bed. The place felt magical, like the cottage home of a kindly witch in a storybook.

It will take a lot of boxes to move all these jars.

She stopped before two large suitcases and a few milk crates filled with jars. She didn't turn to face him.

"I've already packed all of my clothes and anything I'll need right away," she said softly.

Whit couldn't decipher the emotion in her tone.

"Do you think we'll be able to move the rest of this out this weekend?"

He glanced around the space more critically. "You won't need to bring any furniture, so yeah, I think we can get it all in a few trips especially if we use both my truck and your van. I've brought some boxes. Do you want me to go get them?"

She spun around to face him. "Let's go down together."

He wanted to reassure the worry in her eyes. Did she not think he could take her brother should it come to a fight? But then he thought better of it. This was a no-win situation for her. She would lose no matter who won.

He took up the heavy suitcases, and she lifted a milk crate into her arms, the jars softly clinking together.

When they reached the ground floor, they found Clover's mother and father sitting on the couch. Her brother and her friend—whom Whit had recognized as the fairy from the party—were nowhere in sight. Her father was speaking quietly to her mother. They both stood when they saw Clover and Whit.

Her mother's expression was much tighter as if she was damming up a flood of emotions. She held out her hand palm up. "Give me the keys to the van."

The blood drained from Clover's face. "Are you firing me?"

Her mother scowled. "How is Llew going to make deliveries without the van?" she snapped.

After lowering her crate to the floor, Clover produced her keys and removed the key in question.

Whit tried not to squirm in the uncomfortable atmosphere. Clover's mother refused to look at him, but her father leveled a serious yet inscrutable stare at him.

"I'm… Well, obviously I'm moving out. I should have everything done by Monday, so I'll be back to work then."

"Maybe you should take more time," her father said, his tone hard.

Clover blinked, and her mother's expression saddened as she looked at her husband.

"What do you mean, Dad?"

"What I said. Don't come to work Monday. We all have a lot to think about, and some time to ourselves will only do everyone good."

Clover bit her lip. "So you *are* firing me."

"We're not—" Clover's mom started.

"Actions have consequences, Clover," her dad cut in.

Clover lowered her eyes to the floor. Without another word, she picked her crate back up and went out the front door.

Whit hesitated, meeting both of his in-laws' eyes in turn. *This isn't the time for a discussion,* he decided. Dipping his head at them, he followed Clover outside.

After loading her suitcases and crate into the bed of his truck, Whit turned his gaze to Clover. Her hands clutched her elbows, and her shoulders were hunched. She seemed very small to him in that moment.

"Do you want to take these boxes upstairs and fill them?" he asked.

She shook her head. "Do you mind"—her voice broke and was shaky as she tried again—"Do you mind if we just take this stuff and come back when they're gone?"

His eyebrows crinkled. And when she looked up at him, her eyes shimmered with tears like fresh rain on cornflower petals.

His heart squeezed, and his stomach rolled. He didn't like that look on her face at all. Everything within him screamed to do something. But what? He stood frozen.

Finally, swallowing a lump in his throat, he nodded.

But his response did not seem to relieve her. Tears spilled down her face.

Hesitatingly, he reached out and brushed his fingers against one of the hands that clutched her elbows.

Without warning, Clover burst into sobs. Throwing herself at him, she wrapped her arms around him and buried her face in his chest.

A flurry of emotions cycloned inside Whit as his heart raced. Gently, he encircled her in his embrace, hoping this was what she needed.

Chapter Twenty-Two

Clover peeked over at Whit from the passenger seat of his truck, clutching the handkerchief he'd given her.

He'd been so sweet, wiping her tears after holding her while she sobbed her eyes out. It was as if he'd known just what she needed. He didn't say a word. He didn't need to. His protective embrace had said it all.

She wasn't embarrassed or surprised by the way she'd reacted to her family's outburst. She'd never fought like that with them before. Oh, sure, when she was a teenager, she'd sneaked out or gotten the odd test score that was too low for their liking. But overall, she'd always had a good relationship with her parents. She didn't cause trouble like Llew, so she'd never experienced their disappointment.

Llew's reaction wasn't a shock to her either. They may bicker and tease—the way all siblings did—but he'd always been protective of her, of both his sisters but Clover in particular.

If only she'd had enough time to break it to them before Ari had busted in, she was sure they would have taken it better.

She frowned down at her hands in her lap. *Or maybe not.* At the moment, she couldn't tell whether it was the fact that she'd kept the whole thing from them or whether it was whom she'd decided to marry that had upset them more.

Taking another furtive look at her new husband, his eyes on the road, she hoped it was the former.

"I'm sorry you had to witness all that," she murmured. "I should have prepared them before you arrived."

Whit shook his head. "I suppose it was to be expected."

"Still, I didn't think they'd go so far as to fire me. I'll find a new job as soon as I can." Clover sighed heavily. "After I get a car…"

Whit glanced over at her, his gaze sympathetic. "There's no need to rush. You're making a lot of changes in a short amount of time. New marriage. New house. We have time for you to find a new job."

"But I don't want to be a burden. I planned on paying half the bills."

Whit smiled in a way that looked too professional. "I'm not saying not to find a new job. I'm just saying get settled first. You don't have to rush."

Relief washed over Clover, but she pursed her lips

in a faux pout. "Are you always this reasonable, Husband?"

His eyes flicked to her, and he swerved a little on the road before righting the wheel.

Clover giggled under her breath. "It's going to take me some time getting used to the idea of having a husband, so I thought I would call you that way. Does it bother you?"

He adjusted his shoulders as if the word lay heavy across them. "No, why should it?"

Grinning, Clover tapped him with her elbow. "Are you being honest with me, Husband?"

She leaned toward him, and she was glad she did, or she might not have seen the slight blush rise to his face.

Whit cleared his throat. "Just like it's going to take you some time getting used to the idea of saying it, it will take me some to get used to hearing it."

She settled back into her seat with a smile. "I promise never to use it in anger."

A comfortable silence settled between them, and Clover watched out the window as the south side of town and then the woods passed by. Once they were on the north side, it only took fifteen minutes before Whit pulled onto a residential driveway.

Compared to the rest of the neighborhood, Whit's house had more land, which was surrounded by naked trees. The house looked old even from the road—symmetrical and square like a Georgian colonial—and was set back with plenty of front yard to insulate it from passersby.

As they climbed out of the truck and stared at the house, Whit lifted his chin in an expression of pride.

"It's a very nice house," Clover complimented. "Has it been in your family for a while?"

Whit rewarded her with a smile, and her heart stuttered. *I need to compliment him more often.*

"My family has been here since the factions moved from the Massachusetts Bay Colony upon making the treaty. The first house, which was much simpler, is still on the property, and this house was built later. I've done most of the restoration work by hand myself."

"Wow! I'm impressed. You didn't even use magic? I didn't know my husband was so handy."

"Well…mostly by hand. Some things can't be fixed without magic. Come on, let's grab your things, and I'll show you around."

Whit handed her the milk crate she'd filled with her favorite tea blends, and he grabbed her suitcases.

As they made their way to the front door, she admired how easily he carried them. She'd packed every article of clothing she owned into those two cases, and she knew how heavy even one was.

He set down her luggage to unlock the door. "I'll get you a spare key before we head back," he said.

Picking her luggage back up, he went in.

But something made her hesitate on the threshold. Her legs suddenly felt heavy, and a chill ran down her spine.

Whit glanced behind him when he realized she wasn't following. "Come on in," he encouraged. "The heat is on."

Clover hesitated, then stepped into the front hall. Her eyes swept the space. There was a long hall in front of her with a staircase that led upward. On her left, an opening led to a parlor, and on her right, a dining room.

"Is…is this place haunted?" she whispered so any potential ghosts wouldn't hear.

Whit snorted a laugh. "Occasionally."

Her eyes widened, and she stiffened.

Setting down her suitcases, Whit approached her. "Don't worry, Wife. We have wards. The only spirits allowed in here are the ones that mean the inhabitants no harm." He smiled reassuringly.

Her heart raced, and it had nothing to do with ghosts.

Chapter Twenty-Three

Whit smiled down at Clover, then glanced around at the ghosts hovering around them.

It was no big shock that they wanted to see the new witch who'd come onto the premises. Even though he didn't blame them for wanting to take a peek at Clover, Whit was a little surprised by just how many had chosen to greet them. He hadn't seen some of these ghosts in years.

There were ancestors from generations back and limbs of the family tree he couldn't even place. Cousin Lacey—he didn't know how far removed— who had died as a child; Great-Great-Grandmother Aneira, who could often be found knitting in her chair by the fire; Great-Uncle Andri—Grandfather's brother—who was known to be somewhat of a trickster in life and in death; and even the patriarch himself, Edur, who had signed the treaty and moved the family to Forest Haven.

The ghosts crowded the parlor and dining room on either side of where he and Clover stood in the hall. This seemed to be an epic event for them. Among those present, though he could not see them, he felt Grandmother—so recently passed—as well as his father and uncle—Caldwell's father.

He'd put feeling, and a little magic, behind his words to Clover. And by emphasizing that she was his wife, and they would not be permitted to harm her—summer witch or no—many of them dissipated.

Once they'd left, she visibly relaxed. Though it was clear she could not see them, she certainly could feel their presence.

Whit marked that only Lacey, Andri, Grandmother, and Dad had remained.

Looking back at Clover, he saw her cheeks were pink and her eyes bright as she stared up at him. His breath caught, not knowing what he'd done to earn such an expression.

"Let's…take these upstairs first," Whit said, tearing his eyes from her face to go back for her suitcases. He nodded toward the stairs. "You can head up first."

A blur rushed past them up the stairs, and when he glanced around, he saw Andri was gone.

Dread pooled in Whit's stomach. *What's he going to do?* He didn't think Andri would hurt Clover, but he would have no compunctions about scaring her.

She moved toward the steps, and he called out in a hurry. "A-actually, I'll go first."

At the top of the stairs, Whit found Andri with

his ghostly hands on the frame of a painting near Clover's room, ready to pull it from the wall.

Whit glared at his great-uncle, shaking his head in warning. Andri squinted, then drifted farther down the hall as if he were the most innocent spirit the world had ever seen.

For her part, Lacey followed Clover quietly, analyzing her auburn hair and manner of dress.

Clover seemed none the wiser, glancing around at her new home, admiring his craftsmanship.

"I love this wallpaper and these sconces! Gorgeous."

"The sconces are electric, but they're the same style as the gas ones that were there before. My grandmother picked out the wallpaper," Whit explained as he motioned her into the first door at the top of the stairs. "This is your room."

Clover frowned as she entered, and he grasped at any reason she might not like it.

"I'm sorry it isn't as big as your room at your parents' house, but we can find space for anything that doesn't fit."

In the light of day, while Clover took in her new bedroom, Whit suddenly felt it looked very plain.

She turned her blue eyes back to him, a reserved look on her face. "And…your room?"

He motioned toward the other door. "Through there is a shared bathroom. My room is on the other side."

"Oh." She nodded slowly.

"If there's anything you don't like, you can change

it. This is your home now, too." The longer she frowned, the more his chest tightened.

She tilted her head at him. "It's a lovely room. But thank you. I'll keep that in mind."

Before Whit could puzzle out why she would look so disappointed if she liked the room, he heard a chuckle from the hall and saw Andri peek into the doorway. Stepping closer to the door, Whit grabbed the handle just as Andri tried to slam it shut. It was a favorite prank of his—slamming doors when one least expected it. The door pulled a bit in Whit's hand, but he held it in place.

"My grandfather's room is across the hall. I'll show you the downstairs before we head back." Whit yanked the door from Andri's grasp, then closed it gently once Clover was in the hall.

"Your grandfather…" Clover started down the stairs. "Does he know about me yet?" She glanced back at him when she reached the ground floor.

Whit nodded. "I posted our wedding photo to my family group chat, so they all know."

Her eyes widened. "That's a bold move. And the rest of your family didn't care?"

Whit felt uncomfortable with how impressed she sounded, given he'd done it by accident. "Most of them were happy for me even though they were surprised. My grandfather is very pleased."

Whit moved into the parlor, and Clover followed.

"Even though I'm a summer witch?" She sounded shocked.

Whit frowned. "Well, they don't know that part yet."

"Oh. No wonder." She laughed a sad little laugh. "I was starting to think the winter faction had far exceeded us in open-mindedness."

Whit quirked a smile. "Maybe we have. I asked you to marry me knowing you were a summer witch, did I not? Would you have kissed me knowing I'm a winter sorcerer?"

He glanced over to find her looking him up and down. She grinned. "I might have."

Heat radiated from Whit's chest, traveling down his limbs and stiffening his manhood. He tamped down on the feeling before it could get away from him. The glint in those cornflower blue eyes of his new wife said she was only teasing him back. Nothing more.

A loud creak traveled through the parlor, and Clover gasped in surprise, nearly jumping out of her skin. If Whit hadn't been so distracted by her suggestive words and expression, he would have seen Andri putting ghostly pressure on a place in the floor that always creaked.

Whit glared at the ghost of his great-uncle, who grinned and disappeared.

Chapter Twenty-Four

Clover lay in her new bed with her eyes squeezed shut. It had been a long day, and her body was sore in ways it hadn't been for a while. They'd moved quite a bit of her things, and she was confident they would be able to get the rest tomorrow.

Her new home was beautiful. Whit had done a wonderful job of restoring it. The rooms were cozy though not too small. But it was cold here, like living in a museum. Everything was just so. There was no life, just memories.

Clover recalled the sideboard in the dining room —an ancestral altar to Whit's family. There were pictures on the walls of those who'd passed with trinkets and offerings on the table. It was a very winter faction thing to do—having the eyes of dead relatives watching while the living ate.

The summer faction was pretty Oregon Trail about death. It was a thing that happened to everyone. But when someone died, they were buried and the rest sort of moved on. Different summer sorcerers and witches had different responses to where the dead go once they were gone based on their personal traditions and pantheons, but overall, the summer faction was all about living in the present above all else.

A chill ran over Clover's skin as if something unseen was breathing on her neck. She squeaked a muffled yelp and sat up in her bed. That was the last straw. She'd heard all manner of bumps and creaks since she'd lain down to sleep, and nothing would convince her that this was natural.

She jumped out of bed and hurried to the bathroom, her bare feet padding heavily on the wood floor. Once there, she hesitated. But as she glanced back over her shoulder, she felt that same heavy looming presence she'd felt since she'd walked over the threshold for the first time. She tapped on the door to Whit's bedroom.

"Huh?" Clover heard a confused question from the other side of the door.

"Um…Whit? Do you mind if I come in?"

"Clover? Yeah, sure."

Clover opened the door and rushed in before he even had the chance to finish his short sentence.

As she ran across the room, Whit turned on the bedside lamp, blinking his tired eyes against the sudden light. Clover leapt onto the bed beside him as if some horrible, grasping creature would grab her ankle.

She felt immediate relief to have him beside her.

"What's wrong?" he asked her.

Now that she felt calmer, she was a little embarrassed to admit what had brought her here. Clover glanced over at him. Whit—to her surprise— wore proper pajamas: long-sleeved blue plaid with white piping.

She felt improperly dressed in her old holey concert tee and mismatched bottoms that looked like seventies gym shorts.

She dropped her gaze to her hands in her lap, her legs folded atop his bedspread. "I think there's something in my room..." she mumbled.

Clover winced, waiting for Whit to mock her fearful imaginings.

"Do you want me to have a look?" he asked.

Clover shook her head. "No, can I just stay here for a little while? Maybe talking will help ease my mind."

Whit sat up straighter, scooting back to lean against the headboard. "Sure, what do you want to talk about?"

Clover shrugged. "Oh, I don't know. Anything. Tell me more about you. What do you like? What are your goals?"

Whit frowned, but Clover didn't know why a question like that should upset him. He didn't answer for a long time.

"I'm a simple man," Whit said finally. "I want a quiet, honest life. I like history and working with my hands. I like to fix things, and I like to learn about the objects that come into my shop."

He met her gaze, and Clover thought she saw

some anxiety in his eyes. She smiled easily at him, lifting up her leg to rest her cheek on her knee.

"That sounds nice—a quiet, easy life. No drama. No hustle to get to some imagined finish line that's forever out of reach."

The tension in his eyes eased, and a small smile tugged at his lips.

"That's kind of why I left social media," Clover continued.

Whit tilted his head. "You don't have social media?"

"Nope. I used to. I mean, of course, I did. That's where all my friends were. That's how you stayed informed." She shook her head. "But not anymore. I found myself wasting hours of my time scrolling, and I was angry at people I barely knew or didn't know at all. I still stay informed about the news and stuff, but I pick my sources better than some post on a friend's uncle's page. Also…"

Clover analyzed Whit's expression. *Is he interested? Should I go this far into it?* But he seemed to be listening attentively, his eyes unwavering on her face.

"I've started to notice that social media, and maybe the internet in general, is taking something from us."

"What do you mean?" he asked.

Clover pursed her lips, casting her mind for the right words to describe feelings she'd never expressed. "Do you remember when we were younger and we would go to the grocery or something with our parents before everyone had cellphones? I remember my mom talking to people in line, people she didn't even know. It was usually just pleasantries and stuff, but now, people don't talk to each other at all. It's almost discouraged. It's like we forgot how. I also remember when I was in my early twenties getting into deep discussions with people about anything and everything. But now, it's like the world has turned into the worst of internet forums. We don't know how to disagree; we don't have nuance. We don't want to listen. We hear a trigger word and pile on, discussion over. Maybe I'm just getting old, but that truly scares me. Humans are social creatures. If we don't know how to even talk to each other or interact with each other, how are we going to survive? And even if we do survive, it won't be in a healthy way."

"So you're saying…it's like human culture—not language or race or nationality culture, but the thing that makes us *all* human—is dying?" Whit asked seriously.

"Yes! Yes! That's it! Human culture is dying. What happens when there's no one left who remembers?"

Whit was silent for a while. "That *is* scary."

"Right! So I canceled all my social media accounts. I still use the internet, of course, when I can't avoid it. I still live in a digital age, after all. But I try to get my information from books whenever I can —bloggers don't seem to have any responsibility to truth or facts these days. They never cite their sources. I have a dumbphone, and I only check my email twice a day. When I left social media, I said anyone who wants to be my friend in real life can send me their phone numbers."

"And did they?"

Clover nodded. "A few did. I can't believe how much more time I have in my day. And I'm less angry overall. I even branched out and made some new in-person friends. I joined a knitting group. We meet on Monday nights. They're ordinaries, but they're nice ladies. I do miss out on some events I probably would like because I don't hear about them. And I recognize that social media is very useful in some ways—like giving voice to people and issues that regular media wouldn't give any air time, but overall, I'm happier. In any case, your quiet, honest life sounds perfectly lovely to me."

Chapter Twenty-Five

Whit huffed a soft laugh as he stared down at the summer witch beside him. Over the last few hours, she'd slowly sunk down into his bed. It was past two in the morning, and the house was still. Whatever ghosts had been messing with her—Great-Uncle Andri most likely—had called it a night.

After he'd pretended not to know that she didn't have social media and she'd given her reasons, she'd asked him to tell her all about the work he'd done on the house. He couldn't believe she was interested. He'd almost declined to answer when she'd asked what his goals were. But he saw now that he was only nervous because of how Faustina would have responded.

Carefully, he flipped the top blanket off his legs and over Clover's sleeping form.

She was not Faustina. There couldn't have been two women more unalike.

At first, he'd talked adamantly about his passion, and Clover had listened with rapt attention. She'd even asked questions. But as the hours had ticked on, he'd noticed her eyes starting to droop. So he began going into long explanations with unnecessary details in a soft, low voice until she eventually fell asleep.

Looking down at her one last time, Whit smiled. Then he flicked off the light and settled in to get as much sleep as the rest of the night would allow.

It was the smell of bacon that awoke him. He thought something was burning. But when he popped up and took a deeper breath, he recognized the scent. His mouth watered.

Glancing around him in the predawn light, he saw his bed was empty. He ignored his disappointment at not waking up to Clover's sleeping face. *Of course, it's empty,* he scoffed. *Who else would be cooking bacon?*

Whit pulled on his robe and shoved his feet into his slippers before heading downstairs. He paused in the upper hall, hearing Clover's voice carrying a tune from the kitchen.

Slowly and quietly, avoiding all the creaks in the floorboards, he crept toward the sound. Eventually, he recognized the song as Billy Joel's "The Longest Time."

Standing in the lower hallway, Whit peeked around the doorway to the kitchen.

"Oh oh oh oh!" Clover sang loudly, swaying her hips and clicking the tongs to the timing of the snaps in the song as she stood at the stove, bacon frying in the pan in front of her.

Whit's chest warmed. It was such a mundane sight—someone's wife singing as she cooked breakfast. But she wasn't just someone's wife. She was *his* wife. *His* wife who had slept in *his* bed, and this was their first morning together.

No, that's not right. He stepped back from the threshold and turned his back to the wall. *She's just my housemate who got scared and fell asleep on my bed. And she's just making breakfast because she happened to be up earlier than me. Who said any of that bacon is for me? No one has cooked a meal for me since I left my mother's house.*

Quietly, so as not to startle her, Whit slipped back toward the stairs. Then he shuffled his feet as he approached the kitchen through the dining room.

Clover glanced over her shoulder at the sound, smiling at him cheerfully as he entered the kitchen. "Good morning!"

Her greeting did funny things to his stomach. Whit dipped his head. "Morning."

"I hope you don't mind, but I took the bacon from the freezer. You didn't have a lot in there except premade foods. But there was enough for me to start our first morning off right. Do you and your grandfather not cook?"

Whit shook his head. "Not really, no. We're both pretty busy, and we usually eat at different times."

Clover shrugged. "Oh, well, I don't mind cooking, especially until I find a new job and get new hours. We should go to the grocery store tonight after we move the rest of my stuff."

She reached out and turned off the burner, then placed the bacon on a paper towel.

Whit watched as the summer witch efficiently moved about his kitchen. Somehow, she already seemed familiar with where the plates and silverware were.

He frowned as her words sank in. He didn't mind it on the whole, but would he really have to work around having meals together? How often did he stay late at the shop to finish fixing or categorizing a new acquisition? How often did he rush off to some estate sale in the next county without so much as a word to anyone? Did a housemate require so much energy that he had to tell her where he was going and when he'd be home?

But when Clover grinned and offered Whit a plate of bacon, buttered toast, and the fluffiest scrambled eggs he'd ever seen, the effort required to send a text now and then—when his usual routine changed—didn't feel like so much effort after all.

They took their plates to the dining room, and Clover sat beside Whit rather than at the far end of the table.

"I'm sorry I fell asleep last night while you were talking," she said. "That was rude. I don't want you to think I wasn't interested because I was."

Whit suppressed a smile, knowing he was being boring on purpose. "It's fine." He brought a forkful of eggs to his mouth, nearly moaning at the texture.

"Are you allergic to anything?" Clover asked. "I don't want to start making meal plans if there's something you can't have."

Whit shook his head, swallowing. "These are the best eggs I've ever had in my entire life."

Clover beamed over at him. "I knew marrying you was a good idea. But be careful, you keep praising me like that, and I might get too full of myself."

Whit's world seemed to blur as a surreal feeling washed over him. Here he was with a beautiful woman smiling at him—his wife—eating a delicious meal she'd cooked for him at the table where only a few days ago he was eating instant oatmeal.

Could life change so fast?

Chapter Twenty-Six

Clover considered the many, many jars crowding the dining room table. *I didn't think I had so many.* She and Whit had managed to move all her things from her parents' house, but now they had to figure out where to put them.

Whit picked one of them up and read the label. "For abundance? What are all these?"

Clover put her hands on her hips, peeking into the kitchen even though she already knew there wasn't enough space there.

"Herbs, spices, and tea blends," she answered, distractedly. *Maybe we could bring one of the bookshelves from home? But we built them upstairs. We'd have to take it apart.*

Whit placed the jar back on the table. "Well, I see two reasonable ways forward. Either we put shelves in the dining room, or we find space in the root cellar. If we put them in here, they would be close at hand.

But the root cellar is a cool, dark place, which I'm assuming is better for them?"

Clover nodded, then glanced around the room. "Yes." She hummed in thought. "Would it be too cluttered in here, do you think?"

"We can figure something out. Why don't we just move them to the root cellar for now so they're out of the way. The entrance is outside. I'll show you."

As they started refilling boxes with jars, a knock—hesitant and light—came from the other room. Clover's skin tightened. *Is the ghost back?*

"Someone's at the front door," Whit said before moving toward it.

Clover's tension didn't ease. She'd almost rather it was a ghost. What if it was one of Whit's relatives? What if they reacted even worse than her family when they found out Whit had married a summer witch?

But as Whit opened the door, Clover heard a familiar voice. "Oh, h-hello, you must be Whittaker. I'm Erie, Clover's sister. Is Clover here?"

Clover rushed across the room into the hall where Whit held the door open. Her ears had not deceived her. Erie stood on the doorstep, a bouquet of white and yellow daffodils in her arms.

Erie smiled a warm but embarrassed smile. "Hey, little sis. So I heard you got married."

Clover's eyes watered. She should have known that out of everyone, Erie would be the one to reach out. She was the most likely to listen and not jump to conclusions, the family peacekeeper.

"Would you like to come in?" Whit asked.

"Yeah, come in, Erie. I'll make some tea."

Erie nodded and handed Clover the flowers as she stepped inside.

"Pick the jar you want, and I'll take the rest to the root cellar," Whit said while closing the door.

Clover grabbed the jar of hibiscus, knowing it was her sister's favorite, then told Erie to follow her to the kitchen.

Clover had familiarized herself with the kitchen earlier that morning, so she knew there weren't any vases. But she had seen a large beer stein that should hold the flowers long enough for her to get a vase. Erie glanced around the space as Clover filled the stein with tap water.

"Thank you for the flowers and for coming out," Clover told her sister. "How did you find me anyway?"

Erie snorted. "As if I can't always find my wayward sister. I heard everything from Ari and Mom. Ari mentioned Whittaker's name, and it sounded familiar to me. Then I remembered the order for camellias that came in a few days ago. I went to the antique shop first, but it was closed. Anyway, his address is public record."

Without a proper tea kettle, Clover put a pot of water on the stove to boil. "Have you thought about being a private detective?"

"Should I?" Erie laughed.

Clover scooped hibiscus leaves into her favorite tea pot, which she'd packed from her family home, and finally turned toward her sister. "How's Mom and Dad?" she asked, afraid to hear the answer.

Erie sighed. "They just need some time, Clover.

You dropped a bomb on everyone, me included, by the way. How did you expect them to react?"

Clover drooped at Erie's words. "I know… But I didn't know what else to do. They would have tried to stop me, and I'd already made up my mind."

Erie was silent for a while, watching Clover's sad expression. "So how long has this been going on? I was as surprised as everyone else. I didn't know you were seeing anyone, let alone a winter sorcerer."

Clover peeked up at her sister. "Not long…five days?"

"Five *days*?" Erie shouted.

Clover winced. "Okay, but listen. I met him at the end-of-summer party, and we kissed, and it was perfect. And when I was leaving, I talked to a crow. Then he ordered those camellias. And when I delivered them, he asked me to marry him. So I said yes. It felt right. I've felt stuck for months now, and I asked the summer gods for change. This is what they sent me."

Erie listened carefully to Clover's rushed explanation. "He crashed the end-of-summer party?"

Clover nodded meekly.

"Well, he's got a set of balls on him; I'll give him that. And even for a winter sorcerer, he isn't bad to look at. I could imagine falling in love with a pretty face like that at first sight," Erie snickered.

Clover blushed. "That wasn't the reason," she muttered.

Erie bumped Clover with her shoulder. "But it doesn't hurt, though, right?"

A slow grin spread across Clover's face.

Sighing, Erie wrapped her arm around her little sister. "You've gotten yourself into a pickle this time, sis. But I trust you. If all the signs told you this was the right decision, who am I to argue with the gods? Trust your intuition. It's never led you astray."

Clover rested her head on her sister's shoulder, relief spreading through her. "Have I told you how great of a sister you are?"

Erie gave her a squeeze. "Tell me again. I never get tired of hearing it."

"You're a great sister."

Erie laughed. "Well, while you're so worried about what Mom and Dad think, you should be worried about Llew. I've never seen him so upset. He nearly destroyed an entire wedding order by squeezing the heads off stems."

Clover groaned.

Erie patted her back. "Let's have some of this tea, shall we? I'd like to meet my new brother-in-law."

Chapter Twenty-Seven

Whit replayed the visit from Clover's sister the day before as he prepared to open the shop. Outwardly, Erie had seemed polite and curious about him. But he hadn't missed the hint of hardness in her stare or the stiff way she'd sat as if she were uncomfortable even being in his presence.

One thing was for certain, though. She loved her sister, and she'd come to comfort and support her decision to marry him. That was good enough for Whit. He'd overheard their conversation in the kitchen, and he hoped the rest of her family would come around eventually.

Clover hadn't said anything to Whit. Why would she? But he'd heard how sad her voice was when she'd talked with Erie. And he'd seen the shadow in her cornflower blue eyes when the sisters had chatted over tea.

As he wiped fingerprints from the glass jewelry

case, he heard a knock on the window. He glanced at the clock. It was still another ten minutes before he was set to open.

I did lose two days of revenue. If they're so eager to get in, maybe they'll buy something.

But when he looked through the door, he saw it was only Alexandre. He unbolted the lock and flipped the sign to open.

Alexandre burst in, bringing a blast of cold wind from the otherwise warm day.

"I don't have much time," he said in a rush. "I told your mom I was going to visit my mom before work, and you know she talks to her, so I have to actually go."

Whit braced for impact as Alexandre turned his dark eyes on him.

"Do you know what the last three days have been like for me?" Alexandre asked with an uncharacteristic seriousness.

Whit swallowed. He could imagine.

"Your mom was positive I knew something about your sudden marriage."

"Did you tell her anything?" Whit asked.

Alexandre scowled. "Who do you take me for? I played dumb, of course. But let me tell you, when she showed me that wedding picture of you and that summer witch, it took every ounce of my acting skills to pretend."

Whit sighed in relief. He knew he would have to tell everyone about Clover. But it was far better they heard it from him. As usual, Alexandre came through in a pinch.

Alexandre crossed his arms, pursing his lips in displeasure. "Dude, a summer witch? I know your grandfather wanted you to get married fast, but did it have to be a summer witch? She's the one you ditched me for at the party, right? I'd almost rather you'd married Faustina than her."

Whit's hackles rose. "That's uncalled for."

"No, man, what's uncalled for is you putting me in a tough spot between you as my friend and your mom as my employer. Your whole family is going to flip when they find out. You know that's not what your grandfather meant when he said marry a witch."

"Then he should have been clearer with his word choice if he was going to make a magical pact. I thought you'd appreciate the loophole I found, being the resident trickster."

But Whit's comment had no effect on Alexandre's mood.

"I might have if you weren't now married to a summer witch for the rest of your life. Ugh, was it really worth it for a house?"

"She's not that bad. And you said it yourself—no winter witch would get married in a rush like that."

Alexandre huffed through his nose. He knew Whit was right. He had said marrying a winter witch before the solstice was impossible. He'd even been the one to drag him to the summer party. So in a roundabout way, Clover and Whit never would have met without Alexandre.

"How mad is she?" Whit asked, seeing Alexandre's irritation ease a bit.

Alexandre clicked his tongue. "Her rage wasn't as

bad as her sorrow. She's heartbroken. Think about it. Her only son, the only real family she has left, didn't even include her in such a big moment."

Whit's heart squeezed. "I'll call her." But even as he made the promise, he didn't know what he was going to say. He could explain everything to her in detail. He could tell her about Grandfather and his demands. But he knew that would only upset her more. She would see what he'd done as trading his life's happiness for a house. He had to make her believe he'd married Clover because he loved her, or his mother would be considerably more heartbroken than she was now. Not to mention it would affect her relationship with Grandfather and her treatment of Clover.

A wave of exhaustion rushed over Whit. This was why he'd always acted so carefully, why he wasn't spontaneous and thought his decisions through. In less than a week, his whole life had been turned upside down and inside out, and there was no end in sight.

What had ever convinced him this was a good idea?

An image of Clover—bathed in moonlight, her cornflower blue eyes dark in the hushed winter woods, tilting her face upward, inviting him to kiss her—came to his mind. *Was that when I lost my mind? No.*

He wouldn't have even been in that situation had he not felt the intrigue of her magic.

Recalling it now, warmth spread through him. And though he still knew he was in a topsy turvy version of his life, he somehow had the hope everything would work out. The feeling was completely foreign to him. Things didn't just work out on their own. It took work and planning to make life what he wanted it to be. But even so, even though he knew that to be true—had lived his whole life by that principle—it didn't affect the feeling.

He knew that if he threw seeds down now—even if they had to stay dormant for months under the Cailleach's tartan of snow—they would grow because that was what seeds did. That was their purpose.

"Everything will be all right," Whit assured Alexandre.

Alexandre raised an eyebrow at his friend. "If you say so… Just take care of it."

Whit nodded. "I will. And thanks for covering for me."

Finally, Alexandre quirked a smile. "Who do you think I am? You think I don't have my boy's back?"

Chapter Twenty-Eight

Clover carefully slipped the glass bottles into her jacket pocket along with the drawstring pouch. The house still smelled of freshly baked bread even though it had been done for over an hour. She'd already left a slice—generously buttered—on the dining room table to make friends with the house spirits of her new home.

She breathed deeply, the autumn air swirling softly around her as she stepped out of the kitchen door. It was the perfect day for a walk outside, with only a hint of bite on the wind. She knew the resurgence of warmth wasn't likely to last long, and she was determined to take advantage of the dying embers of summer.

After closing the door behind her, Clover started toward the thick woods that surrounded the backyard. Whit had already shown her around the property, but he hadn't given her a thorough tour. She'd seen the original house—a modest one-room cottage that likely belonged in a museum. But that wasn't what she was after today.

There wasn't much of a lawn behind the house; it was made up of mostly trees and dirt paths. *If I'm to have a garden,* Clover thought, following a path that led deeper into the woods, *it will have to be in the front yard.*

Clover's gaze swept across the trunks around her, looking for a good place to make her offering to the land spirits.

The rustle of leaves made her freeze, and a flash of white caught her eye.

She gazed at a fox, not ten feet from her. It had white fur with red ears and red eyes. A tingle ran over her skin. This was no ordinary fox. This was one of the Other Crowd.

Clover dipped her head to the creature. "Good afternoon," she said softly.

The fox turned its back on her and started farther down the path. It paused, looked back at her, then trotted ahead.

Normally, Clover wouldn't follow a fae she was unfamiliar with. Who knew where it might lead her? But then again, the winter faction didn't interact with the Good Neighbors. And any good will she could show them would only benefit her in her new life, especially if this one lived nearby.

Clover blinked, and the fox was gone. Still, she followed the path where it had been headed. To her surprise, the trail led to a small clearing, a tree standing in the center. It wasn't a large tree, but it was already naked for the winter.

Clover bent down and picked up one of the many leaves at its base. *A lone hawthorn.* She smiled. This had to be where the fox had wanted her to go. Taking out the pouch she'd put in her pocket, she untied the strings. Then she knelt atop the fallen hawthorn leaves.

"I make this offering to the land spirits of this place. My name is Clover. I honor you this day. May there be friendship between us." Clover then gently poured the birdseed from the pouch into a crevice made by the tree's roots.

She cleared away some of the leaves to expose the bare soil beneath. Pulling out the larger of the two bottles, she twisted off the cap. It was peppermint and eucalyptus tea for clear and open communication. She took a sip of the brew, cooled before she'd bottled it, and poured the rest on the bare ground.

Finally, she removed the last of her offerings.

"Ancient Ones of the Otherworld, I make this offering to you now so you might know me and my goodwill. May there be friendship between us." Clover poured the honey from the small jar onto the roots of the fairy tree.

She knew they were there; the fox was a clear sign they were watching. And she hoped her offerings might smooth over any disturbance her sudden appearance on this land might cause. Of course, the Gentry wouldn't be much fazed by her having moved. They moved around themselves. But the land spirits didn't know her.

Her goal accomplished, Clover said her goodbyes,

pocketing her empty containers and promising to visit again.

But as she moved to return to the house, she paused. She didn't have much to do there. She'd put the pasta sauce to simmer in the slow cooker, and she'd already unpacked. Whit wouldn't be home until dinner, and knitting group wasn't until after that.

Turning back toward the lone hawthorn, Clover continued her walk. It had been a while since she'd just enjoyed a nice, quiet day outside. Most of her free time was spent with family and friends or running errands.

A sudden sadness made her stomach heavy, but she pushed it aside. *Just because I'm alone, doesn't mean I have to feel lonely.*

And though she knew it was true, the fact was she didn't know how long the fallout with her family and Ari would last.

She'd tried to call Ari that morning, but the line went to voicemail after one ring—telling her Ari had rejected her call.

Clover's steps slowed as she continued to think about the situation, the crunch of leaves softening in volume. But as she let her feet wander, the carpet of leaves gave way to still-green grass.

Looking up from the ground, Clover found herself in a cemetery. A green plain stretched out before her, waving in gentle hills. A two-story house sat at the top of a hill, and a mausoleum stood on the far side near the road.

The tombstones near Clover were a mixture of old

and new—some weathered and hard to read while others shined in the afternoon sun.

The unmistakable tingle of magic hung in the air, not strong but easy to recognize. Clover glanced around to find its source.

"Oh!" a woman exclaimed, standing from a crouch. Her hand was full of leaves she'd just swept from a sunken gravestone.

Clover jumped at her exclamation, just as surprised. She smiled in embarrassment. "I'm sorry," she stammered. "I was just out for a walk. I didn't even know this was here."

The woman's dark eyes analyzed her as if trying to place someone they'd seen before. But Clover was certain they'd never met. The woman had long salt-and-pepper hair tied at the base of her neck and dark eyes—shiny and sharp like a crow's. She wore a long purple skirt and a thick sweater, and the magic Clover had felt wafted off her.

Clover nodded politely at the winter witch—for no summer witch would willingly hang out in a graveyard.

"Would you like any help?" Clover asked. She didn't want to disturb the woman, who'd probably come to visit her loved ones' graves. But she didn't know what else to say with the witch's eyes on her so keenly.

The woman tilted her head, blinking in surprise. "What?" Then she looked down at her handful of leaves and dropped them. "Oh, no, thank you."

Clover dipped her head, awkwardly shifting her weight from one foot to the other. "Well, I'm sorry to have disturbed you. I'll just be going. Oh, and I'm sorry for your loss."

"Wait—" the woman said, her protest cut off by the sound of her cellphone ringing. She pulled her phone from her pocket and stared at the screen but didn't answer, letting the phone ring.

"Aren't you going to get that?" Clover asked.

Frowning, the woman shook her head. "Not right now."

Chapter Twenty-Nine

Whit's eyes widened as he stared down at his phone. His mom had just ignored his call. In his living memory, he couldn't think of a time his mother had done such a thing. His stomach twisted. *I'll go see her tonight.*

To keep his mind off something he couldn't change at the moment, he threw himself into work. He had a stack of bills to pay and a workshop bench full of items to research and price.

He was using his magic to feel out a Japanese tea cup—tears streaming from his eyes as he shook with the terror and suffering the previous owner felt as the atomic bomb was dropped on the nation—when the door chimed.

He opened his mouth to call that he would be right out, but his voice had no sound. He placed the delicate cup back in its saucer, wiped his face with his hands, and cleared his throat before standing from his stool.

Though still shaken from the emotions of someone long dead, he forced a polite smile as he returned to the main shop.

"Good afternoon," he greeted his customer, who was waiting at the counter with her back to him.

She turned at his voice, and he clamped down on a reflexive groan.

"Good afternoon, Whit," Luisa Ornett returned in that suggestive way she always used when she spoke to him. "I've brought you something I know you won't be able to resist."

Whit suppressed a sigh as he approached the counter where the ordinary waited, leaning forward to display what else she had to offer. The fact was that she usually did sell him good stuff, so even though he wasn't interested in everything she wanted to give him, he usually bought her garage sale finds.

Coming around the counter, Whit beheld a transparent yellow compote dish with inlaid facets and scalloped edges. He knew right away from the color that it was uranium glass.

"Where did you find it?" Whit asked, carefully taking off the lid and examining it for damage.

Uranium glass was all the rage at the moment. He had collectors come in nearly every other day. He'd even put UV lights in a china cabinet to show it off.

"Oh, just a garage sale I happened upon while I was driving home from work last week. I thought of you when I saw it."

Whit didn't bother to look at her, keeping his eyes on the dish.

"And how much are you asking for?" he said.

"I'll tell you what"—Luisa stood on her toes and rested her elbows on the counter, leaning toward him —"I'll give it to you for free if you take me out tonight."

Whit eyed Luisa with a frown. The dish she'd brought him was indeed unusual, and even without research, he thought he could get a couple hundred dollars for it. For the last year or so, Luisa had been coming in to his shop and making passes at him. Though this was the first time she'd outright asked him on a date, he wasn't so oblivious as to not know what she'd wanted the whole time. And it wasn't that she was unattractive. She was perfectly good looking. She seemed nice, if a little forward.

But still, he'd never considered the thought of being with her for more than a moment. She was an ordinary. He'd been on dates with ordinaries before. No, it was more than that. She, like all women, just seemed like a lot of work to him. Romantic relationships were a lot of work. It just never seemed worth it. For what? A night's passion? Oh, it would feel good—great, in fact—but would it be worth the emotional fallout? Sex was never just sex.

"Will forty dollars do, then?" Whit asked Luisa. "That's about what I would spend if we went out to dinner."

Luisa pouted her lips. "I wanted your time, not your money. Why? Do you have plans tonight?"

Finally, Whit met and held the woman's gaze. "I do. I'm going home to have dinner with my wife."

Luisa's eyes popped. "Your *wife*? Since when are

you married?" Her eyes shifted to his left hand. "You've never worn a wedding ring before today."

Whit smiled warmly. "That's because I was only married last week."

Luisa blew out a heavy breath, her bangs fluttering as she did so. "Well, that explains a lot," she muttered.

Then she cocked her hip, placing one fist on it. "You should have just told me you were involved. I don't hit on taken men. I've a mind to tell your new wife that you don't shut women down right away."

Whit doubted that Clover would much care. He frowned at the thought.

"Yeah, you wouldn't like that, would you, mister?" Luisa said, mistaking his expression. "You better get your act together and treat her right."

Whit blinked at how quickly the situation had turned. He nearly laughed at Luisa's absurdity. "I'll be sure to do that," he responded dryly.

Luisa analyzed him, then nodded firmly once. "Good. So back to the dish, I haggled the seller down; forty should be fine."

Whit opened his cash register to pay her. As he handed her the bills, he said, "I hope this news won't stop you from bringing me your finds."

Luisa smiled. "Of course not. Even if you belong to someone else, you're still pretty to look at. Besides, you give me a better price than the other dealers in town. See you around."

Stuffing the money into the pocket of her skin-tight jeans, Luisa swished her hips as she went to the door.

Belong to someone else, huh? The phrasing hit his mind in a particular way. *I suppose it is true in a way. We're bound together if nothing else.*

Whit wondered what it meant to belong to someone. Did that make him Clover's responsibility? What part of him? Conversely, did that mean Clover belonged to him as well? He didn't like the idea of having to take responsibility for someone else.

Clover is a grown woman. Surely, she doesn't need anyone to take responsibility for her. He nodded to himself, staring into the yellow glass of the compote in front of him. *I just need to be a good housemate and a good friend. The promises I made were nothing beyond what friendship would entail.*

Chapter Thirty

Clover's phone dinged. Even though she was at the dinner table and always made a point of making it a phone-free zone, the fact that she hadn't heard from Ari or her family all day made her reach for it anyway.

The text was accompanied by another that included the time and address. Clover frowned at the phone. It wasn't the message she'd been hoping for.

"Something wrong?" Whit asked from beside her, his plate of spaghetti nearly clean.

Clover shook her head. "No, but do you mind

giving me a ride tomorrow night? I promised to attend this volunteer orientation at a cat rescue."

Whit nodded.

"I'm really sorry. I'll get another car as soon as I can. I hate having to ask for a ride. I feel like a teenager again."

"It's not a problem. I was planning on going somewhere tomorrow as well, so I'll just drop you off on my way."

"Oh? You have plans, too?"

Whit averted his gaze. "Just going to work out. You were telling me about someone you met today?"

Clover swallowed down another mouthful of spaghetti. "Yeah, I went wandering around today. I wanted to make myself known to the land spirits. Did you know we live next to a graveyard?"

Whit dipped his head.

Clover laughed. "That's a silly question. Of course, you know. Anyway, I popped out of the woods into the cemetery. And there was a lady cleaning off one of the graves. She was there visiting her relatives, I think. She looked so sad and lonely. I think she must have lost someone pretty recently. I apologized for disturbing her, but when I went to leave, she asked if I might stay and keep her company for a while. We didn't talk much, just sat on a bench enjoying the warm weather. But I felt so bad for her when it was time for me to leave—and she said she came to the cemetery most days—that I invited her to tea later this week. Is that all right?"

Whit tilted his head. "Why wouldn't it be?"

Clover carefully twirled noodles onto her fork.

"Well, I didn't want to just invite someone over without telling you. Besides, do you think it's safe? She's a winter witch."

"What's her name?" Whit asked, his face suddenly very serious.

"Lina."

Whit frowned in thought. "I don't know the name. But if you felt comfortable enough to invite her over, it should be fine. And you don't have to tell her you're a summer witch until you feel it's safe. I mean, we never tell ordinaries we're friends with who we are, right?"

Clover quirked her mouth. "Yes, but isn't that a little different? Ordinaries don't believe in witches. After they took over Forest Haven and started outnumbering us, we stopped being so open. They hear the Founder's Day story every year, and they think it's just a silly legend. But you're right. I'll wait until I think she'll be all right with it. Thanks."

Clover's phone chimed again, and she glanced at it. "Oh, shit. That's Rachel from my knitting group. She said she's outside." Her head swiveled toward the door and back to her plate.

Whit waved his hand. "Go ahead. I'll clean up."

Clover smiled. "Really? Thanks. Sorry." Scooping up one last bite of pasta, she shoved it into her mouth as she stood.

On her way to the front door, Clover grabbed the tote bag with her latest knitting project in it—a sweater for Crane.

"I'll be back in two hours," she called out to Whit while she pulled on her coat.

"Okay," he answered from the kitchen.

The night wind carried a chill that promised tomorrow would not be as warm. Clover hurried to Rachel's car and slipped into the passenger seat.

"Thanks for the ride," she said, turning to the ordinary.

Rachel lowered her head to look out the windshield at the house. "I thought you lived on the south side."

"I did."

"You moved?" the woman asked, putting her car in reverse to head back to the road.

"I've got a big announcement. I'll wait until we get there to tell everyone at once."

The elder smiled. "Oh, I wonder what it is."

It took only fifteen minutes to get to the stables, a shorter distance than if Clover had been coming from her parents' house. Rachel parked the car in the gravel lot beside the others.

Clover had been surprised upon her first visit to the group. She didn't think horse stables were the usual place to sit around and knit. But she was told that the group had started from an equestrian therapy class for elders. Apparently, some of the ladies had gotten to talking about knitting and decided to start a knitting circle. Because the stables were open late on Mondays after their class, the owner had agreed to let them use the tack room for their circle. They called themselves the knitting unicorns.

Clover followed Rachel into the room, and everyone greeted their arrival with enthusiasm.

"We thought you weren't coming," Sue said as Clover took the empty chair beside her.

"All right. I'm dying to know. What's the big announcement?" Rachel asked.

A murmur of confusion traveled around the circle.

"Clover said she had something to tell us," Rachel updated.

All eyes fixed on Clover.

Clover stared back at her friends. Everyone there was at least thirty years older than her. The youngest at sixty-five was Belle, who everyone called Darling. Josephine—known as Joey—had just turned ninety; they'd had a big party for her and everything. Rachel, Sue, and Frances were somewhere in between.

"Well?" Joey urged, her voice hoarse and a little shaky as usual. "We aren't getting any younger."

With a smile, Clover held out her left hand. "I got married!"

Chapter Thirty-One

Whit glanced over his shoulder at the cemetery his mother's family had run for generations. This was where he'd grown up—playing peek-a-boo with ghosts among the graves, traipsing through the woods between here and his grandparents' house. Taking a deep breath, he knocked on the front door of his childhood home before heading inside.

"Mom?" he called out, announcing his presence more thoroughly than his knock.

She didn't respond.

But considering the door had been unlocked, he knew either she or Alexandre was home.

He tried the den first. If her habits hadn't changed, she was usually reading by the fire this time of night.

And that was exactly where he found her—a book resting on her bent knees, her bare toes peeking out under her long purple skirt at the edge of the armchair.

"There you are," Whit said from the doorway.

Slipping a bookmark between the pages of her book, his mother turned her dark eyes on him, the firelight reflecting her mask of reservation.

She didn't speak, which was somehow worse than a biting remark.

"I asked if you trusted me, and you said you'd hear me out at least," Whit reminded her of her words from the week before.

Mom lifted her chin, reluctantly signaling he should go ahead with his explanation.

"I'm sorry I didn't tell you before I got married, but Clover and I worried that our families would try to stop us if they found out."

"Was this the bad news you were referring to before? The reason you didn't want to be around family for the ritual?" Her question was soft, her tone tired.

Whit frowned, hesitating. He didn't like to lie to his mother, and she was pretty good at knowing when he did. "It's related, yes."

"But why keep it from us?" she asked, her tone hurt while trying to understand. "We've all wanted to see you settled for a long time. I, for one, am thrilled to finally have a daughter-in-law though I can't say she's ingratiating herself by not inviting me to the wedding."

"It's not her fault," Whit defended. "She didn't invite her family either, and they're just as upset as you are."

Mom's brow furrowed. "Does she not value family? Family is the most important thing for the winter faction."

Whit sighed heavily. "She's not a winter witch. She's a…summer witch."

Mom's eyes bulged, but she clamped her mouth shut. She was showing restraint, holding back her emotions, swallowing them down. Whit knew the expression well.

"That's why we didn't tell anyone. She was afraid her family would stop her, and I…"

"B-but she didn't seem—I mean, from the picture I saw, she didn't look like a summer witch."

Whit raised an eyebrow. "The green dress and the flowers in her hair weren't a clue? In any case, she's a witch same as us. She's not an alien. Why would she look different from any other witch?"

Mom frowned, deep and thoughtful—her eyes losing focus as she considered something far away.

The sound of thumping on the stairs announced Alexandre's approach before he popped his head into the room. "Hey, Mel, I'm headed to the store. Do you need—? Oh, Whit. I'll, uh, I'll give you two some space to talk. Do you need anything while I'm out?"

Mom shook her head, and Alexandre retreated as quickly as he'd appeared.

The soft hiss and crackle of the fire were the only sounds in the room as Whit waited for his mother to say something—anything.

"I'm trying to understand," she said quietly. "My mind is whirling with so many questions. I didn't even know you were seeing anyone. I'm upset that I'm so far out of your life that I didn't know that for so long. I don't even know how you would have met a summer witch, but I suppose that hardly matters now."

Whit relaxed a little, relieved she didn't press for more information. He didn't want to tell her he hadn't dated Clover, and he didn't want to lie about or expose Alexandre's part in the whole thing.

She sighed heavily. "I might have guessed a summer witch was involved," she murmured. "You would never have made such a big decision without forethought. You wouldn't have chosen to hide it from the family."

Whit held up his hand. "I'm going to stop you right there. I don't want you blaming Clover for any of this. I know we've stood on the opposite side from the summer faction for a long time, and we all have our biases. But the fact is I proposed to her. And even though she agreed, she was very surprised. And I'm the one who suggested we keep it a secret first. So don't accuse her of something that was my doing."

"I…I don't know what to say, Whittaker," Mom said flatly. "This is just so unlike the boy I raised. I taught you to be thoughtful and to plan things thoroughly. It doesn't seem like you thought this through. If I laid undue blame on the summer witch, it's because I couldn't imagine the son I know doing something like this."

"Her name is Clover, not 'the summer witch.'" Whit kept his tone calm. "And I can understand that you feel this was unlike me. To be honest, I haven't felt quite like myself since I met Clover. But then, she's unlike anyone I've ever met before. She told her family she knew with everything in her that marrying me was the right thing to do. From where I stand now, the divide between the winter and summer factions seems artificial and forced. None of us are ordinaries. We all worship the old gods. Why is there a distinction between summer and winter? We don't draw lines by pantheon. You're training Alexandre to take over the cemetery even though he doesn't worship the same gods as us."

Mom stared at Whit in silence as the moment drew out uncomfortably. He resisted the urge to squirm under her steady gaze. He believed in what he'd said, but her stare still had a way of making him feel like he'd done something wrong.

"You love her," she said finally.

A thrill ran up Whit's spine.

"That's the only explanation for this behavior. Love makes people do strange and out-of-character things. It makes you feel like a different version of yourself. It makes you believe anything is possible, even closing the rift between warring factions."

Whit fought the urge to correct her. This was what he wanted. If his mother believed he loved his wife, that would only be good for everyone involved. So without a word—which could betray him in tone or quality—he dipped his head in a single nod.

"I'm glad," Mom said though she didn't sound glad at all.

"So…would you like to meet her?" Whit asked. "I think she'll be happy to know someone approves of us."

Mom shook her head. "No, not yet. I need to sit with this for a while. And I didn't say I approve. I said I'm glad. I'm glad you've finally found someone who makes you feel the way she does. It's like nothing else. And I hope it will open up the facets of winter witchcraft that have eluded you until now. But that is a far cry from approval, Whittaker. I want you to grow and learn and feel everything life has to offer. But I never would have wanted you to know the hardships you've just thrust upon yourselves."

Whit wondered what facets she referred to. If there were things about being a winter sorcerer he didn't know, he certainly wanted to know. And since he didn't actually love Clover, he wondered if he could learn those things his mother meant.

Rising from her chair, Mom approached Whit and lifted her hand to his cheek.

"Don't look so worried," she said, misinterpreting his expression. "I'll meet her soon enough. Let me get used to the idea first, and let her settle in. It's a big change getting married and moving into your husband's house. She'll need your attention now. She doesn't need a meddling mother-in-law."

Wrapping her arms around Whit, Mom whispered to the spirit of his father, "I can't believe our little boy is finally married, Grady."

Chapter Thirty-Two

Clover grinned as a flurry of congratulations burst from the knitting circle. Everyone leaned forward to ooo and ahh over her ring, and Darling demanded to see her wedding picture.

As she pulled the photo up on her phone and began passing it around, Sue turned to her seriously.

"As someone who's been married for nearly thirty years, I have some important advice I'd like you to take. Remember that the man is the head of the household."

Clover flinched at her words. Politics and religion were off-limit topics in the group, so she didn't know where everyone stood, but she could see where this was going. "Shouldn't it be more like a partnership?" Clover asked.

Darling shook her head seriously. "No, Sue is absolutely right. The man is the head... But the woman is the neck!"

Everyone but Sue laughed.

As their chuckles died down, Frances said, "I have some advice, too. If you ever ask your husband to do something around the house, and he takes forever to do it, go find the loudest power tool you can, and just turn it on. You don't even have to do anything. The sound will bring him running like a squirrel to a full bird feeder."

"The best advice I have," Rachel added, "is if you really want him to do something, make him think it was his idea. Don't get caught up on taking credit. As long as it gets done, it doesn't matter."

"What about you, Joey?" Darling asked. "You've survived three husbands in your time. Any advice for the newlywed?"

Everyone turned to Joey, and Clover felt the full force of the elder's blue eyes on her. "We are all liberated women here. In our time, we've marched for our rights and equality. Half of us burned our bras."

"I haven't worn one since," Darling chimed in.

Another chuckle from the group.

"So when I say this, I want you to keep that in mind," Joey continued. "Give him opportunities to feel strong. It doesn't matter if it's asking him to open a jar or reach for something on the top shelf, even better if you can make him feel like he's protected you in some way. Men want to feel needed. They want to feel manly—just like we want to feel needed and appreciated for our womanly qualities. So even if you can do it yourself, ask him for help sometimes and praise him by telling him he's strong and you feel safe with him."

"You make men sound like they're children," Clover said.

"Well…" Darling trailed off. Her suggestion was accompanied by more chuckling.

"It might sound simple and silly, but we all just want to feel appreciated and needed," Joey commented. "Perhaps it's childish, but there it is. And"—She paused for emphasis to make sure everyone was listening—"tell him what you want honestly. Don't do the 'you should just know' thing. They don't know. They need to be told clearly. So tell him what you want…especially in the bedroom." Joey smirked.

Giggles erupted from the elders as though they were a bunch of schoolgirls talking about their first crushes, and Clover couldn't help but join in.

As the laughter died down, the chatter veered off to other topics.

Sue and Rachel started talking very seriously about how the Rangers did over the weekend. Clover turned to the others. It wasn't that she didn't like hockey—she did. It was just that Sue and Rachel talked about it on another level—player stats and projections and details she didn't much care to follow.

"Oh, I wanted to show you all," Frances said, reaching for a USPS box beside her chair. "I finally finished crocheting that unicorn blanket I was making for my granddaughter."

"Let's have a look!" Clover encouraged while Darling and Joey agreed.

Frances stood and unfolded the white blanket, pulling one corner up over her head like a hood. The hood had horse ears and a crown of flowers along with a long, pink shaft standing up at the center of the forehead.

Darling burst out laughing as Joey murmured, "Oh my…"

Clover bit her lips.

"So how does it look?" Frances asked with pride. "I messed up the edge a little, so I had to rip it out and do it over. But it turned out pretty good, right?"

Rachel and Sue dropped their discussion to take in Frances's creation.

"Um…how old is your granddaughter?" Sue wanted to know.

"She's in her twenties," Frances responded. "Why?"

Rachel nodded. "It looks great, Frances. But maybe just don't share it on social media."

Frances frowned, worry scrunching up her face. "Why not? Is it bad? What's wrong with it?"

Clover knew how hard Frances had been working on the blanket, and she wanted to save her feelings.

"Nothing!" Clover assured. "It's fine. Rachel is just trying to save you from the worst of people online."

Frances looked around the group. "Do I need to redo it? What's wrong with it?"

Darling motioned for Frances to come closer, and Frances dipped her head toward her.

Even though she whispered, everyone could still hear her. "The horn looks like a giant dick."

Frances's face flushed, and she let out a horrified

sound. "Oh my. I didn't even notice! I'm going to have to redo it."

"No, you don't, Frances," Clover said quickly, seeing how upset Frances was becoming. "Darling just has a dirty mind. I'm sure your granddaughter will love it."

Clover shot Darling a glance.

"I've been accused of worse," Darling said. "She's right, though. It's fine. Your granddaughter probably won't even notice."

"But seriously," Rachel said again. "Don't share it online."

It took more coaxing and compliments for Frances to perk up again. In the end, she decided that everyone there just had their minds in the gutter, especially after Joey's reference to the bedroom. She said she would send it to her granddaughter the next day.

The rest of the meeting was filled with general chatter about what everyone had been up to and the state of everyone's health.

Chapter Thirty-Three

Whit glanced at the dashboard of his truck, checking the time once again. He was cutting it pretty close. But at least Pets and Scritches was on the same side of town as where he was headed.

He pulled into the small strip mall with only five minutes to spare. He hated being late. And as this was his first time, he was sure there were things he was supposed to do beforehand.

Sacred Fire Yoga was squished between a local barbecue grill and a dentist's office. He shut off the truck, grabbed his water bottle, and rushed inside.

The yoga studio was small but cozy. The calming sounds of water emanated from a large glass water fountain nearly as big as the back wall. Close to the entrance, there were hooks to hang coats—half of which were full with shoes beneath them—and to one side, there were shelves filled with yoga mats, hand weights, blocks, and rolled up straps.

The lighting was low, the space lit purely by LED candles around the edges of the room.

The atmosphere was soothing and calm with the unmistakable undercurrent of summer magic.

There were six yoga mats already laid out on the floor—five lined up parallel to one another while one was perpendicular to the rest.

The woman at the mat closest to the door glanced over at him as he removed his shoes to place them beneath his already hanging coat. "You're just in time. Have you been here before?"

He looked up to see the woman was Rania—the summer priestess. Her eyes widened as she sucked in a breath. Whit smiled kindly at her. "No, it's my first time."

"Y-yes, I guess it is," she giggled nervously. "Does, um, does Llewellyn know you're coming?"

"Do I know who's coming?" Llewellyn asked, appearing from behind a folding screen that must have hidden a door.

Llewellyn's welcoming smile dropped from his face as pure rage took its place. "What are *you* doing here?"

Whit shrugged. "Taking a class… Why? Am I not allowed to do yoga?"

"Not here you're not," Llewellyn spat.

A few of the ordinary women murmured to each other, clearly confused about what was happening.

"Aw, why not, Llew?" one ordinary with a very long ponytail asked, looking Whit up and down. "You were just telling us last week that you needed new students. You asked us to bring our friends. I'll vouch for him."

Llewellyn clenched his jaw as a vein in his neck pulsed. Whit knew it was underhanded to approach his brother-in-law in his place of business, where he had a reputation to uphold and ordinaries to appease. But he also knew Llewellyn was the main obstacle to Clover and his life gaining some semblance of peace—he'd heard what Erie had said to Clover in the kitchen. And when they'd mentioned over tea that their brother ran a yoga studio, he thought it was the perfect way to approach him—well, the safest anyway.

"Fine," Llewellyn snapped. "As it says on my website, the first session is free. After that, you can either—you know what? Actually, don't bother coming back."

Llewellyn turned on his heels and stormed to the perpendicular yoga mat at the back of the room. The woman with the long ponytail approached Whit with a warm smile.

"Excuse him, he isn't usually like that. I'm Merry."

"Whit," he said with a nod.

"It's nice to meet you, Whit. Did you bring your own mat?"

Whit shook his head. "This is my first time doing yoga."

Merry's smile brightened. "Well, then, welcome! You can grab a mat from over there." She pointed to the wall of shelves. "Then why don't you roll your mat out next to mine. You can watch me if you get confused by Llew's instructions."

Whit did as she suggested though he wasn't too comfortable with placing his mat at the farthest place from the door.

"Stand at the top of your mats in mountain pose," Llewellyn instructed.

The women moved with smooth, practiced motions, and Whit tried to mimic their stance.

"Stand with your feet shoulder-width apart, weight equally distributed, shoulders down, arms at your side, palms facing forward. And our heads lift," Llewellyn said.

Whit glanced toward Merry, whose eyes were closed. He followed suit.

"*Oṃ Oṃ Oṃ*," Llewellyn chanted.

"bhūr bhuvaḥ svaḥ
tat savitur vareṇyaṃ
bhargo devasya dhīmahi
dhiyo yo naḥ pracodayāt"

As Llewellyn instructed the class to raise their hands above their heads into prayer position and bring them down to their heart centers, Whit opened his eyes.

He glanced at his brother-in-law. All of his animosity was gone. And in that moment, Whit felt respect for the man. However much Llewellyn didn't like him, this was his job, and part of his job was to create a healing environment for his students.

For the next hour—as Whit struggled through poses he wasn't sure his body was meant to twist into—they existed in the same space in harmony. Summer sorcerer, winter sorcerer, clandestine handfasting aside.

And when it was over, and Llew repeated the chant he'd started with, ending with an "*Oṃ Oṃ Oṃ*," that magical bubble popped. And like a delicate soap bubble, Whit was left with slimy, sticky hands as the only proof it had ever existed.

Merry approached Whit as he carefully cleaned his mat with a disinfectant wipe.

"So what did you think? Will you be back?"

Whit already felt sore in muscles he didn't know he had. He glanced over at Llewellyn, who stood talking to Rania in hushed tones.

"Yes, for as long as it takes to feel comfortable," Whit told Merry.

Merry smiled. "That'll be a few weeks at least. It takes a while for your body to get used to yoga unless you do it more than once a week."

"I don't know if my body can handle more than once a week at this point."

Merry giggled. "You'll get there. Take a hot bath when you get home. Will Tuesday be your regular class? I usually come on Tuesdays." Her ponytail swished as she tilted her head.

Whit shrugged—his left hand suddenly feeling very naked without his wedding ring. "I'm not sure."

Llewellyn started toward them, Rania drifting behind.

Merry clasped her hands behind her, shifting her weight from one foot to the other. "Well then… Are you busy now? I usually go get a smoothie after class. I know a great place not far from here. Or, if you're busy now, we could go next week."

Llewellyn crossed his arms, lifting his eyebrows as if he was just as interested in Whit's response to Merry as she was.

Whit dipped his head at Merry in apology. "I'm sorry, Merry. I have to pick up my wife soon. In fact, she's probably waiting for me now."

Merry nodded in disappointment—even her ponytail seemed to droop. Still, she managed a smile. "Oh, no worries, then. Maybe I'll see you in the next class."

Quickly, her ears pink, Merry gathered her mat and scurried to put on her coat and shoes.

With all the ordinaries gone, Whit finally turned to his brother-in-law. Llewellyn's eyes were not the same cornflower blue as Clover's. They were a few shades darker—more like a stormy-ocean blue-grey.

Rania cleared her throat. "Would you like me to stay?" she asked Llewellyn softly.

"No," Llewellyn replied stiffly. "Thanks, Rania. I'll see you later."

Whit knew, magically at least, Llewellyn would be no match for him this time of year, not without another of the summer faction to help him. So while the tension inside him did not ease, Whit took him telling Rania to leave as a good sign.

Chapter Thirty-Four

Clover smiled at the familiar face. "I didn't think you'd be here," she said to Orion as she approached him.

He was rearranging a rack of T-shirts. The main room of Pets and Scritches was a small merchandise shop with two doors at the far end—one of which led to the hallway she'd just left.

Orion's gaze warmed as he returned her smile. He shrugged. "I just happened to be scheduled tonight."

The orientation had been short, and only herself and one other volunteer had attended. It had covered the organization, their mission, and what they needed from volunteers. They'd also taken a tour of the facility, which wasn't very big.

There was a kitten room on the premises as well as a room for new rescues, but most of their furry charges were in foster homes.

Clover had left the orientation with decisions to

make. There were many ways she could help out, but she had to decide how she wanted to give her time.

Behind her, the other new volunteer, Shona, and the presenter, Amy, exited the hall.

"Orion?" Amy said, "I thought you were too busy to help out tonight."

Orion's cheeks flushed, but he continued to smile. "I was just stopping by," he replied. "I'm leaving right now."

Amy turned to Shona and Clover. "I'll send you a link to the schedule portal where you two can sign up for whatever you'd like."

The women nodded and wished each other goodbye.

Clover looked down at her watch. Whit wasn't supposed to pick her up for another half hour. She frowned.

"Are you late for something?" Orion asked.

Clover shook her head. "No, but I'm not getting picked up for a while. What are you doing? I could help you organize."

Orion spread his palms. "I'm already done. But, hey, there's a café the next block over. We could go there to wait, or I could drop you off somewhere."

Being that they were on the south side, Clover knew exactly the café he was referring to. They made a great iced butterfly pea flower tea called arctic purple with mint and lemon. She felt thirsty just thinking about it.

"Sure. Let me just send a quick text, and then we can go to the café."

Pulling out her phone, Clover sent Whit a message telling him where she would be when he was ready to pick her up.

"Ready?" Orion asked, pulling on his coat.

Clover nodded and followed him out into the cold night.

As they walked, she glanced over at him. "You weren't really scheduled for tonight, were you?"

She stifled a laugh when he winced.

"The truth is I was worried Amy would scare you away. She's so passionate about the mission, and it either motivates people or intimidates them. I wanted to encourage you."

Clover quirked her mouth, shoving her hands into her coat pockets as they waited at the crosswalk. It would be cold tomorrow, and she feared it wouldn't warm up again until spring.

"So you think I'm easily intimidated, do you?"

He analyzed her face with a furrowed brow. "You're teasing me, aren't you?"

Clover laughed. "You catch on quickly."

As the light turned green, and they started across the street, Orion asked, "So what are your thoughts about volunteering? Any idea of where you want to spend your efforts?"

Clover hummed in thought. "I'm not sure. The truth is, what I really need is a new job. And anything I sign up for might have to change when I get a new schedule."

"Are you looking for a job? I think my company is hiring. Do you want me to look into it for you?"

"What is it you do?"

Orion opened the door of the café for her. "I'm a microbiologist."

Clover's eyes widened. "Wow, that's impressive. Do you work at a lab, then? I doubt I'm qualified for anything at a lab."

Orion shook his head. "No, I work at a brewery. There are tons of different kinds of jobs though I don't know what they're hiring for at the moment."

Clover smiled. Brewing beer had long been associated with Brighid. *Perhaps the gods aren't done blessing me just yet.* "I might not be qualified for any of the openings. But, sure, check it out for me. Thanks."

"No problem."

As Orion considered what he wanted to order, Clover stepped up to the counter and asked for an arctic purple. Ten minutes later, they were sitting at a table at the back of the café where it was warmest.

"So tell me about yourself, Clover. I feel like you know more about me than I know about you."

Clover tilted her head. "Why do you feel like that?" With ordinaries, witches always had to choose their words carefully. She couldn't blather on about herself in the same easy way she would do with another witch or sorcerer.

"Well, you know about my job and that I like cats so much I volunteer at a rescue. You know I'm civically minded since we met at city hall. I spearheaded that whole petition."

"Do you think you'll have enough signatures before you need them?" Clover asked.

Orion smirked. "Are you avoiding talking about yourself?"

Clover took a deep drink of her purple tea. "Not at all." She played with her straw, moving it in and out of the plastic lid. "I like flowers and teas. I like to grow herbs and flowers and dry them so I can make tea blends."

"Oh, that sounds interesting. I'd like to try one sometime."

"Sure." Clover nodded. "What do you like? Sweet? Spicy? Earthy? Fruity?"

Orion's blue eyes warmed as he flashed her a smile. "Surprise me. I'm sure I'll love anything you pick for me."

Clover's cheeks heated as she recognized the look he gave her. She rubbed her thumb across the base of her left ring finger. She'd forgotten to put her rings back on after doing the dinner dishes—still unused to wearing them.

Clover nodded distantly. "I'll pick something most everyone likes, then. Let's see… What else about me… I've been really busy lately because I just got married—that day we met at city hall, in fact. You remember the man who called out to me, right? That's my husband, Whit."

Orion's warmth mellowed, but his smile did not. "Did you? Well, congratulations. I can see why you'd be so busy after that. Will your husband be volunteering at the rescue with you?"

His nonchalant response made Clover question whether she'd read the situation right. She shrugged.

Either way, it wasn't strange for her to bring Whit up at this point. "I don't know. I didn't ask him." She chuckled. "I don't even know if he likes cats."

Orion's brow furrowed, but his tone was teasing. "Well, if he doesn't, I'd say it's time for a divorce."

Chapter Thirty-Five

Whit stared unflinchingly at his brother-in-law, who stood with his arms crossed and a look of naked hostility on his face.

"It isn't enough that you seduced my sister onto your path of death and darkness. You had to come around here and invade my only place of peace? What do you want from me?" Llewellyn demanded.

"Clover isn't happy—"

"And she never will be with the likes of you," Llewellyn interrupted.

Whit sighed through his nose. He was a patient man, but Llewellyn was trying that patience. His skin prickled with irritation.

"She's unhappy with how she left things with you and your parents."

Llewellyn sneered. "Simple, then. Send her home."

Whit sighed in exasperation. "Why are you being

like this? Look, you don't have to like me. I couldn't really care less. But I'm not going to turn my wife out of the house because you don't approve of her choice of me as a spouse. Get real, man, and grow up."

The strike came so fast that Whit couldn't avoid it. He saw Llewellyn's fist coming toward him. And after the shock of finding himself on the floor waned, pain radiated from his cheek into his eye and jaw.

Whit blinked his blurry vision, trying to focus on Llewellyn, who stood over him—his stance and loose limbs ready for a fight.

"Why am I being like this? Because I don't like you. I don't like people like you. And it makes my skin crawl to think that you would ever even look at my sister let alone touch her. She deserves someone who will light up her life. She deserves to laugh and sing as if every day is summer. Call me fantastical and childish all you want—like I give a shit what someone like you thinks of me. The sun will shine at night before I ever approve of you. So as I see it, you didn't just steal my sister. You killed her."

Whit's stomach twisted at his words, but he wasn't thinking about that. As anger pumped through his veins, all his rational thoughts turned to whispers in his mind. Picking himself up, he sucked his teeth.

Then he threw himself at Llewellyn, tackling him to the ground.

The fight that ensued was not pretty. It was not those glorious action shots in the movies with dramatic music that show off the human form at its fiercest. No, it was ugly and clumsy. Hair was pulled, clothes were torn, blood was drawn. And in the end, the two men were left lying on their backs staring up at the ceiling—the only sounds their heavy breathing and the gentle tinkle of water from the fountain.

"I hate you," Llewellyn huffed.

"Yeah? Well, I don't like you much either," Whit responded.

Llewellyn turned his head to look over at Whit. "You better not tell my sister we got in a fight."

Whit snorted and the blood that had begun to coagulate in his nose started dripping again. "I hadn't planned on it."

Llewellyn pointed his gaze back toward the ceiling. "She hates violence." He smiled, then hissed as the motion pulled at his split lip. "Actually, she's probably going to be pissed at you for getting into a fight. She always lectured me while she patched me up."

"I guess I'm in for it, then."

Sitting up, Llewellyn looked down at him. "You told Merry she was waiting for you. Clean yourself up in the bathroom behind the screen before you leave."

Whit rolled to the side to push himself up with his arms.

"Ew, dude, you're getting blood on my floor," Llewellyn complained.

Whit glanced around the space. There were already specks of blood on the floor. Now he was just being picky.

Llewellyn groaned. "This is going to take forever to clean up."

"Do you want help?" Whit asked, now on his feet.

Llewellyn leveled a glare at him. "Are you going to keep my sister waiting? Clean yourself up, and get the hell out of my studio."

Whit didn't have the energy to argue, nor did he really want to. Stumbling into the bathroom, he stared at himself in the mirror. His nose was bleeding but didn't seem broken. It was still straight anyway. His eye was swelling, and he knew it would be black soon enough. As bad as his face looked, his body was worse. He already felt exactly where bruises were forming on his abdomen and back. And his hands were the worst of all—cut and scraped from the punches he'd gotten in.

Leaning over the sink, he rinsed his face as best he could with cold water. Then he stuck some rolled up toilet paper into his nostrils and washed his hands. The soap stung his cuts, but the pain seemed far away at this point.

After washing up, he still looked like shit. He had no idea what he was going to tell Clover. She would surely ask, and he had no way of hiding it from her. Shaking his head at himself, he couldn't believe he'd let his emotions get the better of him.

Llewellyn was mopping the floor with a strong-smelling disinfectant when Whit came out of the bathroom.

Whit crossed the room and stuffed his feet into his shoes. As he pulled on his coat, he said, "I'll be back next week."

"Don't you dare," Llewellyn barked.

Whit left without another word and turned on his cellphone as he climbed into his truck. There was a text from Clover telling him she was waiting at a café near the shelter. He buckled his seatbelt and started to drive, his mind grasping for any excuse he could give her.

Chapter Thirty-Six

Clover glanced at her watch yet again. Whit was late, and she was starting to get worried. She'd long since finished her arctic purple. She was down to drinking the ice as it melted.

"Are you sure you don't want me to give you a ride somewhere?" Orion asked. "It's not a problem—not that I mind hanging out with you here."

Clover shook her head. "You don't have to wait with me. I'm sure you have some place to be. It's getting late."

Orion chuckled. "It's not even nine yet."

Clover shrugged. "If the sun is down, it's late."

"Even so, I can't in good conscience leave you stranded here. Let me take you home."

"I'm not stranded." Clover frowned. "But I am getting worried," she admitted. "Maybe I should just call him."

But as she dug her phone out of her coat pocket

—pushing her thick mitten aside—it chimed with a text from Whit telling her he was in the parking lot.

She sighed in relief.

"That him?" Orion asked.

She nodded, standing from her chair to put on her coat. "Yeah, he's in the parking lot."

Orion frowned. "He didn't even come in to get you?"

Clover ignored the implied criticism in Orion's tone, smiling tightly. "Thanks for waiting with me. You didn't have to."

"I wanted to." Orion zipped up his coat to head out with her. "And I'll let you know about any jobs at the brewery. Text me your email address, and I'll forward them to you."

Clover nodded as she dropped her cup into the recycle bin on her way out.

The wind blew colder on her face than it had just the hour before. There weren't many cars in the parking lot, so she spotted Whit's truck right away.

She turned to Orion. "I'll talk to you later."

"Wait," he stopped her as she moved to leave. Bending down, he picked something up off the ground. And when he straightened, he stood much closer than she expected.

He smiled a smile that she was certain worked on many a woman's heart. "You dropped this," he said, his voice softened at this distance.

She took the mitten he offered, nodded, and stepped away from him. "Thanks."

"Goodnight!" he called after her as she bustled to the truck.

The cabin was warm and cozy when she climbed in. Whit faced away from her.

"How was your workout? I was starting to get worried." She reached for her seatbelt.

"Who's that?" Whit asked, his voice sort of stuffed and nasally like he was catching a cold.

Clover followed the direction of his gaze to see Orion shuffling down the block toward Pets and Scritches.

"Oh, that's Orion—one of the other volunteers. He's the one who told me about the rescue. Did you meet him outside city hall when we were picking up our marriage license? He was asking for signatures for his petition."

"I didn't, no," Whit answered.

"Well, the orientation got finished early, so he offered to wait with me at the café. If I'd have known your workout would take so long, I would've asked him for a ride."

Whit glanced over at her. "I'm sorry. I—"

Clover gasped as she met his eyes—well, one eye since the other was swollen shut. Even in the dim light of the dashboard, she could see something awful had happened to him. Rolled up tissue hung from his nose, and a bruise was blooming down the side of his face.

"Jesus Christ! What happened to you? Are you all right?" She leaned toward him but was stopped by her seatbelt.

He held up a hand. "I'm fine."

"You're clearly not fine." She frowned severely while worry churned her stomach. "The car isn't damaged, so you didn't get into a wreck. What happened at your gym? Do you box or something? Did you get mugged?"

"I got into a fight," Whit said simply.

"With *whom*? Did someone attack you? Did you file a police report?"

Whit shook his head. "With a friend."

Clover was silent for a heavy minute as thoughts raced around her head. *Does he fight a lot? He didn't seem like the type. But then, I hardly know him. Did he fight with another winter sorcerer? Would they have used fists? Was it because his friend found out he married me? Is he hurt because of me?*

"Does this happen often?" she asked.

"No."

Clover sighed heavily. "Do you have a first-aid kit at home?"

"Yes."

"All right. Get out. I'll drive. You shouldn't be behind the wheel with your eye like that."

Clover didn't speak again until they were home. She didn't know what to say. She didn't approve of violence, and she didn't think Whit's friend was one worth having if he would bust up his face like this. But she also had the strong feeling this had something to do with her, and that made her sick with worry.

"This will sting," she warned before she pressed a peroxide-soaked cotton ball to the cuts on his knuckles.

He winced, hissing through his teeth as she pressed a little harder than she needed to.

"Well, you should've thought about that before you tried to solve your differences with violence."

He didn't argue.

Silently, she cleaned his wounds, showing him no mercy.

But when she was finished, she sighed. "All right. I don't know if this will work, but it's worth a try. We can't have you scaring away customers with your face looking like that."

"What?" Whit asked—his first word since she'd sat him down at the dining room table.

"I don't have the amount of magic I need to heal you right now, but if you lend me some of yours, it might work. Then again, it might not. Do you want to try it or not?"

Whit frowned. "But if you were going to try to heal me, why did we go through the pain of cleaning my wounds?"

"To teach you a lesson," she answered sternly. "Fighting is not the answer."

Stepping closer, she leaned over him, analyzing his face. "We'll start with that eye. That's got to hurt. Give me your hands."

Chapter Thirty-Seven

Whit's pulse jumped as if he'd just heard the shot at the beginning of a race. Clover stood over him—her knees on either side of his, their fingers laced palm-to-palm. Her eyes were closed with her head hung forward, her hair tickling his face.

"Repeat after me," she said in a hushed voice.

But he hardly heard her words, so enthralled was he by her proximity.

"*Willow, rowan, elder, and ash,*" she murmured.

He felt the soft flicker of her magic spark, beckoning his toward her—inviting him in. "*Willow, rowan, elder, and ash,*" he repeated, taking a deep breath to lend her his power.

Her scent, like a hidden wildflower meadow, teased him. He leaned toward it.

"*Summer winds blow and waters lash,*" she said.

He said the same. His face warmed as if he were under the sun on the brightest of summer days. He wondered if it was her magic working or if it was his reaction to her.

"*Primal forces of sun and sea.*"

As he repeated her spell, his knuckles began to itch.

"*Bless and heal him, we ask of thee.*"

Once he said the last line, Clover's eyes flicked open and stared into his.

She started the spell again, slowly this time so he could say it with her.

Their whispered syllables mingled together, harmonizing into something almost physical.

Clover's eyes were bright and clear—urging, willing the magic she wielded to do her bidding.

With every word, the dull pain in his face seemed to subside.

Suddenly, her eyes started to dim and lose focus. She pushed through to the end of the spell—her words forced as if squeezed out of her.

She wobbled a bit and swayed backward. Whit tightened his grip on her hands so she wouldn't fall. Her knees buckled, and she plopped onto his lap.

"Hey," he said urgently, leaning his head back to try to get a better look at her face. "Are you all right?"

Clover nodded slowly. "Yeah, maybe I'm just not used to channeling winter power into summer magic."

Whit frowned. "Or maybe you used up all of your own and didn't take enough from me."

A smile tugged at one corner of her mouth. "Well, you might need it. What if you get into another fight?"

Whit scowled but didn't respond.

Releasing his hands, Clover reached for his face—her sleepy eyes analyzing the work she'd done.

The brush of her fingers was gentle and sent a tingle through him.

Clover leaned toward him and pressed her lips to where her brother had so recently punched him in the eye. A hot shiver went right to his manhood.

"There," she whispered. "All better."

Her heat on his lap, her scent in his nose, and the tender light in her eyes—Whit froze as desire mounted inside him.

He couldn't afford to mess this up. If he was reading the situation wrong, he could ruin everything. He was the one who'd drawn the platonic line. He couldn't rightly promise one thing before he married her and then go back on his word immediately after.

But, gods, did he want her. He wanted her like a starving man wanted food, like a stranded sailor wanted fresh water—like a man who hadn't known the feel of a woman in too many years.

He trembled against his compulsion to press her to him—to make her truly belong to him. He wanted her so much that it honestly scared him. Was his blood still hot from the fight? If her magic hadn't been low since the day he'd met her, he might have thought she'd bewitched him—love magic was summer magic after all.

"Whit?" she whispered.

His name on her tongue nearly broke him.

"You're shaking. Are you—?"

But as she pressed her hand to his abdomen to push herself back in order to look at his face, he hissed in pain. She snatched her hand away from him.

"What? What happened?"

He winced.

Leaning back, she carefully lifted his shirt, gasping when she saw the bruises that would no doubt be even worse later.

"I'm sorry," she fretted. "I didn't know. I can't believe they're this bad. That's got to hurt. Give me a moment, I'll heal—"

Whit put his hand atop hers, which still held his shirt up. The action cut off her words.

"I'm fine," he insisted. "You're exhausted enough as it is. You need to replenish your magic, and that could take a while."

"But…"

Whit shook his head, then gave her a gentle smile. "I'll live. It would have been much worse if you hadn't healed me already." He squeezed her hand. "Thank you."

Clover frowned but nodded. Standing from his lap, she slowly pulled away from him. "I'll go get you some ice."

As she made her way to the kitchen, Whit stayed in the dining room chair—mourning the absence of her weight on his knees.

Whit wrestled to leash his own desire. He knew that if she'd been near him for even a moment longer —if his abdomen hadn't been bruised and her touch had been hot and firm—he wouldn't have been able to stop himself.

He clenched his jaw and tightened his hands into fists. He couldn't remember the last time he'd felt so out of control, and he didn't like it.

How many women had he turned down? How many times had he stopped his primal urges from taking control of his mind? He was a winter sorcerer. He was nothing without logic and reason and considering the consequences of his actions.

Whit's gaze fixed on Clover as she returned from the kitchen, an apologetic smile on her face. She held a bag of frozen peas out to him. "We didn't have any ice. Put this on for twenty minutes over your shirt, then put them back in the freezer."

What makes her so different? Whit wondered, accepting the peas as a shock of cold ran up his arm.

Chapter Thirty-Eight

Clover paused her scissors mid-way through cutting a strip of paper from a grocery store sales advertisement. She sighed, and the sound seemed loud in the middle of the parlor.

She'd started making paper chains from junk mail because she'd wanted to take her mind off Whit. It was a tradition her family had done for as long as she could remember. They would save all their junk mail and bits of sting and yarn through the entire year. And the weekend after Halloween, they would cut the paper into strips, punch holes in the ends—which they would later use for confetti—and tie them into paper chains to decorate the house.

She'd thought the activity would cheer her up and occupy her mind, but it had the opposite effect. While her hands were busy, her mind was free to replay the events of the night before. One look at Whit's expression as she'd sat on his lap told her he'd wanted her. If he hadn't still been injured, she would have instigated him even further—no matter how exhausted she was from using up her magic.

His healing was more important than her scratching the itch she'd felt since she'd first kissed him.

Not only that, but the fact that she was sitting alone doing the activity she normally did with her family—who were still not talking to her—made her sadder than she'd expected.

She finished cutting the paper and was punching holes in the ends when she heard a knock on the door. Rising from her place on the floor, she carefully stepped over her piles and went to answer the summons.

Realization crashed down on her when she found Lina standing on her doorstep. She'd gotten completely sidetracked. The winter witch she'd befriended at the cemetery was coming over for tea today. Clover had even baked cupcakes that morning, which were long-cooled but yet unfrosted.

Lina tilted her head, staring at the long strings of yarn Clover had draped over her shoulders. "Is now a bad time?"

"No! Of course not." Clover smiled embarrassedly. "I just got a little distracted. Please, come in."

Clover stepped aside so Lina could enter, then closed the door behind her.

Lina looked at Clover's piles in the parlor.

"Please excuse the mess. I was in the middle of a

craft project." She pointed toward the dining room. "Let's have tea in here. I'll put the kettle on."

Clover rushed through the dining room into the kitchen, cursing internally that she'd forgotten to finish the cupcakes. *At least I thought ahead enough to set out a selection of teas.*

As she waited for the pot of water to boil—again reminding herself she needed to buy a kettle—she put a few unfrosted cupcakes on a plate.

When she entered the dining room with her teapot of hot water and the plate of cupcakes, she found Lina gazing at the photos on Whit's ancestor altar.

Lina frowned, a wistful look in her eyes. "It's been nearly thirty years since my husband died," she said softly. "We weren't even married for five though I'd known him practically my whole life. To this day, I've never met anyone who could compare to him."

"You must miss him a lot," Clover responded gently.

Lina turned to her with a sad smile. "Every day."

"I'm sorry for your loss."

Approaching the table, Lina took a seat. "Thank you, but even though I miss him, I don't feel lonely. I feel him around me quite a lot, especially while our son was growing up. And he visits me often in my dreams. It's not the same, of course, but it gets me through the hard times."

Clover motioned toward the selection of teas she'd laid out on the table, telling Lina to pick whatever she liked.

"You have a son together? That's nice, but it must have been hard to raise him on your own."

Lina smiled that smile only mothers could. "At times, but my husband's family was there to help, as was mine. And he wasn't a terribly difficult child. He's much more like me in personality than he's like his father, so we usually understand each other...until recently, that is."

Clover felt her words keenly. She and her parents had always gotten along until recently, too. She didn't ask Lina to elaborate. She didn't want to pry. After putting leaves into her tea sieve, she poured hot water into her cup.

"How long have you been married?" Lina asked, pouring water into her own cup.

Clover rubbed her thumb against the rings on her finger. "Not long. I'm still a newlywed."

"And what's your husband like? How did you meet?"

Lina's dark eyes seemed eager to hear her story, so eager that Clover couldn't just brush off her questions. Something about this witch's strong yet quiet presence made Clover want to confide in her. Still, she chose her words carefully.

"We met at a party." Clover couldn't help but smile to herself. "He was wearing this mask, so I couldn't even see his face. Anyway, there was this guy there—not really an ex-boyfriend, more like a guy I went on a date with. He was pestering me—you know, following me around and stuff. And Whit sort of swooped in and saved me. That pretty much covers who he is as a person, I think. He's quiet, serious. He worries a lot—too much if you ask me. But I know he'll always be there when I need him most. We might be different, but I know we're meant for each other."

Lina stared at Clover as if trying to internalize every word.

Clover felt a little uneasy under the older woman's steady gaze. She smiled and offered her the plate of cupcakes. "Would you like a cupcake? I'm sorry they're unfrosted… I didn't get the chance to make the frosting."

Lina nodded, returning her self-conscious smile with a gentle one of her own. "That's all right. I prefer them this way anyway. I don't like sweets very much, so that would have been too much sugar."

"Oh, would you like me to get you something else? I think there are some crackers in the cupboard."

Lina shook her head. "This is fine. Thank you. But that reminds me, I brought you something."

Clover blinked. "Something for me?"

Lina reached for her purse, which was hanging on a dining room chair with her coat. "Of course. It isn't polite to show up empty handed, is it?"

On the table, Lina placed a small wooden box. "Go ahead," she said, nodding to Clover.

Clover gasped when she opened it. Resting on a bed of blue satin was a silver comb, the swoops and swirls of a Celtic knot beside the thick tines. "Oh my gods, it's beautiful." She gently ran her finger along the edge, then glanced up at Lina. "But this is way too much. I only gave you tea and an unfrosted cupcake. I can't accept this."

Lina shook her head in a way that would take no refusal. "Think of it as a token of friendship, not as a mere visiting gift."

Clover's heart warmed at the gesture, and she thanked the woman with all the sincerity she could muster.

Chapter Thirty-Nine

Whit's jaw dropped open when he walked into the house. His stomach rolled. What had happened to his parlor? The place looked like a kindergarten classroom without the parental pride. A paper chain had been tacked—*tacked* into his pristine walls!—near the ceiling like a garland. It didn't even go all the way around, stopping halfway and making the room look incomplete.

Clover bounced down the stairs, her flouncy skirt fluttering as she grinned at him.

"Surprise!" she said, coming toward him. She lifted her chin in pride, her hands on her hips as she surveyed her day's work. "It's my family's tradition. Unfortunately, we didn't have a lot of junk mail, but I might be able to get it all the way around the room before Thanksgiving."

She smiled over at him, but as she took in his expression, her smile faltered. "You hate it."

He blinked, the disappointment in her voice

shaking him from the shock at seeing his house so defiled. "No, no, I don't hate it… I'm just surprised. You said you used junk mail?"

His voice didn't sound convincing to his own ears, but she didn't seem to notice because her smile returned.

She nodded. "Of course! I'm not going to waste paper. We usually save mail through the whole year just to see how long we can make it. So stop recycling it from now on."

Whit imagined the ugly paper chain with its bits of different colored yarn hanging down around every room of his house. He internalized his groan.

She bounced on the balls of her feet. "Anyway, dinner is ready. I made Irish Stew. Oh! And I made cupcakes today as well."

Seeing how happy her project made her, Whit wrestled with his own instincts. *I told her this is her home from now on, too. There's no way she could have known not to put tacks in the walls. If this is a family tradition, she has the right to do it here. But did she have to use tacks? I don't even keep tacks in the house. Where did she even get them? She must be missing her family if she's doing this now.*

"How was your day?" Clover asked as she set a steaming bowl of stew in front of him.

"Busy, but not in a good way. Customers came in practically one at a time but didn't buy much. So I didn't get any back room stuff done and didn't have the sales to compensate."

Clover frowned in sympathy. "That stinks. I got some maybe good news, though."

He glanced up from the potato on his spoon to look at her when she paused.

"Orion sent me an email with job listings for the brewery he works at. I'm not really qualified for most of them, but there's one I might be able to do."

Whit clenched his jaw as he replayed the last time he'd seen the man—the way he'd stood so close to Clover, the way he'd smiled at her. He forced his mouth open to shove the spoon in.

"It would be really great if I got a job someplace where I know someone. Then I could get a ride while I save up for a good car."

Whit imagined her climbing into the car with Orion, smiling over at him as she thanked him for the ride. Even if they worked in different departments, they would probably have lunch together. Whit's stomach burned, and he didn't think it was from the hot stew.

"I thought you were going to wait a while before getting another job? Didn't you want to adjust to all the changes?"

Clover pouted her lips, and the look disrupted the irritation growing in Whit's gut.

"I was…but I mean, what am I supposed to do all day? I'm so used to being on the run. I can only cook and clean and do crafts so much. Plus, if I get used to a slower pace, what if I have a hard time adjusting when I do get another job?"

"Why don't you come help out at the shop, then?"

Clover blinked rapidly. "At your antique shop?"

Whit shrugged. "You don't have to do it every

day. But you helping out at the counter would give me time to do the other things I need to do."

Whit wasn't prepared for the force of the smile she beamed at him. It hit him right in the chest.

"Okay!" she exclaimed, her excitement clear and infectious.

Whit's pulse quickened.

The rest of the meal passed pleasantly. Whit thanked Clover for making dinner and dessert, then helped her with the dishes.

Afterward, they moved to the parlor. Clover settled in the rocking chair while Whit sat on the couch. He picked up his latest little project—what would be a hand-whittled cat when he was done with it. Whittling wasn't his favorite pastime, but it was a relaxing hobby. And his customers often purchased his carved animals.

"Do you mind if I put on one of my programs?" Clover asked him, her tablet in her lap.

"Go ahead. But don't you want to use the television?"

Clover tilted her head. "This is easier."

She tapped her tablet a few times, and then set it on the table as the sound of an old-time radio announcer came through the speaker.

"Old Dutch Cleanser, famous for chasing dirt, presents Nick Carter, famous for chasing crime."

Organ music blared through the little speaker as Clover pulled a nearly finished sweater from her knitting basket.

Whit glanced at her. He didn't think her program was an old radio crime drama. *She's full of surprises.*

She grinned at him. "*Nick Carter, Master Detective* is my favorite. Have you ever listened to radio dramas?"

Whit shook his head.

"They don't always age well, but I still like them. Sometimes they have commercials for war bonds and stuff, too. It's so interesting—like stepping into the past. You'll love it since you like history."

Chapter Forty

Clover rested her face in her hands as she propped her elbows on the glass case at Crawford Antiques. She'd been so excited when Whit had invited her to come to the shop the night before. She'd thought this was the perfect opportunity to get to know each other better, to spend time together.

But after he'd explained how to write receipts and check people out—it had been a long time since she'd seen this type of cash register—he'd disappeared into the back room. He had said that was why she was here, but that didn't stop her from feeling a little disappointed.

At least he let me pick the music. She glanced over at the record player as "Put Your Head on My Shoulder" disseminated through the deserted shop.

Still, it was better than sitting at home. They'd gotten to eat the lunches she'd packed together, and she did get to chat with the customers. When she'd been a delivery girl, she'd met all kinds of people every day.

Taking out her phone, Clover reread the message she'd drafted for Ari. Her friend was still not answering her calls, so she'd written out everything she wanted to say—telling her there were omens and explaining why she hadn't told her she was getting married beforehand. Clover had written it the day before, but she'd still held out hope Ari would answer her call that morning. No such luck.

If nothing else, she knew Ari well enough to know she would at least read the message. She was compulsive that way; she even read junk emails. And though she was angry right now, Clover knew Ari was also curious. She pressed send.

As the bell above the door chimed, Clover put away her phone and adopted her customer-service smile.

"Welcome!" she said to the woman who entered.

The dark-haired beauty pulled down her Gucci sunglasses to grace Clover with a glance of her large brown eyes. She was absolutely gorgeous—her blow-out perfectly fluffed and her makeup on-point. She wore a long-sleeved black turtleneck dress that ended well above the knee and four-inch heels that made Clover trip just looking at them.

She was not your average customer, at least not from what Clover had gathered from her half-day's work. This woman had the air of someone who had places to be.

"Is there anything special you're looking for

today?" Clover asked, impressed by the woman's commanding presence.

The woman gave her a serpentine smile. "Yes, is Whit here?"

Clover nodded. "He is. I'll go get him for you. What's your name?"

"Faustina."

"All right. I'll be right back." Clover bustled to the back room.

Whit had his back to her, sitting at his work bench.

"Hey, Whit," she said softly from the door so as not to startle him. She came fully into the room as he turned toward her. Clover threw her thumb over her shoulder. "A customer is asking for you. She said her name is Faustina?"

The blood drained from Whit's face as his mouth dropped open. He didn't move or make a sound, but Clover knew he'd heard her. For whatever reason, this was not someone Whit was expecting.

"Do you…want me to send her away?" Clover asked.

Whit looked horrible—like he was going to pass out. His Adam's apple jumped as he swallowed. "No," he replied hoarsely. He rose from his stool, shaking his head.

As he passed her to head into the shop proper, he patted her gently on the shoulder. That soft touch of assurance alarmed her more than anything else. She followed close behind.

Whit stood straight, his shoulders firm and so

wide that Clover had to tilt to see Faustina around him.

"What do you want?" he asked coolly, planting himself in the middle of the main aisle with his arms crossed.

Clover flinched at his tone. She'd never heard him like this before, and she would hate to have that voice directed at her.

"Whit," Faustina said warmly. "I see you're doing well for yourself. This shop was just a dream the last time we talked."

Faustina strutted closer, swishing her hips in a suggestion Clover picked up on right away. Clover stepped out from behind Whit to stand by his side. Faustina fully ignored her presence.

"If you're not here to buy something, I suggest you leave," Whit stated.

"Well…there is something I *want*." Faustina looked him up and down, batting her thick eyelashes as she gave him a heated smile.

Clover's hackles rose, her muscles tightening.

"You're not going to find it here," Whit responded sternly.

Faustina pouted her perfectly painted lips. "I know I hurt you before, but I didn't know any better. I was young after all. I'm prepared to make it up to you."

As she took a final step into Whit's personal space, Clover squeezed in between them.

She smiled up at the woman—who towered over her in her high heels. "Hi, excuse me. I believe he said there's nothing for you here. So if you wouldn't mind, I'll ask you to leave."

Faustina spared Clover only a glance before returning her gaze to Whit. "Whit, honey, we really need to have a discussion about your hired help."

Clover sucked a breath in through her nose, standing as tall as she could. "I would appreciate you not calling my husband honey. Thank you."

Faustina's rich eyes widened, and she truly looked at Clover for the first time—twisting her mouth in a sneer. Her gaze returned to Whit. "You're joking," she said flatly. "You said I was the only woman you'd ever love."

Clover's gut wrenched, but she ignored it. What Whit had told his ex before she'd even met him wasn't her problem.

"Husband?" Clover met Whit's eyes over her shoulder. "Do you have anything left to say to this woman?"

Whit shook his head.

"Good." Clover turned a glare on Faustina. "Look, lady, I don't give a snowball's chance in high summer what my husband said to you in the past. He might have promised you the moon itself for all I care. None of that matters now because *I'm* the one he married. *I'm* the one he comes home to every night. *I'm* the one who he vowed to care for and protect. His children will be *my* children. And from one woman to another, I would very much appreciate it if you removed yourself from our happy situation. If his heart once belonged to you, well, then, I'm sorry for your loss. You squandered your chance, but I'm not about to do the same."

Chapter Forty-One

Whit recognized Clover's magic, whipping into a sandstorm as she gave Faustina a piece of her mind. Silently, he projected his magic outward to envelope hers within it.

He didn't much care if Faustina knew Clover was a summer witch. Everyone would know eventually. But if Faustina was back in town, she would see people he knew. And he couldn't have word getting back to Grandfather just yet, not until he found out the truth from Whit.

Even in her fury, Clover's magic wasn't difficult to mask. Faustina would no doubt recognize that the winter magic that surrounded Clover was his, but it would only appear as if he supported her in her words, which he did.

Whit stared at Faustina, her face flush with rage and embarrassment. She'd likely never been spoken to this way in her entire life. It hadn't been so very long ago that this expression from her would have incited his need to protect. He could remember their good times together clearly though they were overshadowed by the bad ones. He had loved her. He remembered that, but it was as if he were recalling a past life rather than just a few years back. He remembered the words —love, lust, laughter, tears—but he couldn't feel the emotions.

Even now, with his wife ripping her a new one, he couldn't get over the shock of Faustina's reappearance. Had she really expected him to welcome her back— to forgive and forget? If he wasn't so disgusted, he might have wondered what had happened to her in the last few years to make her come back to an unambitious good-for-nothing—as she had labeled him when she'd left.

Whit's mind came back into focus when Clover mentioned their future children. A jolt ran up his spine. *Children?* But he shook himself. *She's just making her point... Isn't she?*

Nearly forgetting Faustina was there, Whit looked at the back of Clover's head, her shoulders tense as she stood before him like a bodyguard.

Bringing a child into a loveless house didn't seem like the best idea. *Does she want children?*

If they had gone about things in the normal way, this was something they would have discussed long before getting married. It was clear his grandfather expected children to come of his marriage; otherwise, he would've willed the house to Caldwell regardless. And it wasn't that he didn't like children. It was more that Whit had given up on the idea a while ago, the same time he'd given up on the idea of a wife.

"You've got some nerve," Faustina growled.

Her words pushed Whit's thoughts from his mind. He rested his hands gently on Clover's shoulders as she lifted her chin.

"I've got every right," Clover said. "You come into my husband's shop, thinking you're going to get back together with him after how long? What did you expect? Did you think his life was over after you were no longer in it? Did you think he'd be waiting for you? He's moved on, and if you have any self-respect, you'll do the same."

Faustina's dark eyes shifted to Whit's over Clover's head. She shook her head in that same disappointed way she had when she'd broken it off with him. "You aren't worth it," she spat. Then she turned on her heels and swished toward the door.

"Why you—" Clover jolted as if to follow her.

Whit tightened his grip on her shoulders. "Just let her go," he said softly.

Once Faustina was outside, Clover spun around —her eyes solicitous with concern.

"I'm sorry," Clover and Whit both said at once.

Clover huffed a laugh through her nose. "You go ahead."

Whit nodded. "I'm sorry you had to deal with that. I haven't seen her in years, and I didn't expect to ever see her again. You shouldn't have had to step in. If I'd have just—"

Clover shook her head. "No. Don't do that. None of this was your fault. I gathered from context she was your ex… I'm sorry if I overstepped. I don't know anything about how your relationship was. But when I saw her reach out to you like that"—Clover clicked her tongue—"I should've let you handle it. You could've had all kinds of things you wanted to say to her, and I—"

"I didn't," Whit said firmly. "I don't."

A soft smile tugged at one corner of his mouth. Was it only a few days ago in this very room he'd thought Clover wouldn't care about Luisa hitting on him? *I didn't know my wife was so fierce.*

Clover's eyes danced like cornflowers in the breeze. "What's that look you're giving me, Husband?"

He shook himself, uncertain of the expression he'd been wearing but suspecting it led someplace they might both regret, someplace that would overcomplicate their relationship while they were still getting used to each other, someplace they couldn't come back from.

She chuckled, and it sounded indulgent to him. Then she sighed, shaking her head. "What am I going to do with you?" she murmured.

But before he could wonder what she meant by that, her phone pinged from the counter at the front of the store. Turning away from him, she went to pick it up.

She frowned at her phone, then glanced up to meet his gaze—uncertainty swimming in her eyes.

"Um, do you mind if I babysit my niece tomorrow night?"

Something about her question made him sad.

"You don't need to ask my permission," he told her. "Your family is my family."

His patient reminder won him a brilliant smile.

"I hope you like mac'n'cheese and dino nuggets."

"Who doesn't?" he asked, smiling at how pleased she was by his simple words.

Chapter Forty-Two

Clover rushed to answer the door when she heard the knock. She blinked in surprise to find Ari holding Crane's hand.

Her friend lowered her gaze. "I offered to bring Crane here."

"Zia!" Crane exclaimed, holding her arms up.

Clover smiled and bent down to give the girl a hug. "Ciao, stregina. Ooof, I missed you so much!"

"I missed you, too, Zia," Crane said.

Standing, Clover stared at her friend awkwardly. They'd never been in a fight before, so she didn't really know what to do. "Will you stay and hang out with us?"

Ari shook her head. "I can't. I haven't seen Rhys most of the week, so I told him I'd spend some time with him tonight."

"Oh, okay," Clover responded, not hiding her disappointment.

"But"—Ari looked up to meet Clover's eyes—"maybe we could get together tomorrow?"

Clover's heart lightened, and she nodded enthusiastically. "Yes, text me in the morning. We can do whatever you want."

Ari gave her a hesitant small smile as she handed over Crane's play bag. "Your sister should be here around nine."

"All right. Thanks."

Turning her attention back to Crane after saying goodbye to Ari, Clover grinned down at the girl. "Are you ready to play pirates?"

Crane pursed her lips in displeasure. "I'm tired of pirates."

"What? How can anyone be tired of pirates?" Clover said, shocked, which earned her a grin from her niece. "What do you want to play, then?"

"I want to play safari!"

"Safari, huh? Okay. Let's take your coat and hat off first, though."

Clover helped the child remove her outer layer. While Clover was pulling off her rubber boots, she said, "Well, we can't use your pirate hat to play safari. Do you have a safari hat?"

Crane shook her head.

"Do you want to make one?"

"Yeah!"

Clover smiled. "Okay. I think we have some paper plates and bowls in the kitchen. Let's go check."

Crane followed Clover through the dining room, her head swiveling as she looked around the space. "Is this your house now, Zia?"

Clover nodded. "Yes, it is. Did your mom tell you I got married?"

"Yes, she said I have another zio now and that he does a different kind of magic than us. But what kind of magic does he do?"

In the kitchen, Clover pulled down two paper plates and two paper bowls from the cupboard. "Why don't you ask him?"

Crane looked around. "Is he here?"

"He's here somewhere. You know what's a great idea?"

"What?"

"I bet he's playing hide-and-seek. Why don't you go find him?"

"Okay!"

As Crane ran from the room, Clover called after her, "Stay inside, and be careful on the stairs!"

"I will," Crane promised.

Goose bumps raised on Clover's arms in what she now recognized as her body's response to the unseen ghosts of the house. So far, they hadn't hurt her though they did seem to get a kick out of scaring her. Thus far, she'd tried to ignore them because reacting only encouraged their shenanigans.

She bit her lips, wondering if they would scare Crane.

But though she felt their presence, there were no accompanying bumps or creaks.

As she took her paper dishes to the parlor where she'd left her scissors, string, and hole punch, she thought, *well, nothing too bad will happen with Whit here.*

Just as she was putting the finishing touches on the two safari hats—threading the chin string—she heard Crane yell from upstairs, "Found you, Zio!"

A few minutes later, Crane and Whit appeared in the living room.

"I won! I found him!" Crane told Clover.

Clover smiled. "I see that. Come here. I finished your hat."

"Did you make one for Zio, too?" Crane asked.

Clover's gaze shifted to Whit, who smiled as he watched the child. Crane always had that effect on people.

"He can have this one," Clover assured.

Approaching Whit, Clover giggled when she slipped the paper safari hat onto his head. "Now, we're all ready for our safari."

"Wow! Look over there!" Crane shouted, pointing at the fireplace. "It's a herd of elephants. Do you see them?"

"I see them," Clover responded. "They're drinking from their long trunks."

Crane looked over at Whit. "Zio, do you see them?"

Whit didn't respond. Clover glanced over at him to find him whispering to himself with his eyes closed.

Whit's unique signature of magic swirled around them like a winter flurry. From out of the mist stepped a giant elephant, raising its trunk as it trumpeted—the sound as loud as if it really stood in the room.

Clover gasped, and Crane squealed, her eyes wide with wonder.

"Zia! Zia! Do you see that?"

Clover could hardly breathe. It really felt like she was standing in front of an elephant. It kicked up dust, and the house seemed to shake with its every step.

Clover had heard of illusion magic, but she'd never seen it. How could she have? It was winter magic, and she hadn't exactly hung out with winter sorcerers or witches until recently.

Cautiously, Crane crept toward the illusion, reaching her hand out. But when the elephant lifted its trunk to meet her hand, she screamed and laughed as she scurried away.

"Don't worry," Whit told her. "It isn't real, so it can't hurt you. It's just an illusion."

That was enough to satisfy her. "I want to see a zebra next!"

At the girl's demand, Whit shifted the illusion to a zebra grazing.

As incredible as it was to see a zebra while feeling the living room floor beneath her feet, Clover didn't look at the creature. Her eyes were fixed on her husband. Her chest tightened, and her stomach fluttered as she watched him entertain Crane with that indulgent smile on his face. It seemed every new side of him revealed to her only pulled her in closer.

Chapter Forty-Three

Whit sprang out of bed when he heard a yelp followed by a loud clatter. He rushed downstairs, not attempting to be quiet in his haste. He didn't know what time it was, but it was still fully dark.

"Clover?" he called, trying to figure out exactly where she was. "Are you okay?"

"Yeah," she said from the kitchen. "I'm fine."

He raced down the hall. As he turned the corner, he found her mopping up a puddle of water with a dishtowel.

"What happened?" he asked, picking up the small saucepan from the floor and putting it on the counter.

She sighed heavily. "I couldn't sleep, so I came down to make some tea. I guess something startled me, and I dropped the pot. Thankfully, it was still cold."

Glancing around the kitchen, Whit caught Great-Uncle Andri peeking at them from the dining room.

Grabbing another dishtowel from the drawer, he knelt down to help her mop. "I'm sorry about that. The ghosts always get a little riled up when there are kids around. They must have really liked having Crane here."

"I didn't know that," she muttered. "But it hasn't just been tonight. Am I imagining things? I feel like I haven't slept well since my first night here."

Clover moved to the sink to wring the water from the towel, and Whit followed suit.

"Why didn't you tell me?" he asked gently. *Does she not trust me to take care of it?*

She shrugged, lowering her eyes to her bare feet. "I thought I was just psyching myself out. I didn't want to burden you. I mean, what would you even do about it? The only good night's sleep I've had is when I fell asleep with you. I felt bad enough about that already. You clearly didn't want me there... You wouldn't have given me a separate room if you did."

Whit sighed, running his hand through his hair. It wasn't that he didn't want her in his bed. It was that she didn't belong there. "You aren't psyching yourself out. There have been ghosts present since you arrived. They don't usually hang around so constantly. I thought they were just curious about you, and they would lose interest. And you were so scared that I didn't want to confirm it for you."

"Well, at least I'm not losing my mind," Clover remarked.

Whit shook his head. "You aren't. Here, maybe this will help. Give me your hand."

She slipped her hand into the one he offered her. Smiling softly, she said, "I do feel a little better already."

His pulse quickened at her words, but he pushed that awareness to the side. "Uncle Andri"—Whit turned his head toward the doorway to the dining room—"would you come in here please?"

Great-Uncle Andri sauntered into the room, smirking.

Whit tightened his grip on Clover's hand.

"Spirits of the dead,
spirits I see,
this second sight
I share with thee."

Clover blinked rapidly, likely clearing the fog from her eyes.

"It won't last very long, but take a look." Whit gestured toward Uncle Andri.

Clover gasped, squeezing his hand by reflex. "Oh my gods, he looks just like a person standing there."

Whit snorted. "What should he look like?"

"I don't know. I guess, I assumed ghosts would be transparent or gross looking or something."

Whit shook his head. "Nope. They look just the same as you and me. This is my Great-Uncle Andri. He's a bit of a mischief maker just as he was in life."

Uncle Andri bowed his head in greeting.

"Hello," Clover said. "So you're the one who hasn't let me sleep."

Uncle Andri grinned, not at all remorseful for his actions.

Clover chuckled. "I've met people like you before. Pulling pranks is a great pastime in the summer faction."

Uncle Andri didn't look pleased at the comparison.

"Now that you see the culprit with your own eyes, do you feel less afraid?" Whit asked.

Clover smiled up at him. "Yes, thank you."

"Good." Whit released her hand.

"Can I ask you a question?"

He nodded, covering his mouth as he yawned.

"If ghosts look like regular people, how can you tell the difference?"

Whit shrugged. "You just sort of know, especially if you've grown up seeing them."

"Have you seen them your whole life, then?"

"Yes."

"Did they ever scare you?"

"Not really, no. Sometimes they pop out at you, and that can be startling. But that happens with living people, too."

Clover quirked her mouth. "Can all winter sorcerers and witches see ghosts?"

"Most can. Most children in general can. I think that's why ghosts like being around them. The winter faction is just taught to hold on to that innate ability."

Clover nodded slowly, her eyes unfocused in

thought. "That's not much different from the summer faction and the Good Neighbors. Although, whether or not we see them has a lot to do with if they want to be seen. Can you see them as well?"

"No. We try to stay as far from the Other Crowd as possible."

Clover huffed a laugh. "Good luck with that. They go where they please."

"Well, we have no dealings with them, and we're liberal with how much iron we have around our houses."

Clover tilted her head. "But iron doesn't deter all of them. For instance, house spirits are used to living with humans. They aren't affected by iron. You even have a house spirit here. I won't disclose her real name as that's between us, but I call her Marigold. I made an offering to her my first day here."

Whit's stomach dropped. "You…you invited a *fae* into our house?"

"What? No! I mean, well, yes. But Marigold was already here. And if you don't want their attention, I suggest you refrain from using the word fae aloud."

A cold fear settled into his gut. Winter sorcerers and witches were warned against the fae their entire lives. They were unpredictable and dangerous. They didn't follow the same rules as humans or ghosts. And if offended, even by accident, they could steal all a person's luck. They could even cause sickness or injury.

Whit was very uncomfortable with the idea of a fae living in his house.

He met Clover's eyes. "Can we get rid of it?"

"Of Marigold?" Clover asked, frowning. "But why would you? She's been here for longer than you have. This is her home. She doesn't hurt anything."

"But I don't want it here," he whispered.

Clover straightened her spine. "It's not right to throw her out. She hasn't done anything wrong. I didn't ask you to exorcise Uncle Andri just because he was spooking me. I've already started a tentative friendship with Marigold. I won't let you evict her for no good reason. If you're worried, then try to befriend her. This talk of kicking her out will only upset her."

Whit clenched his jaw. He certainly didn't want Marigold upset, and he'd encouraged Clover to think of this as her home. But he still didn't like the idea of an unknown fae mucking around where he couldn't even see her.

He sighed a sigh that sounded more like a groan. "Will you help me befriend her, then?"

Clover rewarded him with a grin. "She likes cream. I'll show you where to leave it for her and what to say."

Chapter Forty-Four

Clover placed a cup of tea on the table beside where Ari was sitting, then settled on the couch next to her.

Ari's frame was tense as her gaze skittered around the parlor.

"Thanks for coming here. I would've met you somewhere else, but I still don't have a car, and Whit is out," Clover said.

"I know. Llew and I have been covering your shifts all week," Ari reached for the cup and saucer.

Clover lowered her head. "I didn't know that. I guess my parents haven't hired someone else yet."

Ari clicked her tongue. "You don't really think they're going to replace you, do you?"

Clover's eyes snapped to Ari's.

"They told me when they asked me to cover it would only be temporary until you came back."

Clover scrunched her brow. "But they told me not to come back to work."

Ari shook her head. "Do you not know your family at all?"

Clover's heart squeezed, and she dropped her gaze again. "I thought I did, but then no one would let me explain."

Ari frowned severely, answering Clover with silence.

Clover laced her fingers together tightly. "I'm sorry I didn't tell you before I got married. I know you read it in the text, but I wanted to say it anyway."

Ari sighed heavily. "How long has this been going on? All you said in your message was that there were signs and omens. Is this what you've been so depressed about lately?"

Clover shook her head. "No, all that was really as I told you before. I needed a change—a big one. Something didn't feel right in my life, and I asked the gods for help and charged that good luck charm. Do you remember the guy I asked you about after the end-of-summer party?"

"The one you thought might be one of the Good Folk?"

Clover's face flushed. She still couldn't believe she'd actually thought that for even a moment.

"Yeah, well, he wasn't. That was Whit. That was the first night we met."

"That wasn't even two weeks ago." Ari's tone sounded completely unconvinced.

"I know. But that night, after we kissed, I saw the crow on the van. Then he ordered some camellias." Clover shrugged. "So when he asked me to marry him, I said yes."

The scowl on Ari's face shifted as she pursed her lips in thought. "Why would a winter sorcerer do that? I mean, you'd only just met. I thought they were pretty rigid. I thought they didn't like to do things spontaneously. You know I think you're great. But are you telling me that after one kiss this guy fell so madly in love with you that he could overcome his very nature? Not to mention facing all the hardships that will come from marrying someone from the opposite faction."

Clover bit her lip. But after a moment's hesitation, she told her friend the truth. "No, he didn't fall for me at first sight or anything like that. You can't tell anyone this—not even Rhys. Okay?"

She waited for Ari to nod before she continued. "He was in a tough spot." Clover gestured to the room around them. "In order to inherit this house from his grandfather, he had to get married before the solstice. For whatever reason—maybe the kiss, but I never asked—he asked me. I assumed he didn't have any prospects."

Ari stared at Clover for a long time.

"You're incredible," she said finally, shaking her head in disbelief. "You married a man who you don't even know but you know for sure doesn't love you because of a bird and a flower. I'm honestly impressed. I don't know if I could trust omens with something so important. I mean, what if you read the signs wrong?"

Clover smiled softly. "It didn't really feel like a leap of faith. When he actually asked me to marry him, it felt like agreeing was the only option."

Clover chuckled. "He seemed more surprised than I was."

Ari huffed a laugh. "I bet."

"But you know what? Even though I upset you and my family, even though I've been pranked by ghosts and confronted by his ex, even though I'm having to take things slower than I'd like with him physically—I know we'll get there. Every day, I feel a little closer to him. Every day, I see why the gods led us to each other. He was thorough in making sure I knew he didn't love me when he asked me to marry him—"

"How romantic," Ari grumbled.

"—But I knew then, and I still believe, that it's only a matter of time before we love each other. The summer gods provide, and they wouldn't lead me to a loveless marriage. Every day, I find something new to love about him. I feel like I'm collecting a single dew drop at a time, but when I'm done, my heart will be full."

Finally, Ari smiled. And even though it was strained with worry, it carried her understanding. "I hope you're right, Clover. I love you, and I want you to be happy. If it has to be with a winter sorcerer... well, then I guess that's that. If he's going to be married to my best friend, then I'm just going to have to get used to him. I hope he's as great as you say he is. And I want to apologize, too. I was so hurt to learn you got married without telling me that I just sort of busted into your house without thinking. I should have confronted you first. But, honestly, I thought your family would already know. And I'm sorry I've been silent the last few days. I've been dealing with all the emotions. We've never fought before. And…I was also a little ashamed at how I acted, too."

Clover leaned forward and wrapped her arms around Ari.

"Whoa!" Ari said, her teacup clattering.

Clover giggled. "It's fine. That's what saucers are for."

After settling back into their seats, Ari said, "All right, now tell me everything. I'm sure I've missed a lot. What do you mean you're having to take things slow physically? Are you telling me you two haven't even had sex yet? Even the night of your handfasting?"

"I know!" Clover exclaimed. Pulling her legs under her, she pivoted toward her friend, preparing to tell her everything.

Chapter Forty-Five

Whit returned Eirwen's smile when she opened the door to find him on her porch.

"Whit!" his cousin's wife exclaimed. "What are you doing here? Isn't your store open on Saturdays?"

He nodded. "Yeah, but I have to talk to Caldwell about something, so I closed for lunch. Is he home?"

"He's in his office. Come on in." She stepped aside for him to enter. "I just finished making lunch. Would you like some? Chicken sandwiches."

"No, thanks. I already ate."

"You sure? I always make extra. I never know how hungry the boys are going to be." Eirwen closed the door and turned back to him.

Whit shook his head.

"Congratulations on the wedding by the way."

"Thank you."

"Come into the kitchen. I'll make Caldwell a plate, and you can take it up to him."

Following Eirwen through the hall, Whit entered the kitchen to find Caldwell's kids at the table. The boys—eight and ten—were wearing headphones and staring at their tablets as they ate.

"Boys!" Eirwen called. "I asked you to turn those off at the table. Say hello to your cousin."

With mumbles and looks of displeasure, the boys did what their mother bid them.

"Hey, guys," Whit greeted. "How have you been?"

"Fine," Bryan—the older of the two—said before smothering his crinkle fry with ketchup.

Whit looked at Colin, who echoed his brother's sentiments.

"That's good," Whit said. "Anything new? What have you been up to?"

"Just school," Bryan answered.

It was always like this with Caldwell's boys. Having a conversation with them was like pulling teeth. The only time they were excited was when they were talking about video games.

"Yeah? What do you like about school this year?" Whit asked.

"Math, I guess," Bryan replied, completely uninterested.

"And you, Colin?"

Colin shrugged. "Art."

Whit pounced on this bit of information. "Really? You like art, Colin? What do you like about it?"

"I like to draw." The boy's tone wasn't very convincing.

"Do you? Can I see any of your drawings?"

"Maybe later."

Holding in his sigh, Whit was saved when Eirwen offered him a plate with a crispy chicken sandwich and crinkle fries. "Make sure he actually eats it, will you?" she requested.

Whit nodded. "See you later, guys."

His young cousins didn't bother to answer.

Carrying the plate, Whit climbed the stairs to the second floor, then passed the bedrooms and bathroom to the end of the hall. He knocked on Caldwell's office door.

"Come in," Caldwell called.

When Whit opened the door, Caldwell tilted his head. "Isn't your shop open today?"

Whit nodded, staring at his cousin's desk—so full of papers that he wasn't sure where to put the plate down.

"Oh, give me a sec," Caldwell said, seeing his dilemma. He shuffled the papers into piles, clearing the space in front of him.

Finally, Caldwell took the plate from Whit, and Whit sat in the only other chair in the room—an armchair to one side of the door.

"What brings you here?" Caldwell asked before taking a bite of his sandwich. "Not that you aren't welcome."

"I wanted to tell you something in person… something about my new wife."

Caldwell nodded, and Whit was struck by the fact that his cousin—and Eirwen for that matter—didn't seem nearly as surprised as his mother and aunt had been.

Slightly sidetracked, Whit asked, "Did

Grandfather tell you about our pact?"

Putting down his sandwich, Caldwell adopted his serious lawyer face. "Look, Whit, everyone in the family knows how you feel about the house. And even though I'm older, I never had a problem with you getting it. The fact is I'm way too busy to keep it up, and I told Grandfather as much. I advocated for you. I really did." Caldwell shrugged. "But you know how he gets."

"So you knew about it, then," Whit said flatly.

Caldwell's mask slipped as he flinched. "Yeah, he told me that was his plan."

Whit sighed.

"But, hey, it worked out, right?" Caldwell picked up his sandwich again. "I honestly didn't think you could pull it off. Kudos to you. She must be something else to have agreed so quickly. Have you two been friends for a while or something?"

"Clover is a summer witch," Whit disclosed.

Caldwell's mouth fell open, and the chicken breast in his hands slid from between the buns onto the plate.

"That's right. My new wife is a summer witch."

Caldwell blinked. "D-does Grandfather know?"

Whit shook his head. "Not yet, and I don't want you to tell him either."

Caldwell frowned. "But…don't you think that's going to affect his decision about the house?"

"How can it? We sealed a magical pact. If I married a witch before the winter solstice, he would give the house to me. He didn't specify she had to be a winter witch."

Caldwell quirked his mouth. "Yeah…but you know that's what he meant."

Whit shrugged. "That doesn't really matter, does it?"

Caldwell raised his eyebrows and shook his head. "No, you're right. From a contract perspective, he should have specified." His eyes met Whit's. "Are you really okay with this though? I mean…as far as I know, you've never had any love for the summer witches. And you marrying just anyone isn't why Grandfather conceived all this."

Whit snorted. "I honestly don't know why Grandfather has been so obsessed with me getting married. If he didn't want it to turn out this way, he should have let me alone. As for the summer witches"—Whit sighed heavily—"I'm going to be honest, it's been a challenge. Her family is not happy, which is upsetting for her. It takes a lot of energy to have someone else in my space, to consider what she wants and what she's thinking. And she's…well, she's very different from me. She invited fae into the house, she's afraid of ghosts, and she put tacks in the walls."

"I bet you *loved* that."

When Whit looked back to his cousin's face, he saw Caldwell was grinning.

"Why are you making that face at me?"

Caldwell's grin widened as he chuckled a knowing laugh. "You think that all your problems here are because she's a summer witch"—Caldwell shook his head—"when they're because you're married now. You'd be having these same adjustments if you'd married a winter witch. They would only take a different form."

"Then why would Grandfather try to force this on me?" Whit raised his voice.

Caldwell leaned back in his chair, lacing his fingers with the smuggest expression. "You'll figure it out."

Chapter Forty-Six

Clover waved goodbye to Rachel before closing the front door. She'd finished Crane's sweater tonight at knitting group and was thinking about what to work on next.

As she faced the hall, she realized it was quite dark in the house—the only light a soft glow coming from the dining room. Clover peeked around the corner to see a series of tea lights shining on Whit's ancestor altar.

A moment later, Whit appeared from the kitchen —a bowl in one hand and a plate in the other.

"Oh, you're home. How was knitting?" he asked.

Clover removed her wet shoes and came into the dining room. "Good. What are you doing?"

Whit directed his attention toward the altar, setting the dishes on the sideboard. "It's the dark moon. This is one of the times we make offerings to our ancestors."

Clover crept closer. She'd noticed the altar her very first day but hadn't really studied it. It had felt so strange, if not dangerous, at the time. The table was gleaming with candles, one for each picture. There were keepsakes—a ring here, a set of dice there, even an embroidered handkerchief—carefully decorating the space. There was also a carved human skull, wood by the looks of it, before which a tea light glowed. Whit had just placed a bowl of water and a plate with one of the cupcakes she'd frozen from the week before.

"What's that?" Clover asked, pointing at the skull.

"That's to represent any unnamed ancestors, those we did not know but still want to honor."

"Ahh." Clover gazed at each of the photographs. Some of them were quite old, but others were fairly recent. *Which of these ghosts has been hanging around?* "Oh! Great-Uncle Andri!" She smiled as she spotted him.

Her eyes lingered on another picture of a man she didn't recognize, younger than she was now but still an adult. "Who's that?" she inquired in a hushed voice.

Whit followed her gaze and smiled softly. "That's my dad."

Clover's heart squeezed with sadness. "But he looks so young."

Whit nodded. "He was in his early twenties when he died. I was only three years old."

The air rushed out of Clover's lungs as if she'd been kicked. She couldn't imagine what it would have been like to grow up without her dad. And she was ashamed of herself for not asking until now. "Your mom…is she still around?"

Whit frowned. "Yes."

"Will I meet her soon?"

He shifted his weight uncomfortably. "I've already told her about you. She'll come around in her own time."

At least she'll have time to process me being a summer witch, not like what I did to my parents. "Did your mom raise you by herself, then?"

Whit bobbed his head. "Yes, but she had help from my dad's parents."

Clover peeked over at him. "The grandfather who insisted you get married?"

"Yes."

She looked back at the pictures. The most recent was a photo of a smiling old woman. "This was your grandmother?"

"Yes, she died last year."

"I'm sorry," Clover murmured sadly.

Whit shook his head. "You don't need to feel sorry. Death is a part of life. And just because they're no longer in their corporeal form, doesn't mean they're gone. She's still here. They all are."

When Clover was growing up, death wasn't a thing they really talked about. She remembered when her grandfather had died. She remembered asking her parents what happened after death. They'd told her it was best not thought or talked about. This was the most she'd discussed the topic in her entire life.

A wistful longing welled up inside her. "I miss my grandparents. I wonder if summer sorcerers and witches stick around after death like winter sorcerers and witches do."

"Well, ghosts aren't always around. They pop in and out from the spirit world. So it's reasonable to think summer sorcerers and witches just stay there most of the time."

Clover's eyes lost focus as she stared at one of the candles, but she could feel Whit's gaze on her face.

"Would you like to make an offering to them?" Whit asked gently.

Clover flinched at the suggestion. The dead were gone. And she had been taught that any dealings with them could have terrible consequences. Still, something tugged on her heart. When her gaze fell on the cupcake, she remembered the many afternoons she would bake with her grandmother.

Even though it felt like she was standing on the edge of a cliff, she nodded slightly.

"Would you like to share mine or have your own?" Whit asked.

Clover hunched her shoulders. "I can share yours."

"All right," he said, turning purposefully toward the altar.

Clover waited for his words. She had no idea what she was supposed to do. But as the silence drew out, she glanced over at him.

He gave her a soft smile. "Hey," he said tenderly. "You don't have to do this if you're uncomfortable."

His words bolstered her courage, and she shook

her head. *Nothing bad will happen if he's here with me. He knows how to handle ghosts.*

"I want to," Clover murmured.

"Okay," he said with that same gentleness. "I'll start, and you can add anything if you feel like it."

Clover bit her lip but nodded.

But as Whit took a deep breath to begin, panic zipped through her. "Wait!"

He paused to look over at her.

"Will you hold my hand?"

With an affable huff through his nose, Whit nodded. A shiver of heat ran up Clover's arm as he laced his fingers with hers.

"Better?" he asked.

She wasn't sure whether she nodded or not, so unaware was she of anything other than his hand in hers as he turned back to the altar.

"Ancestors!" Whit called firmly. "Those we have known and loved and those whom we have never met. On this night, the night of the dark moon, when shadows and shades rule, we honor you and your wisdom. You have seen and know things we cannot hope to fathom. As you have done in the past, please watch over us, your descendants, and bless us. These offerings are for you."

Some of the candles on the table flickered and danced while others stayed steady.

Whit gave Clover's hand a gentle squeeze. "Would you like to say something?"

She cleared her throat. "Mam-gu, Tad-cu…" Her face flushed as she addressed her father's parents—the grandparents she'd known growing up. "I…I miss you, and I hope you're doing well."

As Clover took a steadying breath through her nose, she smelled the softest hint of Old Spice aftershave. In that moment, she could almost feel her grandfather's beard scratchy against her cheek as she hugged him. And then it was gone.

Chapter Forty-Seven

Whit chuckled under his breath as he pulled his shirt off over his head. He was still a little surprised Clover had joined in on his offering to the ancestors earlier that night.

As he shrugged into his pajama shirt, he wondered how long it would be before he knew her well enough not to be surprised by her unexpected behaviors.

Before he could fasten the first button on his shirt, he heard a gentle knock on the door that led to the bathroom.

"Whit?" Clover called from the other side.

"Yeah?" he asked.

Without warning, she entered the room, skidding to a halt—her eyes wide—when she saw him only mostly dressed.

"Sorry," she murmured though she didn't look away from his bare chest. "I should have waited for an invitation."

He made quick work of buttoning his shirt, trying to ignore how her gaze lingered as his fingers began to tingle. "Do you need something?"

She shook herself and smiled up at him. "Yes, I just finished Crane's sweater, and I'm looking to start another project. I was wondering if you'd like one, too?"

"You don't have to go to all that trouble."

"It's no trouble at all! I'd like to do it. I make them for all my family members."

Whit's heart swelled at the word, and he dropped his head in a nod. "All right, then. Thank you." He couldn't fight the smile that spread on his face. He looked forward to wearing something Clover had made just for him with her own two hands.

"Great." Clover closed the distance between them with a purposeful step. "Stand straight with your arms at your sides, please."

Whit blinked, his brow furrowing in confusion.

Clover laughed. "I have to measure you to know what size to make." She held up a rolled fabric tape measurer for emphasis.

"Oh, right." Whit did as she requested.

"Do you normally wear an undershirt when you wear sweaters?" she asked, moving to his side and putting her thumb over the end of the tape at the top of his shoulder.

"Yes."

She nodded. "Then I should be able to measure like this."

A shiver ran through him as the cold tape touched his bare arm below where his shirt sleeve ended.

"Do you have a color preference? What's your favorite color?"

"Black."

Clover snorted. "Really?" she asked flatly.

He raised an eyebrow. "Is that a problem? Black is slimming."

Clover stepped in front of him, meeting his eyes. "Is that something you're worried about?"

Whit shrugged, a little self-conscious that she asked so directly.

Her answering smile was warm and reassuring. "Well, I wouldn't worry about that just yet. You look great. Put your elbows out, please."

His face heated at her easy compliment while he lifted his arms.

Reaching around, her arms encircled him as she slipped the tape behind his back. He stiffened. He could feel the warmth of her body close to his. Her freshly washed hair smelled of coconut and cream, and he breathed deep the intoxicating scent.

"One more," she said, completely unaware of the turn his mind had taken.

Moving to the side, Clover placed the end of the tape under his arm and slid it down his side.

Whit flinched, trembling as an involuntary snicker escaped him. When Clover paused, he glanced over to find her grinning.

"Are you ticklish?" she asked, too much mischief in her tone.

He shook his head though the smile he was fighting made the gesture rather unconvincing.

"Oh," she said lightly. "So then"—she wriggled her fingers on his side—"*this* doesn't tickle?"

He bit his lip to silence his laugh as he swerved out of her reach.

For a tense moment, they stared at each other like a showdown in a Western—her grinning with intent and him tensed to run.

"Don't do it," he said in a warning tone.

She tilted her head. "Do what?"

"You know what. Don't."

"But I thought you weren't ticklish?"

"I'm not," he insisted.

She sprang at him, and he only barely evaded her by putting the bed between them. The chase that ensued gave no merit to the fact that they were both adults. Chairs were toppled, pillows were thrown—all as Clover giggled with delight.

But when Clover hopped onto the bed to launch herself at him, she lost her balance. Whit reached out and steadied her before she could fall.

"Okay," he said breathlessly. "That's enough. Come down now before you get hurt."

A little shaken by her near miss, she nodded and sat before him on the edge of the bed. Patting the bed beside her, she urged, "Sit down. I promise I won't tickle you."

Whit eyed her suspiciously but decided she was trustworthy before he sat beside her.

Clover leaned her head against the side of his arm, the weight warm and comfortable.

"That was fun," she said.

"If you say so," he grumbled.

She glanced up at him. "You have something on your face," she told him.

He wiped his face with his palm.

Laughing, she shook her head and popped up on her knees to face him. "I'll get it."

Then, leaning in close, she pressed her lips to his cheek.

His heart jumped as his stomach fluttered. And when he turned toward her, all trace of her mischievous grin was gone.

Her cheeks were flushed and her eyes bright. Her tongue darted out to wet her lips, which were parted in a clear question.

Whit met her gaze, his heart pumping desire to all his extremities. She was so close to him, her lips only inches from his. He could hear her uneven breathing; her alluring scent was all he could smell. He knew she would taste as good as she looked— that she would feel even better than he could imagine.

Her eyelashes fluttered slowly over her blue eyes. He held his breath as she leaned toward him again.

When her lips brushed against his, she yanked on something inside him, straining the chain that leashed his desire for her.

She seemed to have no such restraint.

The moment her lips met his, she doubled down —deepening their kiss with a low sound that beckoned something primal within him.

His head swam, dizzy and drowning in the sensation of her. He wanted this. He wanted this and much more.

But when he felt the weight of her hand rest on his thigh, the shock of reality slammed into him.

"It's late," he whispered, pulling away from her slightly.

She smiled a knowing, heated smile. "It is," she murmured before kissing him gently on the cheek again.

He tried to swallow, tried to order his words into what he needed to say. "We should go to bed."

"I agree." Her trail of kisses reached his throat.

With every touch of her lips on his skin, the tether on his rational mind snapped a thread.

This was his last chance. He had to make her understand, or he would do something he'd regret—something he could not take back.

"In our own rooms," he breathed.

She stopped immediately, pulling away from him as if he'd stung her. She stared at his face.

With a little distance between them, he could breathe, and the oxygen to his brain made the situation clear to him. With every passing heartbeat with her eyes watching him, he felt more and more uncomfortable.

He avoided her gaze to relieve the feeling, but he still saw the frown that marred her expression.

Finally, she sniffed hard through her nose and got to her feet. Her bare heels thumped on the floor while she made her way to the bathroom door.

"Goodnight," he said, his hushed tone drowned out by the door she slammed.

Chapter Forty-Eight

Clover sighed heavily as she swept the floor of the kitten room at Pets and Scritches. It had been nearly twenty-four hours since Whit had summarily rejected her, and she still couldn't let it go. After her embarrassment had worn off, she was left with irritation.

We're married, for goddess's sake! Does he expect me to be both faithful and celibate for the rest of my life?

She clenched the broom in her fists. *I was prepared to take things slow, but I thought I saw his desire a few times.* An unbidden image of Faustina's dark eyes and perfect frame rose to Clover's mind. *We're nothing alike... Am I just not to his taste? I've always been the one to initiate...*

"You all right?" Orion asked, tying up a bag he'd just scooped soiled cat litter into. "You seem... annoyed."

"I'm fine," Clover snapped.

Orion raised his eyebrows. "You want to try that again?"

Clover sighed loudly, putting more sound than air into the expression. Her eyes shifted quickly to Orion. "Orion, you're a man."

"Glad you noticed," he said.

"Objectively speaking, I'm an attractive woman. Am I not?"

Orion took his time looking her over, then he smiled. "I'd argue with anyone who said otherwise."

The feeling of vindication that surfaced within her did nothing to temper her frustration.

Orion tilted his head. "Is there…something you'd like to talk about? Or did you just need an ego boost?"

Clover bit her cheek. "I don't want to burden you with…personal stuff."

Orion shrugged lightly. "I don't want you to tell me if you're uncomfortable. But I, for one, would like to become better friends with you. Unburdening our worries to each other is what friends do, right?"

Clover resisted the urge to blurt out her problem. The fact was this was a conversation she'd normally have with Ari or maybe Erie. But they still had reservations about Whit, and this incident wouldn't help the matter. Plus, they were still all wrapped up in the summer versus winter thing, and she didn't think this had anything to do with being a witch.

Orion is an ordinary and a man… He might be able to help.

Sighing yet again, Clover turned fully toward Orion. "Okay…how do I put this? My husband…

doesn't seem very *interested* in me." She gave him a significant look that carried her meaning.

A line of confusion formed between his eyebrows. "How long have you been married?"

"Two weeks Friday."

"I mean…that seems a little soon to lose interest unless you've been together for a really long time."

Clover shook her head.

"Is he just busy? Maybe he's tired."

"I don't think so," Clover said.

Orion grimaced. "Did you have a fight?"

"No."

"That's really weird, I mean, especially if there has been a sudden change in…interest."

Clover gnawed on her lip, glancing around at the cat trees and beds with sleeping kittens. "And if there hasn't?" she murmured.

Orion snorted. "What are you saying? That you and your husband have never been intimate?"

Clover dropped her head and peeked up at him through her lashes.

"Really?" Orion said louder and higher than before.

Clover shook her head. Saying nothing at this point was preferable to explaining.

Orion wrinkled his nose, his front teeth hanging out as he squinted in confusion. He started as if to say something but only grunted. Trying again, he said, "If that's the case…maybe he's just…nervous? Is he religious or something?"

Not in the way you're thinking. "No, he's not religious. And in any case, we're married."

Orion shook his head seriously. "I don't know what else to say, Clover. It's just as baffling to me as it is to you—more so probably. I mean, if I had a wife like you, I'd have a hard time keeping my libido under control. And I can't imagine any circumstances in which I'd turn you down if you wanted it."

Clover blinked at his words, delivered with such matter-of-fact nonchalance. *Did he just make a pass at me?*

"What I will say for certain," he continued as if he hadn't said anything out of the ordinary, "is that you deserve to be loved and appreciated. As a friend, I suggest you have a conversation with your husband. But, on the other hand, fuck that guy. If he doesn't know how lucky he is, then he deserves to lose it. If he's not careful, he's going to wake up one day and be awfully lonely. A woman like you isn't without options."

He is definitely *making a pass at me.* "Thanks, Orion," she responded in a friendly, purposely oblivious tone. "I probably should talk to him. It's just awkward, you know?"

Orion quirked a smile. "More awkward than talking to someone you barely know about how your husband isn't satisfying you?"

Clover's face flushed. "Hey! You said we were friends."

Orion laughed. "We are. But damn, you just dropped a heavy issue on me pretty early on in our friendship."

Clover lowered her face. "Sorry," she muttered.

"Oh, come on. Don't make that cute, pouty face. I know what will cheer you up."

"What?" Clover asked, her tone suspicious and uncertain.

"Now, that we're done cleaning, we get to play with the kittens."

Clover looked around. "But they're all sleeping. We shouldn't wake them up. Kittens need a lot of sleep."

Orion glanced around at the cat babies. "You're right. Okay, how about this? Someone brought in a new kitten they found under their porch today. It had been crying for days, and the mama never came back. How about you name it?"

Clover beamed as her worries temporarily lifted. "Really?"

Orion nodded.

"Which one is it?"

"I think she's over here." Orion carefully crossed the room to the corner farthest from the giant window and opposite the door. He knelt down near a cat cave and looked inside. "Yep, she's been hiding in there most of the day, according to Amy."

Clover crept closer and dropped to her knees, hunching down to look inside at the sleeping kitten.

She was so tiny with sleek white fur and a perfect pink nose.

"What do you think?" Orion asked. "What should we call her?"

Clover reached out and gently stroked the sleeping baby. "Let's call her Lychee."

Chapter Forty-Nine

W hit offered Llewellyn his credit card. "I'd like the six-session bundle, please."

Llewellyn stood with his arms crossed near the entrance of the studio. None of the other students had arrived yet.

"I told you not to come back here."

"Are you refusing me service?"

"Damn right."

"On what grounds? Full disclosure: My cousin is a lawyer."

Llewellyn raised an eyebrow. "Last time I checked, winter sorcerer isn't a protected category under the Civil Rights Act. Besides, you caused a disturbance."

"If I recall, you threw the first punch. That's assault."

Llewellyn barred his teeth. "There are at least three other yoga studios in Forest Haven. Why do you insist on coming here?"

Whit sighed. "Look, think about this logically. Are you really never going to see your sister again? You clearly love her very much. Don't you think it'll be easier for her if we can at least pretend to get along?"

"So what's your plan? Did you think patronizing my business would endear you to me? Or did you think I'd just get used to you if you stuck around long enough?"

"Will it work?" Whit asked.

Llewellyn pursed his lips as he snatched the card from Whit to run it through his reader. "It will not. And by the way, you look like shit."

Whit knew that already. After Clover had left his room the night before, he hadn't gotten a wink of sleep. He played their exchange over and over in his mind; he couldn't manage to erase the feeling of her lips on his. And even though his logical mind insisted that changing their relationship with physical intimacy was a bad idea—as it always had been in the past—the rest of him wanted to throttle the fucking nerd that called itself his brain. Even after he'd dealt with his raging hard-on, it still hadn't been enough. For the first time since he could remember, his right hand was no replacement for a woman who clearly wanted him.

Whit clenched his jaw against the fresh wave of frustration Llewellyn's insult had elicited. "You're one to talk," Whit grumbled.

Unlike Whit, Llewellyn looked like he'd been in a fist fight the week before. His bruises were yellowing but had yet to heal completely.

"Yeah? Well, I blame you for it. My parents wouldn't heal me unless I told them who I'd gotten into a fight with. Erie won't even let me see Crane until I'm completely healed." Llewellyn handed the card back to Whit and turned the reader toward him to sign.

Whit glanced up at his brother-in-law after he was finished signing. *He kept our fight a secret when he could have used it to turn her family against me even further.* "Thank you for not saying anything," Whit said.

"Shut up and go get your mat."

Whit smiled as Llewellyn turned his back to him and headed toward the other side of the room.

The class was the same as it had been the week before, and the other students welcomed him back— even Rania after a furtive glance toward Llewellyn. And though he was sore afterward—but not as sore as after his fist fight—the poses were more familiar to him.

As he pulled out his phone at Pets and Scritches to tell Clover he'd arrived, movement inside made him pause. He could easily see the bright room through the giant window. Among the cat trees, Clover stood with that guy—whatever his name was —she'd been with the week before.

Sitting outside in the cold dark night, Whit watched his wife laugh at something the man said. Her eyes shone in that way he'd come to recognize as amusement. He sucked in a breath through his nose, his nostrils flaring. But when the man leaned in close to her, Whit clenched his cellphone until the sides ground into his hand painfully.

With black spots floating before his eyes and a burning in his chest, Whit got out of his truck and slammed the door shut. His muscles were tense and his footsteps loud as he stomped into the building.

A cheerful little bell chimed above the door when he entered. Whit tried to sigh out his anger but not much escaped him. At least he managed to adopt a neutral expression by the time Clover and the guy came into the room.

Clover's friendly smile faltered and slipped when she saw him. "Oh, hey, Whit, I'll just get my coat. Are you okay to close up by yourself, Orion?"

Clover turned her eyes to Orion, and Whit hated everything about her attention on another man.

Orion nodded, smiling easily. "Yeah, no problem. You go on home, and…don't forget what I said."

Clover glanced at Whit before looking to Orion again with a frown. "I won't."

As she headed down the hall, Orion turned to Whit, who leveled a glare at the man.

Orion seemed completely unfazed. He offered Whit a smile—stiff and polite as it was. "I don't think we've met." He boldly closed the distance between them and held out his hand. "I'm Orion. I'm the one who told Clover about this place."

Whit resisted the urge to spit at hearing his wife's name in Orion's mouth. He reached out and clasped the other man's hand firmly. "I've heard of you."

Orion grinned. "Oh? Does Clover talk about me?"

Whit clenched Orion's hand tighter so as not to smack the look off Orion's face. "Briefly."

Orion continued to smile that irritating smile and tightened his grip as well.

As they struggled in a silent war—Whit glaring into Orion's annoying pleasantness—Whit realized they were evenly matched. Finally, smirking to himself, Whit injected a bit of winter magic into the effort.

The ordinary winced and pulled his hand away.

"All right," Clover said, rushing toward them. "Let's go." She gave Orion a nod. "I'll see you next week."

"Nice meeting you," Whit said with dark satisfaction before opening the door for his wife.

Once in the truck and buckled in, Clover glowered at him. "What the hell was that?"

Whit lifted his chin and started out of the parking lot. "What?"

"You know what. You used magic on him. Why?"

Whit scowled. "Barely. Only enough to prove a point."

"Which was?"

"Now he won't forget you have a husband."

Clover crossed her arms and turned toward the passenger window. "Oh, now you want to act like a husband," she grumbled under her breath.

"What was that?" he asked.

"Nothing," she snapped.

A strained silence settled between them—laden with tension from the night before and her fresh anger at his behavior toward her friend. Whit frowned, his insides churning. He didn't want to fight with Clover. He'd resisted his desire for her in order to maintain the peace of their relationship—a relationship that was still fresh and fragile.

"Did you have fun volunteering?" Whit nudged gently with his words.

"It was fine."

He tried one more time. "Would you tell me about it?"

Clover sighed heavily. But when she began talking about the last few hours, especially when she mentioned the little white kitten she'd named, she seemed to let go of her anger and cheer up a bit.

Chapter Fifty

Clover placed the plate of shortbread cookies on the dining room table in front of Lina.

"I didn't put chocolate on them, so they shouldn't be too sweet."

The older woman smiled. "It's kind of you to remember."

Clover shook her head. "It's nothing."

Clover had invited her new friend to visit the week before, but she wasn't feeling in a very social mood. She wasn't as upset with Whit as she'd been before talking to Orion, but she still didn't know what to do about the situation.

It was clear to her that unless she avoided her husband, her desire for him would resurface at some point. What was she supposed to do about it? Denying it would only make her frustrated and resentful.

Orion was right in that she should probably talk

to Whit about it, but she still felt too raw and vulnerable from his rejection to bring it up.

She also needed to talk to her family. She'd told Ari she would. But she'd never gone such a long time without checking in with them, and the longer she waited, the harder it felt.

"Something on your mind?" Lina asked gently.

Clover jumped at the question, realizing she'd long since stirred sugar into her tea but just kept going. She glanced up and met Lina's dark eyes.

The woman had a calm assurance about her. A presence that said she'd seen some things and come out the other side with an understanding few had.

Clover tightened her grip on her teacup. *Maybe this stuff with Whit has more to do with us being from different factions than I thought. Lina is a winter witch, and she's a third-party observer. Maybe she can help.*

"Can I ask your advice about something?" Clover inquired softly. "I need an uninvolved perspective."

Lina sat up straighter in her chair, then dipped her head slowly. "I'll try my best."

Clover quirked a smile, but she didn't feel the emotion. "The truth is"—she dropped her gaze into her tea—"I'm a summer witch."

She peeked up at Lina through her eyelashes to see her reaction. The woman sat with the same openly listening expression as she had a moment ago.

"I know," she said. Then she tilted her head. "Did you need a perspective on being a summer witch? Because, as a winter witch, I can't really help you with that."

Clover blinked rapidly. "You…don't mind? How did you know?"

"I wouldn't be here if it was a problem for me," she divulged.

Clover nodded. "Right. That makes sense. Well, the problem is…that my husband is a winter sorcerer."

Lina frowned. "Why is that a problem?"

"Oh, it's not in and of itself. I don't mind. But… well, the thing is, we got married without knowing much about each other. That didn't really bother me because I thought we would get to know each other as we went along. And we have…sort of. But sometimes, I can't understand him."

"That's often the case with married people even if they aren't from different factions. What don't you understand?"

Clover pursed her lips. "My husband won't have sex with me, and I don't know why."

Lina's face flushed. She cleared her throat uncomfortably. "Well, um…you said you don't know each other well yet, right?"

Clover nodded.

Lina adjusted her shoulders and squirmed a little in her seat. "Winter sorcerers aren't usually as…free with their intimacy as summer witches are. Perhaps he doesn't feel close enough to you yet?"

Clover frowned. *Could that be it? I thought it might be that first night, but then I thought we'd gotten closer since then. It seemed like he wanted me…* Clover's stomach soured. *Was I forcing myself on him the other night, then?*

"If you're worried about it, why not just ask him?" Lina suggested.

Clover nodded slowly. "Yeah, I know I should. I just…feel hurt and embarrassed."

Lina cleared her throat softly and took a sip of tea.

Clover's swirling emotions made her unaware of the silence that settled between them.

"And your family?" Lina queried, her tone steadier with the change of topic. "How are they taking your marriage to a winter sorcerer?"

Clover puffed her cheeks as she blew out a breath. "They were surprised for sure. I didn't tell them I was getting married beforehand because I thought they would try to stop me."

"Are they so against the winter faction?"

Clover quirked her mouth. "I don't know. I didn't think so. I mean, my brother's anger wasn't a surprise. He's always causing trouble. But"—she shook her head—"I was really shocked by how bad my parents took it. My sister told me they just need time, and my friend said I should reach out to them. I just…a lot has changed in such a short amount of time. I don't regret my decision to marry my husband, but it hasn't been as easy as I initially thought. If he's the answer to my prayers—like I believe he is— why is it so hard?"

Lina smiled a knowing smile. "I don't know about the summer gods, but the winter gods often answer our prayers with challenge and hardship. It may not seem like it now, but when you look back, it will make sense."

Clover thought about her words, then chuckled.

"Wouldn't that be something? What if the blessing I asked for was answered by a winter god instead of a summer god?"

Lina's eyes warmed. "Could be. Or perhaps—rather than your husband being the answer to your prayers—you were the answer to his."

Clover snorted a laugh. It was a nice thought, but she doubted it very much. Whit had been taken aback by her reasons for saying yes to him. If he'd asked the gods for someone like her, he wouldn't have been so surprised.

As she reached for a shortbread cookie, she thanked her new friend for her advice. She felt much more at ease after talking to her. Asking a winter witch for advice about her winter sorcerer husband had given her an answer she could live with. And the fact that Lina had easily accepted her identity as a summer witch made her feel like everything would work out all right somehow.

Chapter Fifty-One

Whit scratched his head in confusion. He knew he'd left them here. He always left them here.

Clover came downstairs, pulling her sweater on as she descended.

"What's wrong?" she asked, stopping when she reached him.

"Do you know where my keys are?" he inquired, looking around.

"Don't you leave them here by your wallet?"

"Yes." He knelt down to see if they'd fallen under the table.

Clover hummed. "Did you check your dresser or the pants you wore yesterday?"

"Yes."

She chuckled softly to herself. "Maybe Marigold is playing a little prank on you."

Whit frowned. "I don't like pranks. We're going to be late opening the shop."

"Says the guy who blew out our fire."

"I told you that wasn't me. That was my friend, Alexandre."

Clover raised an eyebrow. "I've never met this friend. Is he a ghost?"

"Gods forbid. I can only imagine the trouble he would cause if he were."

Clover grinned. "In any case, if you don't want to be late, I suggest you make an offering to Marigold."

"That's extortion."

"It's more like key-napping."

Whit pursed his lips at the sudden, bitter taste in his mouth. *I knew I didn't want anything to do with the fae.*

Clover laughed a chiming little giggle, and the situation didn't feel so bad anymore. It was nice to hear her back in good spirits.

"Don't be so glum. Think of it as her playing hide-and-seek with you. She must like you. Go on. Go put out a pat of butter and ask for her help. The keys will turn up in a place you've already looked, or she'll lead you to them somehow."

Grumbling to himself, Whit did what Clover suggested. And lo and behold, the keys turned up on his bedside table.

"Thank you, Marigold!" Clover called to the quiet house before shutting the front door behind them.

It was unseasonably warm again today. The forecast said it would top out at seventy degrees. The tug-of-war between seasons seemed fierce this year. The trees were naked and ready to sleep, but the grass was green and happy.

Once in the car, Clover cracked the window even though they'd not yet hit the full warmth of the day. Whit did the same to control the cabin pressure.

"You know, I was thinking," Clover started, looking over at him while he pulled onto the main road to head to work. "Maybe we should invite everyone for Thanksgiving next week."

Whit's skin prickled. "By everyone, you mean…?"

"I mean, our families. Maybe our friends, too, if they have no place to go. What about this so-called Alexandre?"

Whit shook his head. "Alexandre celebrates holidays with his mom and sisters."

"Well, everyone else, then. Your mom and whoever else. You said your grandfather won't be back for a while. What other family usually comes to your gatherings?"

"My Aunt Cheri, my cousin Caldwell, his wife Eirwen, and their boys Bryan and Colin." Whit glanced over at his wife, who frowned in thought. "Are you sure inviting everyone is such a good idea? Have you even talked to your parents since…you moved out?"

Clover shook her head. "No, but I was going to see them today if you wouldn't mind taking me." She sighed. "I think we need to trust our families, trust that they care about us. They didn't get to come to our wedding because we were worried about how they would act. We need to give them a chance to get along at least. Don't you think? They could surprise us. This could be the best Thanksgiving ever."

"Or the worst," he countered.

"Do you think so? Have you told everyone about me? Did they take it so badly?"

Whit quirked his mouth. "I didn't tell my aunt, but Caldwell can handle that if I ask him. And my grandfather doesn't know, but he won't be able to come anyway since he's still on his cruise." He thought hard about how his family might act. They weren't rash people. "I think my side would be all right. But what about yours?"

Whit had a hard time believing Llewellyn was ready to break bread with a room full of winter sorcerers and witches.

"I'll get back to you when I ask them later, but I think they'll be okay. I'll make them promise to behave, especially my brother. I need to believe that they'll be able to accept you in my life. I need to give them a chance. Does that make sense?"

Whit nodded. "Do you want me to be there with you when you go to see them?"

Clover sighed again. "It might be better if you aren't, but I don't want you to have to sit in the car. I don't know how long the visit will take."

Whit shook his head. "That's fine. If we're going to have Thanksgiving, I'll have to get my hands on a turkey. I'll go to the grocery store before they're all out."

"Good idea. Does your family also have ham on Thanksgiving?"

Whit wrinkled his nose. "*Ham?* On Thanksgiving? Have you lost your mind?"

Clover laughed. "I guess that answers that."

Whit's heart lightened to hear her laugh again.

She'd been so quiet—distant—the last few days that he'd been worried that while trying not to change anything by rejecting her advances, he'd inevitably changed everything in a different direction. But seeing how easily she talked with him now, he knew he'd been over-thinking. They just needed time to get used to each other and learn each other's habits. They would eventually fall into a pattern of behavior where situations like the other night would no longer arise and be a problem.

After opening the shop for the day, Whit retreated into the back room. Having Clover there—even one or two times a week—had really helped him with his work backlog.

But before he jumped into it, he sent a quick message to the family group chat, inviting everyone to Thanksgiving dinner. Then he sent a private message to Caldwell, asking him to explain the situation to Aunt Cheri.

Chapter Fifty-Two

Clover glanced over her shoulder and gave Whit a little wave before turning back to the front door of her parents' house. Taking a deep breath, she blew it out. Then she knocked firmly.

A minute later, her brother opened the door.

Clover squinted at his face. There was something odd about it, but she couldn't quite put her finger on it—a discoloration around the eye. *Maybe he hasn't been getting enough sleep.*

Llew scowled at her. "Since when do you knock?" Then turning on his heel, he walked farther into the house, leaving the door wide open for her to follow.

"Where's Mom and Dad?" Clover asked her brother, who shuffled into the living room.

He shrugged, plopping down onto the couch and grabbing the television controller. "How should I know?"

"Because you're home and so are they. Their cars are in the driveway."

Llew shrugged again.

"Llewellyn?" Mom called from the kitchen. "Who was it at the door?"

"It's Clover!" he shouted back.

Even though her brother had the remote in hand and stared at the movie he'd paused—*Home Alone* by the looks of it—he didn't hit play.

Clover glanced around the living room. It featured none of the holiday cheer it usually had this time of year. There wasn't even one link of the paper chain hung up. She frowned. She felt this was somehow her fault.

Before she could take a step toward the kitchen, Mom came into the living room, drying her hands on a dishtowel. Dad was right behind her, wearing his gardening clothes.

He must be seeding in the basement.

"Hey." Clover raised her hand in a self-conscious greeting.

Her family all stared at her for one heavy moment.

"Who wants cake?" Mom asked.

"Me!" Llew shot to his feet.

"I'll have some," Dad said.

Mom turned toward her. "Clover?"

Clover nodded. "Yes, thank you."

"Good. Come to the kitchen, then."

A few minutes later, everyone was seated at the kitchen table—a slice of spice cake with maple frosting and either coffee or tea before them.

"So where's your husband?" Mom asked, her tone light and curious.

"Whit is at the grocery store. He'll pick me up afterward."

Mom nodded.

Silence wedged its way back in, practically pouring itself a cup of coffee. Clover knew she had to say something, but it felt so surreal to sit at the same table and do the same thing that would have felt totally natural only a few weeks before.

Taking courage from the sweet maple frosting, Clover apologized to her family.

"I'm sorry. I'm sorry I didn't explain beforehand. It all happened so fast. At the very least, I'm sorry you had to find out the way you did. I know you were all surprised."

"We were hurt, Clover," Dad clarified.

"Do you think we didn't want to be there on your wedding day? Do you think we didn't want to celebrate with you? You took that from us," Mom added.

Clover hung her head. "I know, and I really am sorry."

"You didn't trust us." Mom shook her head.

Clover frowned. "Look, I'm sorry I hurt your feelings. But you can't honestly say you all would have just accepted Whit with open arms." She met each of their eyes. "Am I wrong?"

Mom pursed her lips, and Llew slid his gaze to the side.

"How long has this been going on?" Dad asked.

Clover crossed her arms, digging her fingernails

into her biceps. "That's partially why I didn't say anything. I'll tell you everything if you promise to listen quietly."

She glanced at each of them again. Their silence was their agreement.

"We met on the last day of summer."

Mom blinked. "Last year? Have you been keeping this a secret for over a year?"

Clover leveled a pointed look at her mother, who bit her lips.

"No, this year."

It was clearly difficult for her family to stay quiet while she told them everything about how she'd been feeling lost and adrift for a while, about her good luck charm, how Whit had saved her from Rune, about their kiss, about the crow, about when he proposed and the camellias. But they somehow managed it.

"Do you understand now?" she asked them. "You've always taught me that the summer gods will provide. So even though this seemed crazy on the outside, it made perfect sense to me."

Mom and Dad exchanged a glance. Mom sighed heavily, then nodded.

"If your intuition is telling you this is right, then you should trust it," Dad said.

Mom nodded in agreement.

Clover's heart warmed. She turned toward her brother, holding her breath.

Llew sucked his front teeth, then sighed through his nose. "All right. Fine. He's not as bad as I thought he was. At the very least, he cares about you."

Clover titled her head. "What do you mean? You make it sound like you've talked to him."

Llew avoided her eyes and shrugged. "I wasn't going to say anything, but dude came to my studio a few times—bought a full punch card and everything. He's a tenacious little"—Llew's eyes flicked to Clover's—"sorcerer."

Suddenly, Clover recalled Whit's black eye and swollen lip. She analyzed her brother's face again. The discoloration could certainly be a healing bruise.

"Did you fight?" she asked bluntly.

Llew lifted his chin. "No."

He's lying… Why didn't Whit tell me?

But as upset as the thought of Whit and Llew duking it out in a yoga studio made her, Clover knew there was only one reason for Whit to go there. He was trying to win Llew over, and by the sound of it, he'd succeeded.

Clover's chest lightened as butterflies fluttered in her stomach.

"All I need to know is: Do you love him?" her brother asked, staring at her seriously.

A slow smile spread across her face. She dipped her head once. "A little more every day."

Picking up his fork, Llew shoveled a huge bite of cake into his mouth. "That's enough for me," he responded with difficulty.

Clover turned to her parents, who watched her brother with awe. They were just as surprised as she was.

"Mom? Dad?" she asked.

"I agree with your brother," Dad said.

Clover bit her lip while she waited for her mom's answer.

"Summer gods grant me the patience to see these seeds become fruitful," Mom replied finally.

Clover grinned at her family. She felt so light that she thought she might float away.

"So will you all come to Thanksgiving, then?"

Mom blinked at her, glancing at Dad uncertainly. "What do you mean?"

"I talked with Whit this morning. We thought it might be nice to bring the two families together for Thanksgiving next week. Since you didn't get to come to the wedding, you can think of it like a delayed reception."

The hesitation that answered her made Clover a little nervous. "You'll come, right?"

Finally, Mom nodded. "Of course, we'll come."

Clover shot her brother a look. "And you'll be on your best behavior?"

Llew clicked his tongue. "I said we're cool, didn't I?"

Clover beamed. "Great! I'll let Erie know, too. Crane will be excited to come over again. She took a real shine to Whit."

"Is there anything you'd like us to bring?" Mom asked. "Making an entire Thanksgiving dinner by yourself is no easy task."

"Could you make some of Mam-gu's pumpkin pie?"

Mom nodded. "Yes."

"With homemade whipped cream?"

"Is there any other kind?"

"Perfect." Clover happily shoved the last bite of cake into her mouth just as her phone chimed with a text from Whit.

He was asking if she needed more time.

"Is that him?" Mom queried.

Clover nodded. "Yeah, he wants to know when he should pick me up."

"Tell him he doesn't have to," Dad said.

"Oh, you don't have to give me a ride back. He's already expecting to pick me up."

"I'm not giving you a ride. You're taking the van, and I expect to see you bright and early at the shop tomorrow."

"Thank the gods!" Llew groaned. "I hate delivering flowers!"

Chapter Fifty-Three

Whit opened the can of gelatinous cranberry sauce. Even though Clover had gone through all of the trouble to make homemade, which was her family's preference, he knew his family would want canned.

Since Clover had visited her parents the week before, Whit had seen a change in her. She was a constant ray of sunshine from the minute she got up in the morning until she wished him a goodnight. At least that was how she acted around him. As she'd returned to her job at the flower shop, he hadn't seen her nearly as much. But she was there for breakfast in the morning, and they had dinner together when they got home. Making up with her family had clearly been the missing piece in her life.

"Okay. The turkey is in the oven." Clover mumbled to herself as she counted on her fingers a few feet away from him. "Mom is bringing the pies. Bread is proofing. The mashed potatoes are in the slow cooker. Cranberry sauce is in the fridge. Fruit cocktail is chilling. I'll make the gravy when the turkey is done. What am I forgetting?"

"Did you make a list like I suggested?" Whit asked.

"I don't need one," Clover said. "I'll remember."

This was the fourth time Whit had heard his wife go through her list of things that needed to be finished. He'd secretly written them down just in case. But he didn't need to consult the paper in his pocket to know what she'd forgotten.

"Did you set the table?"

"I want to take care of the food stuff first, but the table cloth and dishes are out there already."

"Did you make the cheeseball and mustard dip?"

Clover beamed at him, a light in her eyes that he'd only noticed over the last week. The light was soft but warm, and it had the most curious effect on his heart. "You're so smart, Husband! That's what I forgot. Plus, I have to stuff the celery with cream cheese. Thank you."

He tightened his grip on the can and spoon in his hands, resisting the sudden urge to wrap his arms around her just to feel her close to him.

Returning his attention to his task, he made sure to get every last speck of cranberry sauce from the can before putting the bowl in the fridge.

"Can I help with anything else?" he asked, watching Clover plop goat cheese and herbs into a mixing bowl.

"You can stuff the celery. Have you ever done it before?"

Whit shook his head. "No, but I think I can figure it out."

"Great. Put them on a serving plate. Then cover them and put them back in the fridge."

Whit returned to the fridge, grabbed the celery—which was already cut and soaking in a bowl of water—and a tub of pineapple cream cheese. He'd never had cream-cheese-stuffed celery before. The only appropriate toppings for celery to him were either ranch or peanut butter. But Clover had insisted it was delicious.

Taking up his butter knife, Whit went about his assignment at the counter beside Clover. She took a break from vehemently mashing the cheese and herbs together with a wooden spoon to check his progress.

She giggled. "They don't have to be perfect."

Whit frowned down at the two evenly stuffed celery sticks, each one with a smooth leveled-off top. "Why not do something to the best of your ability?"

Clover grinned at him, bumping him with her shoulder. "It will take you more time than necessary if you do it like that. Also, there isn't enough cream cheese on them. Let me show you."

Clover took the knife and celery stick he was holding and slathered more cream cheese onto it. It was chaotic and uneven, with way more cream cheese than celery, but Whit enjoyed watching her do it—the tip of her tongue peeking out of the corner of her mouth as she concentrated.

"There." She placed the finished stick next to the two he had done.

"I'll try my best," he remarked, picking up one of the finished ones to restuff it.

"I believe in you," she encouraged with a smile. "Get crazy, go wild, see how much cream cheese it can hold before it falls over."

"That is not sound life advice."

"Of course, it is."

"You're a bad influence."

She flashed him another grin. "The best kind."

Whit smiled to himself. He agreed but wouldn't tell her so.

As Clover carefully sculpted her cheeseball onto a small plate, Whit said, "After I'm done with this, I've got something for you."

She glanced over at him. "Something for me? What?"

He kept his eyes on the celery in his hand. "It's nothing big. I got a few picture frames. I thought you might want to include your family on the ancestor altar. We always set out a plate of food for them at big family dinners."

Clover clicked her tongue softly, and Whit looked over at the sound. Her smile was warm and watery—touched. "That's so nice of you. I'd love to do that. After I'm done with the mustard dip, I'll go upstairs and grab some photos from one of my albums. Thank you, Husband."

Picking up her cheeseball with one hand, she stroked his arm with the other as she passed him on the way to the fridge. Warmth radiated from the spot where she'd touched him so tenderly, spreading through his body. He'd always wondered what people meant when they said something made them feel warm and fuzzy, and now he knew. In that moment, everything was pink and hazy with a rosy glow.

Clover returned to his side and placed mustard, sugar, olive oil, and mayonnaise on the counter. "Okay. Last thing," she told herself. "Then I can set the table."

Her mustard dip didn't take her very long. Whit was still filling celery by the time she was finished though he was nearly done. She'd been right, lack of precision did make the task go faster.

Chapter Fifty-Four

Clover rolled her eyes at herself. She should have put the tablecloth down before stacking all the dishes on the table. As she began moving the dishes to the sideboard, a knock sounded on the front door. She tilted her head. They weren't expecting anyone until four o'clock. Surely, it wasn't that late already.

Making her way to the door, she glanced at her watch. Her visitor was an hour early.

Clover blinked, confused to find Lina on her doorstep.

The older woman's pale face was drawn and tense. "I'm sorry I'm so early, but…given the circumstances, I thought we might need some time to talk."

Clover tilted her head, scrunching her brow in thought. *Did I invite Lina to Thanksgiving dinner?* Given the older woman's situation, it was certainly something Clover would have done, but she couldn't remember doing it.

"Sure, come on in," Clover said, stepping aside. *It doesn't matter. We have more than enough food, and I'm not going to turn her away.*

Stepping into the house, Lina's eyes darted around the room as if expecting a ghost to jump out at her. Though that was a real possibility, she'd never acted so skittish before.

"I was just setting the table," Clover said, heading back to the dining room.

"Clover, listen." Lina's voice was strained but urgent.

The tone from her friend made Clover pause and turn toward her.

"I've got something to tell you. Actually—"

Footsteps from the kitchen announced Whit's approach before his appearance. "Did I hear someone at the door?" he asked, entering the room.

Upon seeing Lina, Whit smiled warmly. "I see your track record of being early is yet to be broken." Crossing the room, Whit wrapped his arms around Lina. "Happy Thanksgiving, Mom."

The breath rushed out of Clover. She felt as if she'd just been punched in the stomach. Her head spun and tried to grasp anything about this interaction that made sense to her.

Releasing Lina, Whit turned to Clover. "I know it's overdue, but, Clover, this is my mother, Melanie. Mom, this is my wife, Clover."

Clover could clearly see the apprehension—the guilt—on Lina's face, but she couldn't seem to process it.

"Yes," Lina acknowledged softly. "We've, uh, we've met."

"What? When?" Whit's voice was loud with shock.

Lina cleared her throat. "Before you came to see me at the house. I was out cleaning some of the graves when Clover found her way onto the property."

Whit screwed up his face in thought.

As the situation finally sunk in, Clover felt sick to her stomach. She'd thought this woman was her friend. She'd talked about Whit with her—talked about their marital problems.

"You said your name was Lina." Clover's voice held a sharpness even she didn't expect.

Whit's eyes widened with realization. "Mom… you didn't…"

"Lina is what my husband used to call me," Melanie revealed.

Clover scowled. "I thought we were friends."

Melanie frowned, her face crumbling. "I just…I just wanted to get to know you. I wanted us to be friends. I thought you—"

Clover shook her head. This was all too much. She felt like she would die of embarrassment. *How could I talk to my mother-in-law about how her son won't have sex with me? No wonder she looked so uncomfortable.* "I…I need to go get those pictures. I'll, uh, I'll be right back."

Without another word, Clover raced up the stairs and into her room. She was pacing the space when she heard a soft tap at the door.

"It's me," Whit said from the other side. "Can I come in?"

"Sure," Clover answered softly, stopping in her tracks near the dresser.

Whit approached her and rested his warm hands heavily on her shoulders. "Are you okay?"

Clover sighed, shaking her head. "I feel so embarrassed. You have no idea the things I divulged to her."

Whit nodded though he truly had no clue at all. "What she did was wrong. She knows that, too. There's no excuse for it at all. But we aren't exactly innocent in this either. We got married without her even meeting you. It's not a surprise she would want to get to know you."

"Then she should have told me who she was."

"You're right. She should have."

"I feel…deceived."

"Understandable. But I can tell you she's very upset with herself. She clearly didn't think this through. How was she going to keep that going for any length of time? You would have met her eventually."

Clover lowered her head.

"What's that?" Whit asked.

Clover followed his gaze to over her shoulder. He was staring at the silver comb on her dresser.

"Lina—I mean, your mom gave it to me when she came over for tea the first time."

Whit smiled warmly at the thing before meeting Clover's eyes again. "Do you know what that is?"

"A comb?"

Whit huffed a laugh. "Yes, but this comb has been in my mother's family for over a hundred and fifty years. It's been passed down from daughter to daughter for generations."

Clover's throat tightened at the swirl of emotions inside her. She was still upset at Melanie, but clearly her mother-in-law had accepted her from the very beginning—when everyone else was still angry.

Clover sighed. "I guess I can forgive her, but it's going to take some time for me to adjust."

Whit nodded. "I'm sure she'll understand that. Thank you for giving her another chance."

Clover gave Whit a reassuring smile. "She's your mom, right? You said it before: Your family is my family."

Whit's dark eyes softened as he looked down at Clover. In that moment, she thought he might kiss her. And though she wanted nothing more, she didn't make a move to close the distance between them. Melanie's advice may have been given under false pretenses, but she would know her son better than anyone else.

If Whit needed more time to get close to her, that was what Clover would give him. She would wait for him to come to her—no matter how much she wanted to feel him against her.

Chapter Fifty-Five

Whit glanced between his mom and Clover. After they'd set the dining tables, Clover brought the hors d'oeuvres into the parlor and set them on the coffee table.

The atmosphere was heavy, but at least it wasn't hostile. The repeat of the Thanksgiving Day parade played, muted, on the television as they nibbled on the snacks.

Mom asked simple, polite questions about who would be joining them from Clover's family and if she needed any help in the kitchen. Clover answered with equal politeness. Mom complimented the cheeseball. Clover thanked her.

When another knock sounded on the front door, Clover popped up from her seat.

"I'll get it," she said.

Whit looked over at Mom, who jerked her chin to tell him to go with Clover. He rose from his seat and followed after her.

Clover opened the door, grinning to find her parents and brother there.

"Thanks for coming. Come on in," she invited.

"Welcome," Whit added stiffly with a nod.

As the summer sorcerers and witch stepped into his house, they seemed bright and bursting with energy. It was such a complete change from his earlier interaction with them that Whit wondered if it wasn't forced.

"Where's the kitchen?" Clover's mom asked, holding a tinfoil-covered pie plate in each hand.

"I'll show you," Clover answered.

"Honey, could you bring the whipped cream?" her mom asked, turning to her husband, who carried a grocery bag in one hand.

Llewellyn came in last. "Brother-in-law," he greeted, nodding at Whit. "We made this for the table."

Llewellyn offered Whit a square vase with an assortment of fall-colored flowers; Whit only recognized the sunflowers and orange roses.

"Thank you." Whit accepted the vase. "I'll put it on the table."

As Whit moved toward the dining room, Llewellyn followed.

"Where should we put our coats?" he asked, slipping his jacket off.

Whit placed the flowers at the center of the large dining table. "Oh, right. Um…I'll take them and put them in the library."

He took Llewellyn's coat and grabbed his mother's

off the back of a dining room chair as well. Then he went into the kitchen to collect the rest.

After having put the pies and whipped cream into the fridge, everyone trickled into the parlor.

Clover was introducing Whit's mother to her family when he returned from putting the coats away.

Everyone greeted each other politely, and Llewellyn immediately sat down on the floor next to the coffee table—reaching for the stuffed celery first.

Whit looked around. There wouldn't be enough seating for everyone, but he'd already had to use the folding chairs for the kids' table in the dining room. Still, no one looked uncomfortable. Mom, Clover, and her mom sat on the couch. Her dad settled into an armchair, and Llewellyn seemed content with his place on the floor.

Mom was telling them that she ran the cemetery next door when more visitors arrived.

Again, Whit and Clover answered the door together. This time it was Caldwell, Eirwen, and the boys. Aunt Cheri was walking up the drive. They were promptly on time as usual.

Whit introduced Clover to everyone, who nodded and thanked her for the invite. Aunt Cheri watched Clover with a particularly keen gaze. But it seemed Caldwell had done his job well because she didn't say anything untoward.

The parlor was getting rather full at this point, so some of the visitors overflowed across the hall into the dining room. Except for his mother, it was split by faction, with the winter faction in the dining room and the summer faction in the parlor.

As Whit returned from stacking more coats in the library, he glanced around the space. He didn't see Clover anywhere. He found her in the kitchen, pouring soda into a few glasses.

She looked over at his arrival.

"How's it going?" he asked.

"So far so good. I just basted the turkey, and no one has said anything rude. I think this could actually work."

Whit smiled at her. "Let me help you."

He grabbed some of the glasses and followed Clover into the dining room.

"Here you are." Clover beamed at his family.

Aunt Cheri covered her nose with her handkerchief and sneezed. Her eyes were red and puffy. She sneezed again.

"Aunt Cheri, are you all right?" Whit asked.

"Of course I'm not all right," Aunt Cheri snapped, her voice thick with phlegm. "You know I'm allergic to flowers."

Clover gasped, her eyes darting to the centerpiece her family had so thoughtfully brought. "I'm so sorry. I didn't know. I'll just"—she snatched up the vase—"take this somewhere else."

Clover skittered from the room and headed upstairs.

"Can I do anything to help, Aunt Cheri? Do you want some antihistamines?"

"It's a little late to start thinking about that now," she said miserably.

"Come on, Mom," Caldwell admonished. "It was

an honest mistake. You aren't *that* allergic. You'll feel better after you take the pills."

Aunt Cheri pursed her lips, clearly holding back a lot more she wanted to say. "I have some in my purse."

As Aunt Cheri went to the study to retrieve her allergy medication, another knock sounded at the door. Clover came down the stairs just in time to open it with him.

It was Erie, her husband, and Crane.

"Zio!" Crane shouted, rushing in to hug Whit's leg.

"I see someone's got a new favorite," Clover murmured.

"Zio, I told Mom and Dad all about our safari! You have to show them! Do you think a giraffe would fit in the house? Maybe we should do it outside." Crane tugged on Whit's hand. "Let's go into the yard."

"Crane, we just arrived. Don't you want to say hello to everyone first?" Erie asked.

Crane looked very much like she did not.

"Go on, Zio Llew, Nan, and Tad-cu are in there," Erie coaxed.

"And guess what?" Clover added. "There are even other kids you can play with."

Crane's eyes widened. "Really? Where?"

"Right in there." Clover pointed to the card table covered in an orange plastic tablecloth she'd designated as the kids' table.

The boys were sitting on the folding chairs with their tablets.

Crane rushed into the dining room to engage them.

"Whit, this is my husband, Antony," Erie introduced the short man with dark hair beside her.

Whit shook his hand. "Nice to meet you, Antony."

Chapter Fifty-Six

Clover clutched internally at her hopeful mood. Other than Lina's surprise, everything had started out so well. Granted, the families mostly kept to themselves, but at least they weren't being hostile toward one another.

Sure, Whit's aunt being allergic to the flowers her parents had brought wasn't great, but she looked much better now that she'd taken her pills and Clover had moved the flowers to her bedroom.

Now was the time for the ultimate test. She called to everyone that dinner was ready.

While her side of the family trickled in from the parlor, she watched as each of them noticed the ancestor altar—and the photos of her grandparents.

"Do you mind if I sit on that side of the table?" Mom asked, pointing to the side where Whit's family was settling. "I don't think I'll be able to enjoy the food if my dead mother is staring at me."

Clover tensed, glancing at the winter sorcerers and witches, who frowned.

"Did you not have a good relationship with your mother?" Melanie asked curiously.

Now Mom frowned. "Our relationship was fine."

"You can sit wherever you're most comfortable," Whit chimed in.

A general feeling of annoyance emanated from the winter witches as they all switched to the other side of the table.

"What happened to the flowers?" Llew asked as he sat down between Antony and Mom.

"Someone was allergic, so I moved them," Clover said.

"Allergic to flowers?" Mom commented. "That's awful."

As everyone settled into their chairs, Clover stood at the end of the table. "We're going to make two offering plates before we start: one for the ancestors and one for the Good Neighbors."

The gathered sorcerers and witches all looked equally uncomfortable.

Crane raised her hand enthusiastically. "Can I give the plate to the Little People?"

Clover smiled at her niece. "Of course. What about you, boys? Colin? Bryan? Would you like to help Crane make an offering to the house spirit, Marigold?"

"No," Eirwen said, her voice quick with panic. "My children will not be making any fae contracts."

Erie snorted. "They aren't making contracts. It's just an offering."

Eirwen shook her head firmly. "We don't need to invite them in."

Erie quirked her mouth. "They're already here, though."

Eirwen's eyes widened as she glanced around.

"I'll help Crane make the offering," Whit said. "I know where to leave it."

Clover smiled over at her husband, his words cooling the brewing conflict.

After making up two plates, Clover placed one on the ancestor altar while Whit and Crane took the other to Marigold.

When they returned, Whit finished carving the turkey, and everyone started passing dishes around.

Clover thought that with silverware clinking and mouths full, the atmosphere would gradually get less tense, but the near silence and forced proximity only made it worse.

Crane had no such awareness of the situation. Getting up from her seat at the kids' table, she approached her mother.

"Mama, can I go outside and play?"

Erie glanced over at Crane's still-full plate. "Not until you eat your food."

"But I'm not hungry. I want Zio Whit to show me a giraffe. You said I could ask him when we came over."

Erie was the epitome of patience. "Zio is eating right now. You need to eat before you play."

"But Moooom—"

"Crane," Antony scolded. "This is not a

negotiation. Eat your food, or you won't get to play at all."

Crane pouted her lips and stomped her tiny feet back to her seat.

"You know," Eirwen said conversationally. "I read that children who can't sit still have a hard time in school."

Erie bristled, glancing over at the boys, who were engrossed in their tablets. "And I read that children who have too much screen time lack imagination and social skills."

Eirwen's polite façade slipped as she glared at Erie.

"This turkey is delicious," Whit said. "Thank you for going to all the trouble, Clover."

A nervous tingle ran over Clover's skin, but she forced a smile. "You're welcome. I'm sorry the bread didn't turn out. It collapsed because I lost track of how long it was proofing."

Clover had been completely distracted by Melanie's reveal and had forgotten to put the bread in the oven on time.

"It's fine," Dad stated. "There's more than enough food. You'll have leftovers for days."

Clover smiled. "Everyone is more than welcome to take some home."

"I'm looking forward to the pie," Melanie said helpfully, smiling over at Mom.

Whit's aunt scowled. "Really, Melanie? You hate sweets."

Melanie squirmed in her seat. "Pumpkin pie isn't too sweet."

Cheri clicked her tongue. "How long are we

going to pretend that this is normal? Are we really going to indulge this nonsense?"

"By nonsense, you mean…?" Mom probed.

Cheri gestured between Whit and Clover. "This. All of this. None of us here are comfortable with this. It does no one any good to pretend."

"Mom—" Caldwell interjected, his face flushing.

"No, Caldwell," Cheri snapped. "I can't stay silent. I was just as pleased as everyone else to learn that Whit had finally settled down. Little did I know. And I'll tell you something else: Your grandfather is going to throw a fit. Now, I've agreed to keep my mouth shut—to let Whit tell him the truth. But this is outrageous. They have nothing in common. She brings flowers into the house; they make offerings to the *fae*? There is a tacky paper chain hanging in the parlor for gods' sakes! If I'd have known that this was what Whit would do, I would never have agreed to let him inherit the house instead of you. Your father would be ashamed of you, Whittaker."

"That is not true, Cheri, and you know it," Melanie defended. "My husband would be happy Whit found someone to love, someone who loves him. He wouldn't have cared whether Clover was a summer witch or an ordinary."

"Well, my Charlie would certainly have had had something to say," Cheri said.

"Yeah? Well, your Charlie was as snobby as you are. He always was," Melanie shot back.

Cheri stood from the table. "I refuse to be talked to this way."

Melanie blinked widely. "Feel free to leave, then."

Sniffing hard through her nose, Cheri looked down at her son. "Caldwell, bring me my coat."

Chapter Fifty-Seven

Whit finished putting the leftovers in the fridge but left the dishes for tomorrow. He felt raw as if all his nerves were exposed. He'd been so certain his family would keep cooler heads.

After Aunt Cheri had stormed out, the party just sort of fizzled and died. It was honestly a relief that everyone went home early. If there had been uncomfortable tension before her outburst, it had been unbearable after. The only salve on the wound was that his mother had stuck up for Clover, and no magic had been thrown around. He couldn't imagine the damage that would have caused.

He'd been impressed at how quiet his brother-in-law had been, but then, Clover had made him promise to behave. If only Whit had been so diligent.

The moment the last guest had left, Clover retreated to her room. Whit climbed the stairs to check on her now that she'd had a little time to settle.

He knocked on her bedroom door gently.

"Come in," she called, her voice thick and nasally.

When he opened the door, Whit wasn't prepared for the heart-rending sight of Clover crying. Her beautiful eyes swam with tears, and she clutched the handkerchief he'd given her in her hand.

His heart squeezed, and his stomach clenched. He was going to ask her how she was doing, but the words died on his lips.

The corner of her mouth quivered as she tried to show him a smile. Her accompanying laugh bordered on a sob. "Well, that was an unmitigated disaster."

Whit crossed the room and sat beside her on the bed. "I wouldn't go that far," he said soothingly. "It could have been worse."

"How?"

"Well, your brother could have punched my elderly aunt."

Clover chuckled. "Okay. Yeah, that would have been worse. Remind me to treat my brother to something delicious for being on his best behavior."

Clover sighed, then leaned her head on his arm. Her warmth spread through him, and his heart skipped a beat.

"I guess I should just accept that our families will never get along."

Whit put his arm around her, stroking her shoulder with his thumb. "Don't give up just yet. On the whole, I think everyone did remarkably well."

She was silent for a while. Finally, she turned her head to gaze up at him. "Do you think your grandfather will be as upset as your aunt said? After all, he's why you got married in the first place."

It was Whit's turn to sigh. "To be honest, I don't know exactly how my grandfather will respond. The fact is, I never thought he'd try to pressure me into getting married in the first place. But he doesn't really have a choice but to keep up his end of the deal. We made a magical pact. So unless he's willing to sacrifice all his magic, he'll have to uphold his end of the bargain."

Clover frowned. "That's not exactly the same as accepting me. Even if he gives you the house, he could make our lives very uncomfortable."

The worry that swam in Clover's eyes tugged at Whit's heart. He couldn't help but want to comfort her. Reaching up, he brushed his thumb along her cheek. "Don't borrow trouble. We still have a month before my grandfather returns."

Clover smiled at him, and his efforts felt worthwhile. "What a very summer sorcerer thing to say, Husband."

He huffed a laugh through his nose. "Yeah, well, maybe you aren't such a bad influence after all."

She pouted her lips as she pulled back from his touch. "Damn, and I thought I was doing so well corrupting you."

The light of mischief in her eyes, the curl of a smile playing at the edges of her mouth, even her playful tone, reminded him of the night they'd first met. His heart raced in his chest. The memory of her lips against his had not faded in the least. But suddenly, a mere memory wasn't enough.

Leaning toward her slowly, Whit kissed her.

He retreated only far enough to see her reaction. Clover's face was flushed, and her eyelids were low and heavy. Her slow breath shook.

And though he could feel she wanted him, her eyes seemed to hesitate—a little crinkle forming between her brows.

"Are…are you sure?" she murmured.

His logical mind seemed far away. He wasn't even really comprehending what she was asking. All he knew was that he didn't want her to pull away. He wanted her closer, much closer. And from the look on her face, she wanted the same.

Incapable of forming the appropriate words at the moment, he kissed her again with more fervor. She needed no further assurances.

Clover pushed forward, deepening their kiss. As she whimpered softly, a burning heat shot through Whit—stiffening his manhood and urging him on.

His hand traveled down the line of her body until it rested on her hip. She trembled at his touch, her fist crumpling the fabric of his shirt.

Any thoughts of why he'd been resisting this were long forgotten. It felt good—it felt right.

Grasping her other hip, Whit pulled Clover onto his lap.

She rested her hands on his shoulders, spreading her thighs on either side of his hips. As she slipped her tongue into his mouth, he could taste her faint magic—bright and sweet like fresh strawberries and soft peaches.

Shifting her weight, she ground her core against

his cock. He shuddered—a groan climbing up his throat.

Clover tilted her head back, exposing her neck and gasping for air as she wrapped her arms around him.

"I thought you didn't want me," she whispered.

He pushed her long hair back and kissed along the column of her throat. "You're crazy," he said.

She shivered at the feel of his hot breath on her neck, squeezing her thighs and grinding against him again. She chuckled, her voice smoky with lust.

Then pulling back, she held his face in her hands. Her eyes shined as if they danced in the summer sunshine.

"I love you, Whittaker Crawford."

Chapter Fifty-Eight

Clover watched as the desire on Whit's face slowly drained away.

He flinched, blinking at her. "What?" he asked confused.

Her stomach clenched at his response, but she'd said what she'd said, and she'd meant it. "I said I love you." She shook her head. "But I understand if you aren't there yet." She smiled softly. "You don't have to say it if you don't feel it, but I hope you don't mind me saying it because I do."

Whit frowned, a deep crinkle forming between his brows. "You said you didn't love me when I asked you to marry me, and I told you I didn't love you."

"That was true. At the time, I didn't love you yet." She snorted a laugh. "But that wasn't to say I never would."

Whit's dark eyes wavered. The more she spoke, the more uncomfortable he looked. His hands dropped from her hips. Rising up, Clover climbed off his lap to sit beside him.

Whit's Adam's apple jumped as he swallowed hard. He turned his serious gaze to her, and her guts quivered. She didn't like that look at all.

"I think there's been a misunderstanding," he said.

Clover took a breath with effort. "Such as?" she whispered.

"When I asked you to marry me, it was with the understanding that this was a marriage of convenience. Yes, I made promises to take care of you when you're sick and help you when you need it. But I think of this as if we're roommates, friends at most. Is that not how you see it?"

Clover tried to swallow, but her mouth was too dry. She shook her head and tried again. "I think... that's how it started. But I never doubted that one day we would love each other—one day this would become a real marriage."

Whit looked like he was going to be sick, which completely mirrored Clover's feelings.

He shook his head. "I...don't think that's going to happen."

His words clarified all his previous actions. No wonder he hadn't wanted to get intimate with her before.

"T-then what was that just now?"

Whit frowned, avoiding her eyes. "We're both adults. We have needs. Surely, you haven't loved everyone you've slept with. You're a summer witch after all."

Clover's stomach dropped, and she felt like she

couldn't breathe. Never had being a summer witch sounded—and felt—so dirty.

"I—" Her voice broke, and she took a shallow breath to try again. "You're saying you'll never love me, that I'm stuck in a loveless marriage for the rest of my life?"

His silence was her answer.

Tears blurred her vision. "I never would have agreed to that if I'd known," she whispered as a deep pain gnawed at her chest.

Whit opened his mouth to say something, but Clover shook her head sharply.

"Don't. Don't say anything else. I…I need some time alone."

He didn't make a move to stand, hesitating as he looked at her.

She closed her eyes, shielding herself from the concern in his gaze as tears spilled down her cheeks. "Please," she said.

She felt his weight leave the bed beside her and heard him cross the room. When she finally opened her eyes, he was gone.

A silent sob climbed up her throat, squeezing the air from her lungs. Had she really agreed to marry someone who would never love her? Had she been so stupid as to fall for all his friendly niceties? Why would the summer gods lead her to this painful place?

As she tried to muffle the sounds of her crying, her gaze fell on the flowers her family had brought for the dining room table. The sunflowers, orange roses, rusty mums, and golden poms were bright and cheerful. She suddenly wanted to be home—

home in her cozy attic, surrounded by her loving family.

She hesitated only a minute before rising from the bed and grabbing her coat and purse. In that moment, she didn't care what questions she would be asked or how many times she'd have to hear "I told you so." She just wanted to be around her own people. She wanted the warm embrace of the summer sun, the playful laughter of the Good Folk, the scent of flowers—the atmosphere of love and life.

Without so much as a goodbye, Clover slipped on her coat and left the house, bringing nothing with her but the clothes on her back and the sadness in her heart.

It took longer to get home than it should have. She had to keep pulling over when the tears made it too dangerous to drive. But she eventually got there.

She didn't bother to knock as she came in the kitchen door. She found her parents on the couch, watching television—her brother in the recliner.

They all looked up at her when she shuffled into the living room.

"Clover, what—?"

Her mom cut her question short as Clover burst into fresh tears. Rushing toward the couch, Clover sat between her parents, who huddled in close as if to protect her from all the ills of the unforgiving world.

Llewellyn sighed angrily and stood from his chair.

"Where are you going?" Mom asked.

"To have a nice chat with my brother-in-law," Llew growled.

"Don't," Clover pleaded, her voice thick with

tears. "It's not his fault. I'm just…stupid. It's my fault for being so naïve."

Llew frowned, then moved toward the kitchen.

"Llew—" Clover called.

"I'm just going to make you some tea," he snapped.

Mom and Dad didn't ask Clover what happened. They just wrapped their arms around her and let her cry out her emotions in a safe place. Eventually, she fell asleep.

Her dreams were restless and sad as if she were chasing something just out of reach. She couldn't recall what they were about when she awoke on the couch the next morning—a fuzzy blanket laid over her. But she was left with a feeling of deep loss.

Chapter Fifty-Nine

Whit jerked awake when he heard the sound of a car door outside. He sat up from the couch, his eyelids scraping against his eyes like sandpaper. He was surprised he'd gotten any sleep at all though he doubted it was quality.

Wiping his face with his hands, he tried to look awake for when Clover came inside.

She'd been right. Yesterday had been a complete disaster. Everything had gone wrong. He couldn't believe he'd somehow rationalized having sex with her. He'd known it would only lead to trouble.

But then again, it was probably better to find out what was going on in her head sooner rather than later. When he'd asked her to marry him, he'd thought she was operating under a different set of assumptions. That was why he'd said he didn't love her in the first place. Then he'd thought they were on the same page. Clearly, that wasn't the case.

If nothing else, he was glad he'd thrown cold water on their heated situation the night before. Maybe glad wasn't the word. He could hardly be glad trying to smother the desire smoldering within him. But it was the right thing to do. He'd already been worried that getting physically intimate with her would cause problems. And if he'd gone through with it knowing she loved him and he didn't feel the same? He'd feel even more guilty than he already did.

She'd said she needed time, and he was a patient man. But he still couldn't help worrying about what she might say when she was finally ready to talk to him. Would she come to terms with where he was on their relationship? Would she call the whole thing off and ask for a handparting? He really had no idea because he obviously didn't understand her as well as he'd thought. He pushed his speculations away as the thought of her leaving him hardened his stomach.

He stood from the couch when he heard the key unlock the front door. Fear gnawed at his insides. He wasn't ready to hear what she had to say. But he sucked in a deep breath through his nose to steady himself.

Whit blinked in confusion as the morning light revealed Grandfather—his suitcase in tow—shuffling into the hall.

Grandfather noticed him before he even shut the door. He smiled. "Whit, my boy! I'm sorry I'm late. When you said you and your lovely wife would be hosting Thanksgiving, I decided to cut my trip short." He snorted. "Unfortunately, my flight was delayed by snow in Dallas. Snow! In Texas! Can you believe it?"

Whit felt sick. He swallowed with effort and lowered himself back onto the couch.

"What's the matter? Are you unwell?" Grandfather asked, leaving his suitcase in the hall while he entered the parlor.

Whit covered his eyes and shook his head. Where was Clover when he needed her most?

He could feel Grandfather's analyzing gaze but dared not look at him.

"You look like shit," Grandfather said. He stared at the blanket Whit had so hastily thrown off. "Did you sleep down here?"

Whit didn't respond.

"Ahhh." Grandfather chuckled and rested his hand on Whit's shoulder. "I wouldn't worry about it too much. I've spent many a night on the couch in my time. Don't get hung up on whose fault it is. In the end, it doesn't really matter. Swallow your pride and apologize first. Better yet, make breakfast. She'll appreciate it, and I'm hungry."

Whit hung his head. "She's not here," he murmured.

"What was that?" Grandfather asked though Whit knew his hearing was as sharp as ever.

"She left," he said louder.

"What do you mean 'left?' Where did she go?"

Whit shrugged. "I don't know. She didn't say."

Grandfather pursed his lips, deepening his wrinkles. "What happened? Did dinner not go well?"

Whit shook his head. "It went horribly, but that's not why she left."

Grandfather shuffled around Whit's legs and sat

beside him on the couch. "We'll put a pin in that for later. What did she say when she left? Anything?"

"The last thing she said was that she needed time alone, which I gave her. Then she left the house without telling me."

Grandfather frowned but reached out and patted Whit's hand. "Don't worry too much. It's difficult to get used to living with someone. I can't tell you the number of fights your grandmother and I got into in our youth." He chuckled. "That woman had a glare that could freeze the piss in your bladder. Give Clover some time to cool off. She'll talk when she's ready. You know how winter witches and sorcerers are. We need time to work things out on our own."

In that moment, Whit was glad Clover wasn't there. This would be easier to say with her out of the house. She didn't need to deal with another Aunt Cheri-type situation.

Whit turned his head toward his grandfather. "But Clover isn't like that."

Grandfather tilted his head. "She isn't? Well, then perhaps she went to talk it out with a friend."

Whit shook his head. "That's not what I meant. I mean, Clover isn't a winter witch. She's a summer witch."

The only reaction Grandfather showed was a line between his brows. He hummed softly to himself. "Is she now?"

Whit couldn't tell what he was thinking by his expression. "She is."

Grandfather grunted. With difficulty, he pushed himself off the couch.

Whit wasn't sure whether to be worried or relieved that he wasn't making a fuss. "Do you…have an opinion about that?" he asked, unable to handle not knowing.

"Could you bring my suitcase up before you go to work, please? I haven't showered or slept well in a few days. I'm going to head upstairs."

Whit watched his grandfather's every shuffling step out of the room. He sighed heavily into the lonely parlor.

His gaze caught on Clover's paper chain, which had grown in the last few weeks. Whit tilted to one side and flopped onto the couch, the air rushing out of him in a muffled groan.

Chapter Sixty

Clover yelped as the blankets were suddenly ripped off her and the cold air of her attic bedroom slammed into her like she'd fallen while ice skating. She curled into the fetal position to try to stay warm.

"All right. That's enough," Ari announced.

Clover scrunched her face and peeked at her friend from under her eyelids. "What do you want?"

"Come on. Let's go."

Clover moved to snatch the blankets back, but Ari kept them out of reach. "Where?" Clover groaned.

"Your parents told me you haven't left this room for two days. And while living the cat's life might sound nice, it's time to come back to reality."

Clover didn't feel like leaving her room. She didn't feel like doing anything but hibernating. Even eating what her family delivered to her gave her mind too much time to think. And when her mind had room to think, she thought about Whit. And thinking about Whit made her heart hurt.

"I've cleared the whole day just for you. I sent Rhys to his sister's for the night, too. So you have my undivided attention. I've stocked up on your favorite paste-like foods, and I've pulled out your favorite black-and-white movies. It's a girls' day with your best friend, and attendance is mandatory."

All of that sounded like things Clover didn't want to do, but she and Ari had made a promise long ago that when attendance was mandatory, the other party couldn't refuse.

Clover wiggled her limbs, whining loudly in protest.

Ari grinned. "Your mom said you left some clothes in the dryer when you moved out. Shower before you change. And for goddess's sake, brush your fucking teeth. You smell like a bum. I think we're going to have to burn this blanket. There's no saving it from what it's been through."

Clover laughed, launching herself at her friend. She wrapped her arms around her and kissed her on the cheek.

"Ew! I'm squealing to Dr. MacIntosh when I go to the dentist next. He's going to have sharp words for you."

"I love you so much. You're my best friend."

"Ugh. I love you, too! Go shower, please!"

Her revenge complete, Clover went to shower, change, and brush her teeth. And though her heart stung as her mind replayed Whit's hope-crushing words over and over, she did feel a tiny bit better once she was clean and sitting in Ari's passenger seat.

"Did you really get all the paste foods?" Clover asked as Ari pulled onto the street.

Ari smirked. "I think I know the drill by now. I got canned cheese and crackers, whipped cream and strawberries, hummus and veggies, chocolate pudding, plus guacamole and chips. And don't worry. All of my spoons are clean in case you want to do away with pretense."

"How many cans of cheese did you get?"

"Two because I know you're a little piggy."

Clover smiled. Her friend knew her well.

It didn't even take ten minutes to get to Ari's apartment. Clover was sitting on the couch with a pudding cup in her hand fifteen minutes after leaving her parents' house.

"So did you guys fight about what happened at Thanksgiving?" Ari asked before licking pudding off the back of her own spoon.

"You heard about that?"

Ari shrugged. "I had to know what I was getting into."

Clover shook her head. "No, I was upset about that"—her heart panged—"but he was very sweet."

Ari waited silently for Clover to explain what had happened.

Clover's eyes filled with tears. "I—" Her voice gave out. She cleared her throat to try again. "We started to get hot and heavy, and I told him I loved him."

Ari raised an eyebrow. "And that's…bad," she said in an uncertain tone.

"No. Yes. I don't know." Clover stared down at her pudding cup. "This whole time I thought that we were just sort of doing things out of order, that love would come later. And for me, it did."

"But you can't expect him to reciprocate right away. Can you?"

"I didn't. I told him so. But then he said he would never love me."

Ari's mouth dropped open. "What? But how could he even be sure? I mean, he liked you enough to marry you. It's not like you repulse him. How does he know if love won't come years from now?"

Clover grabbed the can of spray cheese and squeezed it directly into her mouth. She swallowed down the salty cheese-like substance.

She shook her head. "It doesn't really matter. If he says he won't ever love me, I can't just blow that off and hope that one day he will." She sighed. "It's all my fault. I should've known what he meant from the beginning. But now…I just don't know what to do. I know I love him. Do I stay married to him just to be close to him, knowing he'll never love me back? I get everything else I wanted. We're married, and he'd even have sex with me if I wanted him to, I think. Should I just be content with that? Or do I…"

She couldn't bring herself to mention a handparting—her chest aching at the mere thought of uncoupling from Whit for good.

Ari frowned. "That's tough, Clover. But you deserve to be loved."

"But isn't giving love more joyful than receiving love?"

Ari scrunched her nose. "I'd say both are necessary for a healthy relationship."

Clover's heart sank. She knew her friend was right.

"You know what I think you need right now?" Ari asked.

"What?"

Ari grabbed something from the side table behind her. She held up an audio cassette tape.

"What's that?" Clover quirked a brow.

"Do you remember that mixed tape you made me in high school when I broke up with Wayne?"

Clover snorted. "You still have it?"

"What? Of course, I do. My bestie gave it to me after my first love broke my heart."

"He was an idiot. Do you have a way to play it?"

Ari grinned. "Sure. I even still have my Sega Genesis. What do you say we rock out to some breakup songs?"

"Can we play *Sonic* after?"

"Anything you want."

"Deal."

Ari put her cassette into the player. As the screaming guitar of Joan Jett's "I Hate Myself for Loving You" crackled through the speakers, Ari stood up on the couch—holding her spoon like a microphone as she pulled Clover up to stand beside her.

They sang themselves raw, and the pain in Clover's heart became a little more bearable.

Chapter Sixty-One

Whit rewrapped the second half of his turkey sandwich. The half he'd just finished sat like a rock in his stomach. For the last four days, he'd subsisted on Thanksgiving leftovers—when he felt like eating, that was, which wasn't often. Pie for breakfast, half a sandwich for lunch, and maybe the rest for dinner. But none of it tasted quite right. It felt like too much flavor—overwhelming as it forced him to deal with reality.

He hadn't heard from Clover since she'd asked him to leave her bedroom. She hadn't come home, and he had no idea whether she would. Even with his grandfather back, the house seemed empty. Things had returned to exactly how they'd been not even two months before. Yet he felt like a stranger in his own life.

What had he even done with his time before, when he didn't have to think about what or how Clover was doing?

Whit rubbed his palm against the uncomfortable burning that had settled in his chest—probably heartburn from eating pie for breakfast. He took a deep breath, then cleared his throat. But he felt no relief.

He didn't have the capacity to worry about the fact that, after three days, Grandfather had still not revealed how he felt about Clover being a summer witch. He was almost grateful that the old man had masterfully evaded dealing with the topic. Whit didn't ask. Then again, he hadn't talked much at all.

His mind was too full—too full of memories and what ifs. He replayed every encounter he'd had with Clover. He wondered what he could have done differently. But it was the anxiety of what would happen next that truly tormented him.

Whit didn't want Clover to leave, but he also had no right to ask her to stay. He couldn't give her what she wanted. So he waited. He waited for her to work through her emotions, to come to her decision, to deliver a verdict that would determine the course of the rest of his life.

Sighing heavily, Whit looked down at the glass jewelry counter in front of him, where his deck of tarot cards sat beside his phone. He clenched his fist when his fingers twitched toward the phone to text Clover. Was it a bad idea just to see if she was all right? Surely, he was allowed to worry about that.

Instead of picking up the phone, he grabbed the cards and gave them a quick shuffle. He couldn't trust his mind at the moment. He needed guidance.

Flipping the top card over, he frowned at the

three of swords—a bleeding heart run through by three sharp blades.

Whit huffed, rolling his eyes. "You don't say," he muttered to himself.

Clicking his tongue in frustration, he tossed the cards down and picked up his phone. His fingers hesitated on the keyboard. Shaking his head, he typed his message and sent it.

> Please let me know you're okay at least.

He was staring at the screen, waiting for a response when the door to his shop opened.

Whit looked up to find Alexandre with a thermos in hand.

"No wonder your mom sent me," Alexandre said, setting the thermos on the counter.

Whit had not told his mother Clover had left, so he had no idea what Alexandre was talking about.

"How was your Thanksgiving?" Whit asked, reaching for the thermos to look inside.

Alexandre raised an eyebrow. "Amazing as always, but is that really what you want to talk about?"

Whit peeked into the container before taking a sniff. *Banana milk. Mom knows something's wrong. Did Clover tell her?*

"What do you mean?" Whit questioned, screwing the thermos lid back on.

Alexandre raised his lip in distaste. "Have you taken a look at your face lately? I mean, I knew something was up when your grandfather came to visit and your mom shut the study doors. But I thought they were just discussing your wife's status as a summer witch. What happened? Did your grandfather come home early and disapprove? I told you it was a mistake to marry her."

Whit's stomach lurched. "It wasn't a mistake," he snapped reflexively.

Alexandre held up his hands. "If you feel so strongly about it, why do you look like the world is ending? You said you followed the terms of the pact. So you've got nothing to worry about."

Whit hesitated. Was that what he looked like to someone who knew him well? He thought he was handling it. He thought he could handle whatever conclusion Clover came to.

Whit swallowed around the lump in his throat. He didn't meet Alexandre's gaze. "She, uh, she left me."

Alexandre blew out a loud breath, shaking his head. "See? That's what you get from those summer girls. They're flaky. It's amazing that any of their relationships last. At least Faustina was honest. As much as I don't like her, she didn't play around."

Whit winced. Clover and Faustina were polar opposites. How had he ended up in the same place?

"Look, man, I'm sorry. I shouldn't have said that. I just don't like to see you like this. I don't even know the woman. I've been busy, and you were still getting to know each other, so I stayed away. I didn't think you'd get in so deep this fast. Go on. Tell me what happened. I'll keep my mouth shut. Well, I'll try to keep my mouth shut."

Whit scrunched his brow—his mind pushing against his friend's words. It wasn't that he was in deep. He'd been in love before—with Faustina—and this feeling was nothing like that. Loving Faustina had been desperate and all-encompassing. She was everything, and he'd done the stupidest things to please her, to be with her for even a moment longer.

But being around Clover was never like that. He wanted to see her happy, to make her smile. Her laughter gave him joy, and her tears made him sad. She was simultaneously brave and strong—standing up to those she loved most for what she believed to be true, weathering the storm of their disapproval—as well as fragile and scared. At times, he wanted to follow her lead, try things her way and trust that everything would work out. But he also wanted to use his strengths to protect her. If it was stormy, he wanted it to be his coat that sheltered her. If she cried, he wanted it to be his arms around her. If she was hurt, he wanted it to be his fists defending her.

But that wasn't love. That was merely what he'd promised to do as her husband. He'd vowed it before all the gods—both winter and summer—as well as the ancestors.

Faustina had made him vulnerable, exposed like a newborn left in the wilderness, and only she could provide him with what he'd needed. But Clover, she made him strong. She made him want to act, made him want to be more himself than he'd been before.

If Clover left for good, he would still be who he was. He just wouldn't be as bright. He wouldn't be as certain. He wouldn't be as much himself as he was when she was around.

Whit looked up at Alexandre, who was patiently waiting to hear what had happened. But Whit shook his head. He wasn't ready to tell his friend. In that moment, he couldn't bring himself to relive it. He couldn't bring himself to say that she loved him, but he didn't feel the same.

Chapter Sixty-Two

Clover sat in the passenger seat of Ari's car, staring at the house she'd so recently called home. She knew no one was there, that Whit would be at the antique shop at this time. But something inside her hesitated to go in. She wasn't moving out. She just needed some clothes to get her through the week. This wasn't goodbye for good. But going in to get her suitcase felt like a nail in the coffin of her relationship. It was one step closer to her calling it quits.

Her phone chimed with a text message, and she flipped it open.

Husband
Please let me know you're okay at least.

Clover's heart squeezed. Whit wanted to know she was all right. But this was just more of the same.

It held no indication that he loved her, and it certainly wasn't a message asking her to stay.

Her thumbs typed out the message without thought before pressing send.

> I'm alive.

"You don't have to do this now," Ari said gently.

Clover shook her head. "Yes, I do. I need clothes, and I can't keep having you and Llew cover for me at work. Stay here. I'll just be a few minutes."

"All right. Take your time."

Clover climbed out of the car and crossed the short distance to the house. Taking out her keys, she unlocked the front door and slipped inside.

The now-familiar house didn't seem nearly as cold and intimidating as it had the first time she'd entered. There were little traces of herself in every room. She wondered if that bothered Whit or if he even noticed.

Sucking in a breath to push back her tears, Clover made her way up the stairs to her bedroom. She pulled a suitcase out from under her bed and laid it on the floor before heading to her dresser.

"You must be Clover," a low voice said from the open doorway.

Clover gasped, nearly jumping out of her shoes as she spun around.

The elderly man stood in the hall with his hands clasped behind his back, a solemn expression on his face.

She swallowed down her heart. "And you are... Whit's grandfather?"

The man smiled warmly and nodded. "I'm sorry I didn't make it to your first Thanksgiving. But the leftovers were quite delicious."

Clover grabbed a stack of clothes and took a few steps to drop them into her suitcase. "I'm glad you enjoyed them."

"Are you going somewhere?" he asked.

Clover returned to her dresser. "I'm going to stay with my parents for a while."

Grandfather nodded sadly. "Whatever he's done, I can tell you he's sorry for it."

Clover paused, glancing up at the man as she squeezed the stack of clothes between her palms. "I'm not so sure about that."

"It's…difficult to understand each other in the beginning."

"I don't know that we'll ever truly understand each other," Clover muttered.

Grandfather smiled a smile that seemed to hold all the answers. "With a little patience, communication, and a lot of love, a relationship can survive almost anything."

Clover shook her head. "That's the thing, though, isn't it? What if there isn't any love? Is a relationship like that worth saving? Is it worth having? Because it might be fine for him, but I'm not sure it is for me."

Clover didn't know what Whit had told his grandfather, but in this moment, she didn't much care. He was the reason they were in this messed up situation. He had to know love would not be a prerequisite for a hurried marriage.

Grandfather frowned. "You think he doesn't love you?"

"I know he doesn't. He told me to my face."

Grandfather muttered something under his breath that Clover couldn't hear, but the timbre of it sounded like a curse. He sighed. "Let me talk to the boy."

Clover snorted. "To say what? Look, I appreciate you trying to help. Gods know I love him. But he's a grown man. You can't *convince* him to love me back."

Clover dropped a final pile of clothes into her suitcase and knelt down to zip it up. She grabbed the handle and looked seriously at Grandfather again. "No matter what I decide, I hope you'll still give Whit the house. He got married like you wanted him to, and he tried to make it work—he really did." She sighed through her nose, shaking her head. "He was a good husband, too good. If he hadn't been, then I wouldn't have fallen for him so fast and so hard. I know he wants nothing so much as he wants this house."

She rolled her case into the hall, where he stepped aside to let her pass.

She stopped at the top of the stairs though she did not look back at him. "It was nice meeting you. I'm sorry it wasn't under better circumstances. I'll—" Her voice gave way as tears tightened her throat. "I'll see you later."

As Clover carried her suitcase downstairs and out the front door, she hoped Whit had told his grandfather she was a summer witch. She could tell he was a kind man who loved Whit very much. And she wanted to believe someone like that not only accepted her for who she was but wanted her and Whit to be together.

Ari popped the trunk, and Clover lifted her suitcase into it before slamming it shut.

Once buckled into the passenger seat again, Clover faced the house Whit loved so much. She didn't want to leave; everything in her told her to go inside and wait for Whit to come home. She wanted to apologize and tell him she could wait for the rest of her life for him to love her. Hadn't she been happy here? Didn't they have a nice little life together?

Covering her eyes with her hand, Clover let the silent tears flow as Ari pulled away.

Chapter Sixty-Three

Whit took his time wiping down his yoga mat as the rest of the students filtered out of the studio. He looked up at Llewellyn, who stood over him with his arms crossed.

"I didn't think you'd show," Llewellyn said.

Whit tensed at the hard tone in his brother-in-law's voice. He didn't want to fight again. He dropped the disinfectant wipe on the mat and rose to stand.

A pang of guilt twisted Whit's stomach as he met Llewellyn's stormy-ocean eyes. "How is she?" he asked softly. He didn't know how his question would be received, but he had to ask nonetheless. The only reason he'd come was to find out how Clover was.

Llewellyn sighed and dropped his arms. "Not great. She spent two whole days in her room. She barely ate anything, and she wouldn't tell us what happened. Look, I know you two haven't known each other long, so let me clue you in. With my sister, what you see is what you get. She always looks on the bright side, and she tries to see the best in everyone. That makes her too trusting and naïve. Why do you think I'm so protective? She's too kind for her own good. She gets taken advantage of all the time. So when she puts herself out there—which she inevitably does—and something goes wrong—like with your aunt on Thanksgiving—she takes it really hard. I'll always be there for her because she's my sister. But don't you think it's about time you stepped in? You're her husband. Why didn't you comfort her? You fumbled, man."

Whit's chest tightened as a pain formed at the back of his throat. Llewellyn didn't know what happened. Clover hadn't told her family that he didn't return her love. There was no way his brother-in-law would be talking to him this way if she had. He almost wished she had. Another punch in the eye would distract him from the uncomfortable feeling inside him.

Llewellyn stared Whit up and down. "You don't seem to be taking it much better than she is. Have you reached out to her at all?"

Whit nodded. "I did. But she said she wanted to be alone, so I didn't want to push."

Llewellyn snorted. "Summer witches never want to be alone. We shrivel up. We need each other. That's why we sent Ari in to pull Clover out of her funk."

Whit latched onto this bit of information. "So she's...better now?"

Llewellyn looked at him like he was the biggest idiot in the world. "Of course she isn't better. If she were, she would be back at your house. But she's functioning at least. She went to work today, and she's even volunteering tonight. She's still not really eating, though."

Whit's head bobbed on its own.

"Just talk to her. Nothing will get better if you don't. Now, roll up your mat, and get out of here. I still have to clean the floors."

After throwing away his disinfectant wipe, Whit rolled up his mat and put it away on the shelf. As he pulled on his coat, Llewellyn called out a goodbye, which Whit acknowledged by raising a hand.

His mind raced with all of the information Llewellyn had given him. If it was true that Clover didn't really want him to leave her alone, then he should go see her. But then, Llewellyn didn't have all the information. His family making her feel bad wasn't the same as him telling her he didn't love her. He couldn't approach those two problems in the same way. After all, hadn't he comforted her properly once everyone had left? She hadn't seemed bothered by what his aunt said when she was sitting in his lap kissing him.

His heart ached to think of it. Was he really never going to see her like that again? Was he never going to feel the weight of her body, the warmth of her breath, the soft brush of her hair?

Turning on his truck, he started to drive home. But somehow, he ended up on the street where Pets and Scritches was. He pulled up to the side of the road—not in the parking lot but still close enough to see inside.

There were two cars parked in the lot, one of which was Clover's van.

Killing the engine of his truck, Whit turned his face toward the shelter.

And there she was through the large window of the brightly lit kitten room. Her long, auburn hair was pulled up into a messy bun, exposing her pale neck—a neck he'd felt quiver at the touch of his lips. She moved sluggishly, tired and worn as if any little thing could rip her apart.

The burning in his chest increased. It was his fault. He wanted to make her happy, to protect her from the harsh world. But she would have been so much better without him. Her brother had said she was naturally cheerful, and he knew that to be true. Why did he have to drag her down? She was a summer witch. She should live in the sun. She didn't need his winter sorcerer problems. She deserved all the love he couldn't give her.

As Whit watched Clover chat with Orion, she suddenly smiled. It was a sad, pathetic little thing compared to what he'd seen from her before. But it was a true smile, and it was not for him.

An anguished groan escaped Whit's throat as he leaned forward, resting his forehead against his white knuckles on the steering wheel. He squeezed his eyes shut and sucked in cool air when a wave of nausea rolled over him.

He was in no state to drive, but he had to get away. Turning on his truck, he peeled out onto the street, his tires squealing in his haste to put distance between him and the feelings inside him.

Chapter Sixty-Four

Clover hadn't wanted to come to Pets and Scritches tonight. The truth was that she didn't really want to do much of anything. But she was an adult, and she had commitments. This wasn't the first bout of emotional turmoil she'd experienced. It probably wouldn't be the last either. At least she got to play with the kittens.

Lychee had learned to purr. For such a tiny thing, she was as loud as a chainsaw.

"Do you think her eyes will stay blue?" Clover asked Orion, who was waving a feather around while an orange tabby chased it.

"We'll know in a couple of months," he said.

Clover frowned. "Hopefully, she'll have a home by then."

Orion glanced over at her. "You seem awfully attached already. Why don't you adopt her?"

Clover smiled sadly. "I'd love to, but I don't think now is the right time…"

"Well, it wouldn't be right now anyway. We don't let kittens get adopted until eight weeks."

Clover jumped as the sound of tires squealing on the street startled her. Her flinch surprised Lychee, who dug her claws into Clover's chest. Clover winced, then gently unhooked Lychee from her shirt.

"Do you want to talk about it?" Orion asked, keeping his eyes on his playmate.

"About what?" Clover responded, soothing Lychee with gentle strokes.

"About whatever it is that's making your face look like that."

Clover frowned. She'd thought she was doing better today. But it seemed that even without knowing her very well, Orion could tell something was wrong.

"Did you talk it out with your husband like you said you would?"

Clover leaned against the wall and slowly slid down to sit on the floor, Lychee still purring against her chest. "Yeah, we talked. Well, I figured out what was going on at least."

Orion frowned. "Your tone doesn't sound like you worked things out."

Clover didn't really want to talk about it. Talking about it with Orion wouldn't make her feel better nor bring her closer to a decision. After all, even Ari couldn't do that, and she knew the whole story. Orion didn't know about the factions or why she'd married Whit in the first place. But he did seem concerned about her, and he'd lent her an ear last time. It was only natural that he would ask for a follow-up.

"I don't think my husband loves me," she said softly. In fact, she knew Whit didn't love her, but phrasing it this way would make more sense to an ordinary's mind.

"So first you think he's not attracted to you, and now you think he doesn't love you? Is he broken? Why would he marry you?"

Clover couldn't tell him that. "I was wrong about him not being attracted to me. I think this is the crux of the issue."

"Could it be that you're being a little too sensitive? I mean, what's the likelihood he would marry you if he didn't love you?"

This conversation was going nowhere. Orion didn't have all the facts to develop an informed perspective.

"Supposing he did, though. Supposing he had a reason to marry me other than love," Clover said.

Orion sighed and sat down on the floor, facing Clover. His blue eyes bored into hers, searching for something—what, she couldn't say.

"You're making this difficult for me," he replied after a few moments.

She blinked. She knew she hadn't given him all the information, but surely, she'd given him enough to speculate.

"There's no excuse for making you feel unloved, Clover. It's normal to argue and disagree in a relationship. But there needs to be trust. And both people need to have confidence that the other person loves them in order to weather any challenges. If he makes you feel that way, then you shouldn't be with him."

Orion's words plucked at the strings of Clover's heart—ringing true in the worst possible way. A month ago, if her friend had come to her with the same problem, she would have given the same advice.

But now, it didn't seem so clear. A month ago, she wasn't in love. A month ago, she wasn't married. And that wasn't even mentioning the fact that she'd agreed to the marriage already knowing her husband didn't love her. Was there really no hope that he would one day feel the same?

Tears blurred her vision.

"Hey," Orion murmured gently, crawling across the floor to sit beside her.

She leaned against him, resting her head on his shoulder as she swallowed her tears.

"It's not the end of the world," he assured. "Even if this one idiot doesn't love you, you'll be all right. You're special, Clover. I knew it right away. You're beautiful and bright. I can't help but be drawn to your warmth… The point is…you're more than worthy of love. And anyone you're willing to give a chance is lucky to have it. I know a whole bunch of guys who would line up just for a single date with you…" Orion tenderly placed his hand over Clover's on the floor between them. "Including me."

A jolt of panic ran up Clover's arm. Orion wasn't a bad guy. He was kind, attentive, and more than just attractive. But he wasn't who she wanted holding her hand right now.

She slowly slipped her hand out from under his,

using it to stroke the sleeping kitten in her arms. Sitting up straight, she smiled sadly at Orion. "Thank you," she said.

As expected, Orion picked up on her gentle rejection. Returning her sad smile, he bowed his head and nodded.

"Well," he said, huffing a soft sigh through his nose. "I hope it works out for you. I'd hate to think I lost to a lesser man."

Gods of summer, Clover called out in her mind. *Please bless this ordinary with a love who will appreciate him.*

Bumping her friend with her shoulder, Clover smiled over at him. "I have faith you won't be lost for long."

Chapter Sixty-Five

W hit shuffled in through the front door. He was exhausted. All he wanted was a shower and his bed. His mind couldn't think anymore. He was simply coasting on autopilot; the ache in his chest had dulled but wasn't going anywhere.

"Whit, could you come in here, please?" Grandfather called from two rooms over.

Whit moved toward the library, opening the door to find Grandfather sitting at his desk—the reading lamp casting deep shadows on his face.

"What is it?" Whit asked, his voice tired and thin.

Grandfather frowned seriously. "I want to dissolve the pact."

Whit blinked in confusion.

"I will give you the house if you annul your marriage to the summer witch and handpart."

Whit froze, forgetting even how to breathe.

"And if you don't," Grandfather continued. "I won't sign the papers."

"What?" Whit shouted. "So if I don't divorce Clover, you won't keep your end of the pact? You'd sacrifice your magic just to keep the house from me?"

Grandfather straightened his spine. "To keep my family's ancestral home from a summer witch? Absolutely. Who knows how much longer I'll live anyway? What do I need magic for? Ordinaries get along without it just fine. And besides, it wouldn't be a divorce. It would be an annulment. You haven't even been married for a month."

Fury raged in Whit's belly like flames on kindling. "I refuse."

Grandfather tilted his head while raising his eyebrows.

"I don't want to annul our marriage. I made a promise to care for her and protect her. I took that seriously."

Grandfather snorted. "Did you now? Is that why she's coming here in the middle of the day to collect her clothes while you're at work? Do you care for her and protect her all the way from the north side of town?" Grandfather shook his head. "Don't be foolish, Whittaker. This will never work out. You could never hope to understand her, and she will never understand you."

"That's not true," Whit refuted.

"Do you really think a summer witch—one who's used to frivolous days of laughter and dance—could ever love someone who lives in the dark where she would never dare tread?"

Whit clenched his fists to stifle the tremors in his limbs. "She does love me," he growled.

Grandfather sneered at him. "Then she's more of a fool than any other summer witch."

"That's my wife you're talking about, old man," Whit said darkly.

Grandfather shrugged, completely unperturbed by Whit's menace. "You don't seem to give that title much weight. After all, you pretty much sold it for a pile of wood and stone."

"I want to dissolve this pact right now," Whit snapped, holding out his hand. "*I release you from your vow.*" His magic thrummed through the air, cold and strong like the Cailleach's fury.

Grandfather frowned but repeated his words, clasping Whit's hand. Silence reigned as the bound magic dissipated.

"You'll get an annulment, then?" Grandfather asked softly.

Whit jerked his head from side to side. "No. I'm moving out. You can keep your house. Let it burn to ashes for all I care. I'm going to get my wife."

Grandfather's face was stern and unmoved, but there was a twinkle like his brother Andri's mischief there.

Whatever. Whit didn't care anymore. All he knew was that he had to see Clover.

His chest lightened with a sense of purpose as he strode from the room—the burning pain turning to fuel for his determination.

The night was cold, but the wind blew at his back when he stepped outside, rushing toward his truck.

The drive to the south side of town felt like an eternity; he tapped his fingers impatiently on the steering wheel. Every red light was a personal insult.

But finally, he pulled up to Clover's parents' house.

His heart pounded so loud he couldn't even hear his own footsteps, he couldn't hear the sound of his knuckles on the front door.

The door was opened a few moments later by Llewellyn. He smirked at Whit, jabbing his thumb over his shoulder. "She's in her room."

Whit went straight for the stairs, not bothering to greet anyone, not even sure if there was anyone else in the house.

It wasn't until he was standing at the door to the attic that he hesitated. He took a deep breath. The only thought that could make him open that door was knowing Clover was on the other side. He didn't know what he was going to say. He just knew he had to see her.

He twisted the knob and started up the stairs without knocking so she wouldn't have the chance to turn him away.

Though the space was void of Clover's things—every shelf and surface empty—it still felt full. The warmth of her presence, the slightest hint of her magic, was unmistakable.

She didn't notice him at first, and that was just as well. For a blissful moment, he took in the sight of her sitting on the window seat, her eyes unfocused as she stared out at the backyard. Her hair was swept over one shoulder, and she wore a faded Kiss T-shirt that was much too big for her and had a small hole in the shoulder seam.

As if she sensed him there, though he didn't make a sound, she turned her sad eyes toward him. They widened, and she jumped to her feet. But her surprise quickly turned icy.

"What are you doing here?" she asked, her tone cool and distant.

He felt like he could hear his heart squish under the boot of her tone.

"Where else would I be when you're here?" he whispered. Warmth spread through him as the truth of his words sang in his veins.

She frowned, and as she opened her mouth, he was afraid to hear that crushing tone from her again.

"I love you," he declared before she could speak.

Chapter Sixty-Six

Clover's heart jumped into her throat. As she stared back at Whit's determined expression, she knew she'd heard him right.

Her stomach clenched. "What happened? Did your grandfather say you couldn't have the house if you didn't bring me back?"

Whit shook his head, moving toward her slowly. "I told him I was moving out. I dissolved the pact so he wouldn't lose his magic. But I won't get the house. He can do whatever he wants with it. It doesn't matter."

Clover's mouth dropped open. "It doesn't matter? It doesn't matter!" she shouted. "The only reason you married me was to get that house, and after everything, you just throw it away?"

Whit stepped into her personal space but didn't reach out to touch her. His dark eyes stared down at her, soft and enraptured, as if she were the only other living thing in the world.

Her heart skipped a beat. She'd never thought he would look at her like that.

"It's just a house. It's nothing if you're not in it," he said.

Clover's face flushed. "Be serious."

Slipping his hand into hers, he laced their fingers. A spark ran up her arm, setting her aflame.

"Winter sorcerers are always serious."

Her heart raced ahead at his touch, at his words, but she pulled it back and frowned.

"I'm sorry," he murmured, his eyes suddenly vulnerable. "I…didn't understand. I didn't recognize. This doesn't feel anything like last time. And"—he shook his head—"I tried so hard not to make a mistake that I messed up in an unexpected way. Did I…"

His desperate expression tugged on Clover's heartstrings.

"Did I ruin everything? Is it too late? Can you forgive me?"

Clover shook her head.

Whit's expression started to sag before she could clarify.

"There's nothing to forgive, Husband. I didn't expect you to love me right away. I just…wanted to know it was somewhere in our future."

Whit lifted her hand and brushed it with his lips, never taking his eyes from hers. "I didn't know summer witches were so patient," he commented against the back her hand.

Clover shivered. "Of course, we are. We have to wait all summer for our seeds to bear fruit," she murmured, stepping in even closer and lifting her free hand to his chest. She could feel the summer magic warm on her fingertips. Raising her chin, Clover tilted her head back—a clear invitation.

Whit leaned his face in closer, stroking her cheek with his thumb as he pushed her hair away. The trail of his touch left a cool sensation as his winter magic danced across her skin like the first frost on dewed grass.

"I love you, Clover Bronwen," he whispered.

A bright glow pulsed inside Clover, and she smiled up at him. "That's Clover Crawford," she corrected.

Whit captured her mouth with his, his fervent urgency slamming into her. She gasped, dizzy from the sheer intensity of his attention.

He pulled back, huffing a heavy breath as he looked down at her. "Are you—"

She grabbed fistfuls of his shirt to keep him from retreating. "Don't you dare stop now, Whittaker Crawford."

Whit grinned down at her. "Yes, ma'am."

Wrapping her arms around the back of his neck, Clover lost herself in his kisses. His breath was heavy, and his hands burned her hips through her threadbare thirty-year-old T-shirt.

As he pressed her to him, she felt every inch of his manhood through his thin workout pants. She shuddered as desire shot through her. How could she ever have thought he wasn't attracted to her?

Tugging at his shirt, Clover couldn't seem to coordinate what her brain wanted and what her hands were doing. Lucky for her, her husband was smart. The stitches cracked in protest as he hastily removed his shirt.

Clover took a moment to appreciate the sight of her husband—his abdomen and arms a testament to how seriously he took his carpentry hobby.

He reached for the hem of her shirt, bunching it slowly as if he wanted to savor every inch she revealed to him.

She shivered when he lifted it over her head, goose bumps raising on her arms and legs as she stood in only her panties in the middle of her bedroom.

The chill melted as Whit pulled her close. Even if he had the magic of winter, he was still flesh and blood. His skin heated hers as he drew her into another dizzying kiss.

Every stroke, every lick, every breath had her wanting more. But she didn't have the wherewithal to ask for it. She couldn't form the words to move this to the bed.

Her knees started to wobble, and her legs trembled under his passion.

Effortlessly, Whit bent and scooped Clover's knees, lifting her into his arms while never breaking their kiss. He strode purposefully across the room and climbed the stairs that led to her loft bed.

Gently, he laid her down on the bed and placed his knees on either side of her with his weight supported by his hands near her head. His dark eyes fixed on hers were filled with a purpose that both awed and pleased her.

As their lips met again, their magic swirled

together like hot fudge slowly melting vanilla ice cream.

Despite his purposeful trek across the room, Whit didn't seem in any rush. And Clover squirmed against the need pooling in her core. Her thighs rubbed together uncomfortably in her desire for relief.

Cupping her breast with his hand, he rubbed the calloused pad of his thumb across her sensitive nipple. She arched her back, clamping her mouth shut to stifle her moan.

Clover's insides blazed like a bonfire on the summer solstice, her magic heightened as it mixed with his.

She was surrounded by him, by his body, by his magic, by the vehemence of his desire for her. It wasn't enough.

Wiggling beneath him in protest, she trailed her fingers down his torso and slipped them into his pants.

Whit tensed atop her, groaning against her lips when she wrapped her fingers around his heavy cock.

When he pulled out of her reach, she frowned. She liked feeling him stiff and throbbing in her hand. It was solid proof he wanted her. But as he slipped her underwear down her legs, she smirked. He'd gotten the message just fine.

Locking eyes with Clover, Whit slowly trailed his hand up her inner thigh. She trembled, biting her lip and praying to any gods who were listening that he wouldn't stop.

His thick fingers found the slick wetness he'd elicited, and he smiled a reward at her.

She jerked and shivered, whimpering as he rubbed her clit with his thumb. The slow rhythm made her rock her hips, and her mind slipped into the foggy abyss as she closed her eyes.

Clover gasped, grunting an inhuman sound when she felt him lick her clit, wide and slow. Her face started to go numb, and her legs shook as she begged him to enter her.

Trust a winter sorcerer to be efficient.

Whit slid inside her, shuddering as he made space for himself.

As he settled his weight atop her, she smiled, wrapping her arms around him to feel the tight muscles of his back. His moan in her ear, his muscles tensing and twitching under her hands, the throb of him deep inside her—she was doing this to him. She was giving him this pleasure. And that only made the pleasure he was giving her even greater.

"I love you," she breathed in his ear as he thrust inside her again.

"I love you, too," he said, lifting himself up to meet her gaze.

"Come for me, Husband."

With another hard thrust, she gasped while she approached her peak.

"You first."

Her face contorted. "Then don't stop!" she moaned.

Chapter Sixty-Seven

W hit floated in blissful warmth, his wife safely wrapped in his arms. She trailed her delicate fingers across his chest as the morning sunlight lit up her auburn hair.

"What do you think our children will be like?" she murmured. "Do you think they'll be summer or winter witches?"

Whit thought about it. "Have you ever wondered whether being a winter witch or a summer witch is more nature or more nurture?"

She hummed.

"Because it occurs to me that it's more about the gods we worship and the magic we perform. But we're taught magic by our families. So it's possible that, as children, we're capable of all magic; we just learn certain kinds."

"But there are magical children who are innately talented at certain things," she countered.

Whit nodded, his hair ruffling against the pillow.

"That's true. But what about goddesses like Persephone? She's queen of the underworld, but she's also the goddess of spring. Which faction does she rule?"

"There are plenty of stories where winter and summer are at odds. Take Brighid and the Cailleach, for instance. The Cailleach literally holds Brighid captive because she wants dominion, wants it to be winter forever."

Whit was silent for a while. "I've read versions of that story where the Cailleach and Brighid aren't in opposition, where the Cailleach transforms into Brighid after drinking from a sacred well."

Clover tilted her head up to look at him and smiled. "I like that one better."

He returned her smile, lifting her hand to his lips. "Me, too."

"If that's true, then our children could learn all kinds of magic," Clover said. "They could be superheroes."

Whit chuckled. "Or they could just explore whatever magic they're best at regardless of faction."

Clover closed her eyes and snuggled in closer to him. "You're so practical, Husband," she praised.

They were quiet for a while. Whit was just enjoying the feeling of her body's warmth, the sounds of their mingled breathing.

Finally, he sighed. "As someone who's practical, I can't help but think about where we'll live now."

"I'm sure my parents won't mind if we stay here for a while—at least until we find an apartment."

Whit frowned. "There's a room above my shop.

I'm using it for storage right now, but there's a bathroom already. It wouldn't be too much work to put in a kitchenette."

Clover smiled up at him. "I'll be happy wherever we are. A cozy little studio sounds perfect for newlyweds."

"You're so easy to please, Wife," Whit admired.

"Well"—Propping herself up on her elbow, Clover leaned up and kissed him—"I wouldn't say that. You're just up to the challenge."

Desire shot through Whit, and he pulled her closer, kissing her more deeply. He vaguely heard the sound of Clover's phone chiming.

She moved to answer it, but he stopped her with another kiss. "Ignore it," he said, his blood heating further.

Clover giggled. "I'm learning new things about you. Have I unleashed a monster?" But even as she placated him by stroking his hair, she reached for her phone.

She smiled down at the screen.

"Who is it?" Whit asked before pressing his lips to her bare collarbone.

"My brother. He said this is the last time he's going to cover for me at work." She set aside her phone. "He said it's his wedding present to us."

Whit's eyes widened, and he sat up with a start. "Oh shit. It's a work day. I have to go open the shop."

Clover trailed her fingertips down his arm. "Do you though? Because...I have the whole day off."

Whit looked at his wife—completely naked but for the sheet draped over her waist. He hesitated. "I really should take a look at the space. I could start moving things around if it's not busy."

"I have the *whole* day off, though. Won't there be time for that later…like after lunch?"

She fixed him with a heated gaze, pouting her lips in a plea. His cock stiffened.

"You're a bad influence," he scolded playfully, pressing a kiss to her throat.

"The best kind," she breathed.

It was well into the afternoon when they finally made it to the antique shop. But as Clover laced her fingers with his on the short walk from the truck to the door, he was glad he'd spent the morning the way he had. There was nothing better than that satisfied smile on her face.

When he reached the glass door, he found an envelope taped to it. Releasing Clover's hand, he took down the note and opened it.

It read simply: Come to the house after you close.

Whit recognized Grandfather's handwriting. He sighed, offering the paper to Clover to read.

"Do you want me to go with you?" she asked.

He didn't know what to expect, and he wanted to protect her from the potentially hurtful things his grandfather might say to her. But they were in this together now, and she deserved to know the truth of the matter.

"Yes. We can pack up some stuff while we're there."

For the rest of the afternoon, Whit worked upstairs while Clover watched the cash register. It would be at least a couple of weeks before the space would pass for a proper apartment. But he'd managed to clean it up and move some of the stuff to his workroom.

As he drove to his grandfather's house, a pit formed in Whit's stomach. He didn't know what to expect.

Clover rested her hand over his, smiling as he glanced at her.

"It will be all right," she assured.

Turning his hand to squeeze her fingers, he returned her smile. "I know it will."

Whit pulled into the driveway and parked. Then he looked at his wife one more time to remind himself of why he was doing this before climbing out.

Clover rested her head against Whit's arm while they stood on the doorstep, waiting for someone to answer his knock.

A few moments passed before Whit's grandfather opened the door. He stared at them solemnly, the expression making Whit feel defiant.

Without a word, Grandfather stepped aside and motioned them toward the dining room.

Whit entered first, pulling Clover gently by the hand after him. But he stopped short when he saw Caldwell sitting at the table—papers spread out before him.

Whit blinked. "Caldwell? I didn't see your car."

Caldwell smiled tightly. "Grandfather picked me up."

"I didn't want to tip you off. Have a seat," Grandfather said.

They moved to the dining room, and Clover took a seat beside Whit, who sat across from Grandfather.

"What is this?" Whit asked.

Grandfather smiled a mischievous grin. "I'm signing the house over to you right now."

Whit's mouth dropped open in shock.

Grandfather held up his hand to stop Whit from speaking—not that he was even capable of forming words at the moment. "I'm going to move into a senior living community. I had a lot of fun on that cruise. Your grandmother had been right to book it though gods know I resisted her. But you're married now. You have a wife. And maybe one day, you'll have children. You don't want an old man hanging around all the time."

"That's not true," Clover said. "We'd never want you to feel unwelcome."

Grandfather smiled warmly at her. "It's sweet of you to say so, dear."

"I don't understand." Whit tried to wade through his confusion. "This isn't what you said last night."

Grandfather burst out laughing, a full-bellied laugh. "My boy, you think too much," Grandfather remarked. "You weren't always like that, you know. When you were younger, you never hesitated to open your heart and share your feelings." He shook his head. "But along the way, you lost what was important. You only cared about things—the house, your shop, and all the useless trinkets inside. I couldn't leave this plane without trying to help you."

"Are you saying all of this was some joke?" Whit asked flatly.

"Not a joke," Grandfather responded. "A life lesson. My gift to you. I held what you wanted most over your head in the hopes you would learn that it really didn't matter at all. And you did! Congratulations."

Whit sighed, covering his eyes as exhaustion drained him. "You are a troublesome old man."

Grandfather grinned. "Ain't I just?"

Lowering his hand from his eyes, Whit stared at his grandfather, a deep feeling of gratitude filling his heart. "Thank you."

"You're welcome! Now, let's get these papers signed already and be done with this business. I want to get to know my granddaughter-in-law."

Epilogue

The sun shone brightly through the budding leaves of the hawthorn tree. Jars, bowls, and pouches of offerings to the Good Neighbors peeked from every crevice and root of the fairy tree. Clootie cloths, tied into the branches, swayed as the wind caught them. It was chillier than expected, but the breeze carried the warm promise of summer.

They'd set tables and chairs out in the clearing, and upbeat Celtic music played from a Bluetooth speaker. Platters and plates of food crowded the tables —oat cakes, scones, and freshly churned butter sat beside early spring vegetables and beef kabobs. Bright red punch rippled in a crystal bowl, clean cups ready for the filling around it.

Summer sorcerers and witches—young and old— chatted and laughed as many of them greeted each other for the first time since the end of summer.

It was May Day, the official start of summer in

the magical world, and Clover's increasing magic positively hummed within her.

The night before, she'd gathered with Whit's family to solemnly bid farewell to winter. But now was her time, a time for her to celebrate the start of summer with the broader summer community.

This gathering was particularly important to her. It was the first time she'd ever hosted. And it was the first time many of her faction would meet Whit—most hadn't even been told she was married.

Clover smiled as she caught sight of Crane dancing with Antony, the ribbons on her flower crown fluttering behind her. Ari and Erie stood nearby, keeping time by clapping their hands.

Returning to the flowers in her hands, Clover finished weaving a flower crown.

"Excuse me, miss," Whit said low from behind her. "Are you aware you're trespassing in winter faction territory?"

Clover grinned, turning to face her husband. "It's summer now. All territory is summer faction territory."

"Oh? Is that how it works?"

"That's how it works when it's our half of the year." Clover laughed. "Did you find her?"

Whit nodded. "She was in the pajama drawer, which you left open." He held up the end of a drawstring from a set of his vandalized pajama pants.

"Aww, baby cat doesn't know any better."

Whit shook his head. "She does. The moment our eyes met, she ran like her fluffy white tail was on fire."

Clover pouted. "You big bully. You scared her."

"I'm the one who's been wronged here. Lychee has it out for me. How am I supposed to keep my pants up without a drawstring?"

Clover moved in closer to him. "You won't need them tonight," she murmured.

Whit's playful annoyance disappeared as his blood heated. He reached out, easily capturing her hips in his grasp. Leaning down, he brushed his lips against her cheek. "I think I'm going to like summer holidays," he whispered in her ear.

His hot breath sent a shiver through her as her body flushed.

"We have guests," she said, her tone holding no conviction.

Whit huffed. "They're summer witches. They won't care."

"But there are children here."

Whit sighed and let his hands slip from her hips. "All right. But I expect compensation for what your devil child did."

Clover beamed up at her husband. "Look here. I finished it. Bend down a little."

Whit dipped his head, and Clover nestled the flower crown atop his dark hair.

She giggled. "Now you're officially ready for your first summer party."

Whit smirked down at her. "But this isn't my first summer party."

"It's the first one you were invited to. Do you want to tie a clootie cloth next?"

"What's that?" he asked.

She giggled, slipping her arm through his. "Come on. I'll show you."

Clover pulled him toward the hawthorn tree.

As they made their way across the clearing, she smiled and waved at the summer sorcerers and witches she knew. But Whit couldn't take his eyes off her. She was that much more breathtaking with summer magic rolling off her, the sparkling sunshine glistening in her hair, which was topped with a flower crown of her own.

They were digging into the bucket of cotton strips when they heard a splash followed by a strangled grunt.

Clover looked back toward the food tables just in time to see Alexandre laughing as he slapped a cackling Llew on the shoulder. Rune stood on the other side of the table, looking very much like the punch bowl had exploded all over him. A second later, Rune lunged toward them while Llew and Alexandre made a run for it.

Whit chuckled, and Clover stifled a laugh by biting her lip.

"Have you picked one yet?" she asked, drawing his attention away from the commotion.

"What is it again?"

"You pick one of these cloths. Then you tie it to the clootie tree. It's good for healing, or you can make a wish."

They each chose a strip of cloth from the pile of undyed muslin. And together they moved to the tree, picking a branch Clover could easily reach. She tied her cloth to the limb, imbuing her wish with as much summer magic as she could muster. Whit tied his close to Clover's. His magic was waning, but he wished as hard as a child seeing his first shooting star.

As he looked down at her, Clover slipped her hand into his.

"What did you wish for?" she asked.

Whit glanced around, then leaned down, pushing her hair aside to whisper in her ear again. "I wished that you would always know how much I love you."

Clover smiled, wrapping her arms around the back of Whit's neck as she gazed into his eyes. "I wished the same."

Afterword

Thank you for reading! I do so hope you enjoyed it. If you have a moment, I would very much appreciate a review on the store where you bought it. Tell other readers what you thought, and help them make a decision on this book.

If you'd like to stay updated on news about my books and events, you can subscribe to my newsletter on my website: www.dlieber.com

Thanks again! I hope you will travel through my worlds with me again in the future.

D. Lieber

About the Author

D. Lieber has a wanderlust that would make a butterfly envious. When she isn't planning her next physical adventure, she's recklessly jumping from one fictional world to another. Her love of reading led her to earn a Bachelor's in English from Wright State University.

Beyond her skeptic and slightly pessimistic mind, Lieber wants to believe. She has been many places—from Canada to England, France to Italy, Germany to Russia—believing that a better world comes from putting a face on "other." She is a romantic idealist at heart, always fighting to keep her feet on the ground and her head in the clouds.

Lieber lives in Wisconsin with her husband (John) and cats (Yin and Nox).

Links

Website: dlieber.com
Goodreads: goodreads.com/dlieberwriting
Bookbub: bookbub.com/profile/d-lieber